In Golden Blood

In Golden Blood

Stephen Woodworth

A   DELL   BOOK

IN GOLDEN BLOOD
A Dell Book

Published by
Bantam Dell
A Division of Random House, Inc.
New York, New York

This is a work of fiction. Names, characters, places, and incidents either are the
product of the author's imagination or are used fictitiously. Any resemblance to actual
persons, living or dead, events, or locales is entirely coincidental.

Dell is a registered trademark of Random House, Inc., and the colophon
is a trademark of Random House, Inc.

ISBN:0-7394-6085-4

Printed in the United States of America

I dedicate this book to my entire family
and most especially to my beloved wife and partner,
Kelly Dunn, and the wonderful family
we've started together.

Here lay Duncan,
His silver skin laced with his golden blood;
And his gash'd stabs look'd like a breach in
    nature
For ruin's wasteful entrance.
    —*Macbeth*, Act II, Scene iii, 117–120

In Golden Blood

1
A Death in the Andes

AS HE DID EVERY MORNING, NATHAN AZURE ROSE AT dawn, dressed, and shaved in the musty canvas confines of his private tent, scrutinizing the aristocratic severity of his Mayfair face in a travel mirror to make certain that not a whisker remained and that every strand of blond hair was in its proper place. He then opened the carved wooden box next to his cot and selected a pair of leather driving gloves from the dozens of pairs inside. Although he wore gloves as a matter of habit, he donned these with especial care, like a surgeon wary of infection.

He had not touched another human being's skin, nor allowed his to be touched, in more than a decade.

Seated on the edge of his cot, Azure idled away half an hour skimming Prescott's *History of the Conquest of Peru,* lingering over passages that he had long ago committed to memory—those that described the abundance of gold sixteenth-century Spanish explorer Francisco Pizarro and his conquistadors had extorted from the Inca people, who tried in vain to purchase the release of their leader Atahualpa. A king's ransom, indeed.

Azure's gloves made it awkward for him to turn the pages,

however, and he soon tossed the book aside. After snatching the .45 automatic from beneath his pillow, he chambered a round and shoved the gun barrel-down into the hollow of his back between the waist of his slacks and his oxford shirt. He put on a cream-colored linen jacket to cover the butt of the pistol and stalked out of the tent.

Outside, the Andean air, thin and crisp, pricked the inside of Azure's windpipe, as if he'd inhaled a handful of asbestos. The sun had yet to ascend above an adjacent peak to the east, leaving the mountains in a pall of predawn gray. Nevertheless, the camp already bristled with activity, Peruvian laborers bustling to and fro with spades and sifters, men delicately brushing dust off bits of broken metal and stone at makeshift tables. Azure had staged this dig with painstaking detail, accurate enough to fool an expert. Or *one* expert, to be precise.

It was all a sham. Azure had bought the artifacts at auction and then planted them on this Andean slope. The Peruvians he'd assembled to pose as his assistants were actually mercenaries—some of them former Shining Path terrorists, others drug runners from the Huallaga Valley cocaine trade. Men whose loyalty Azure could purchase and whose silence he could ensure. Men to whom all work, whether menial labor or murder, was the same, as long as it paid well. Not unlike the conquistadors themselves.

The performance was proceeding as scheduled, but the audience—the expert for whom Azure had created this mock expedition—was missing. It seemed that Dr. Wilcox, the only true archaeologist on the site, had chosen to sleep in.

The closer Azure drew to his prize, the more impatient he

became with delay. Intent on hastening today's drama to its climax, he made his way down the path his crew had cleared in the spiky brush that carpeted the mountain slope. Erected wherever the ground leveled off for a few feet, the haphazard tent encampment formed a terraced village of canvas and plastic, with Azure's large shelter at the hill's summit. At its base, a medium-size tent rested near the edge of a precipice, where the mountainside abruptly plunged into the valley below. Clouds blanketed the dell, a comfortable illusion that hid the screaming descent.

A bearded thirty-something man in a creased white dress shirt and chinos sat in a director's chair outside this last tent, head bent over a book, legs crossed as if he were lounging at a Parisian café. He must have sensed Azure's approach, though, for he slapped the book shut and hopped to his feet before the Englishman arrived at the tent's entrance. A *gringo* like his boss, he differed from Azure in nearly every other respect: his hair and complexion dark instead of fair, his face broad rather than narrow, his manner expansive, not calculated.

"Looks like I got up before you did today." He displayed the book's cover, smiling. He smiled a lot—a monkey appeasing an alpha male. "Researching my role. See?"

Conqueror and Conquered: Pizarro and Peru read the title copy above an artist's rendering of a composite face—half Pizarro, the other half Atahualpa, the Inca leader he overthrew and executed. Below the dual portrait was the author's name: Dr. Abel Wilcox.

Nathan Azure did not smile. He never smiled. "There'll be plenty of time for that on the plane, Trent," he commented in a clipped Cambridge accent. "Do you have the cuirass?"

With exaggerated flair, Trent snapped his fingers at one of the nearby laborers, who hurried up with a mud-encrusted, rust-stained breastplate in his hands. The men had done an admirable job of simulating centuries of exposure to the elements. The armor had been polished to a museum-ready sheen when Azure had obtained it from an underground "antiquities dealer" in Lima—a glorified fence for grave robbers and artifact thieves.

Azure noted that the center of the breastplate had been rubbed clear of dirt, revealing the ornate engraving of a family crest. He registered his satisfaction by withholding criticism. "What about Wilcox?"

Trent glanced at the tent behind him, shrugged. "Still asleep."

"Wake him."

Trent smiled again and pulled his own pair of leather gloves out of the back pocket of his pants. He put them on and ducked under the black plastic flap that served as the tent's door. A drowsy grumble came from inside, followed by the shuffle and clatter of hasty activity.

A few minutes later, Trent emerged with a man who could easily have been his brother. The latter stood an inch or two taller and lacked Trent's muscular development, but they shared the same almond-shaped eyes, high forehead, and dark widow's peak. Trent had grown the full black beard to downplay the resemblance, but it was not a coincidence; Azure had chosen Trent for his appearance as much as for his acting skills and had even insisted on certain…*alterations* in the confidence man's physiognomy. Trent had demonstrated exceptional dedication to his craft, doggedly researching his role during the months it took his face to heal from the surgery. Even now, he eyed the professor with avid attention, taking advantage of his last opportunity to observe his subject.

"Good morning, Dr. Wilcox," Azure greeted the second man. "I trust you slept well."

"Until now." A day's growth of whiskers darkened the archaeologist's face, the fly of his jeans was only half-buttoned, and his untied bootlaces trailed in the dust. He put on a pair of oval spectacles and scowled at Azure. "I hope you have something worth getting up for this time."

"Perhaps." Azure thought of the string of worthless daggers, swords, coins, and other flotsam he'd tossed in front of Wilcox like a trail of bread crumbs over the past month, gradually luring him to this remote Andean peak. "We just found this piece, and it seems promising—*very* promising. Naturally, I couldn't wait to get your professional opinion."

He held a gloved hand toward the cuirass, which the impassive laborer still held. Wilcox sniffed dubiously and glanced at the breastplate as if scanning the headlines of the morning paper. As he moved close enough to see the crest inscribed on it, his expression flared with stifled excitement—a prospector afraid that the mother lode he's discovered is actually fool's gold. He shot a look at Azure. "Where did you find this?"

Azure's face remained as immobile as a bas-relief. He *asked* questions, he didn't answer them. "Is it genuine?"

Wilcox pushed his glasses higher up on his nose, bent forward, and squinted at the armor's insignia.

"Well? Is it *his*?" The archaeologist's silence rankled. Azure knew at least as much about Peruvian history as this ivory-tower effete, and yet…had he been wrong about the cuirass? Had he blown a million quid on a clever forgery? If he hadn't wanted to be absolutely sure of the breastplate's authenticity, he wouldn't have put up with Wilcox this long. Although Nathan Azure would never admit it, he needed to commandeer the man's knowledge as much as his identity.

The archaeologist did not respond directly to Azure's questions. Instead, he pointed to the design on the breast-plate, mumbling as if to himself. "The family escutcheon… but with the black eagle and twin pillars of the royal arms. And here: an Indian city and a llama. Charles the Fifth's seal of approval for the Peruvian conquest."

"But is it *his*?" Azure pressed. "Could one of his men have worn it?"

Wilcox shook his head, voice quavering. "Pizarro wouldn't have *allowed* anyone else to wear it."

"Then we can use it to summon him?"

"Yes." The archaelogist straightened. "You have a Violet?"

Azure's face returned to its dour placidity, the closest he ever came to expressing pleasure. "We have one in mind."

"But I thought all American conduits were controlled by the N-double-A-C-C," Wilcox said, using the popular acronym for the North American Afterlife Communications Corps.

"Not all." Azure pictured the photos he'd collected of Natalie Lindstrom, the classical contours of her visage turned skeletal by her scalp, which she kept shaved so that electrodes attached to her head could detect the presence of the souls that occupied her brain. Like all conduits for the dead, she had violet eyes, weary yet intense.

She was the only Violet he could find who was not in the employ of one government or another, and Nathan Azure was eager to avoid attracting the attention of any government. Even Lindstrom, he knew, was monitored by the NAACC, but it would take the Corps a while after her disappearance to figure out where she'd gone—long enough for Azure's purposes. To avoid wasting time, he had decided not to bring her to Peru until he possessed a genuine touchstone for her to summon Pizarro. Now that he had one, he knew that she would agree to assist him. Especially after good Dr. Wilcox helped draw her here to these isolated Peruvian peaks. A pity the archaeologist would never get to meet the Violet...at least, not until Azure had finished with her.

"If you're right about Pizarro's gold, this could be the biggest find since King Tut." Wilcox's words grew heavy with a kind of lust. He did not appear to notice the two Peruvian workers who flanked him from behind, gloved hands clenched into fists. "Everyone's going to want a piece of it. Customs, the Peruvian government—everyone."

"I agree. That's why they mustn't find out about it." With a shift of his eyes, Azure signaled the men, who seized the archaeologist's arms.

Wilcox wriggled in their grasp, more from astonishment than fear. Then he laughed.

"You can't be serious." When Azure didn't smile, the archaeologist's own grin failed. "I'll be missed. If I die, *they'll bring me back.* I'll tell them all about you."

Azure sniffed to indicate his amusement. "You're under the mistaken impression that I care."

He pulled the .45 from the small of his back and emptied it into Wilcox's chest.

The impact of the shots threw the archaeologist backward, but the men holding his arms kept his body from falling. Wilcox lifted his head, gurgling and hacking as if struggling to utter a final curse.

"*Madre Maria,*" one of the superstitious Peruvians gasped.

In the instant before they dropped him, Wilcox spat in Nathan Azure's face.

"*Bastard!*" Azure recoiled, dropping the gun and slapping at the viscous spittle on his cheek. A film of crimson mucus smeared the palm of his driving glove, and he tore it off his hand and flung it in the dust at his feet, nearly doubling over with nausea. He'd gone to great lengths to avoid establishing any quantum connection with Wilcox, but now the man's soul would adhere to him with the tenacity of a lichen. He'd have to keep that dead-talker Lindstrom from touching him, or Wilcox's spirit might ruin everything.

The Peruvians laid out the bleeding corpse while Trent rushed up to put his gloved hand on Azure's shoulder. "You okay, boss?"

Azure swatted his hand away. "*Don't touch me!*" He pointed at the dead archaeologist. "Find his passport. Then get rid of him and everything else he came in contact with. We're moving camp by nightfall."

Trent essayed a grin, but his Method technique failed to conceal his unease. Azure staggered away from him, compulsively wiping his contaminated cheek.

As commanded, Trent and the other men gathered everything Abel Wilcox had touched—his tent, his bedroll, his books and notes, his campfire cookware—and tossed it all over the cliff's edge into the valley below. Last of all, they pitched the body itself off the mountain. Before it dropped beneath the cloud cover, the drifting limbs of the corpse spread-eagled in the air, as if the archaeologist were about to take flight.

They never heard the body hit ground.

2

Wolves at the Door

NATALIE LINDSTROM DID NOT RECOGNIZE THE CORPS Security agent who followed her to the movie theater that May afternoon: a man not much taller than she, of Southeast Asian Indian extraction, with slick black hair and sideburns. His gray suit seemed to blend chameleonlike into whatever background he passed.

She sighed and pretended not to notice him as she purchased her ticket, for which she used one of the few credit cards she hadn't already maxed out. *The N-double-A-C-C must be having higher turnover these days,* she thought. They must also have instructed their people against becoming overly familiar with the Violets they were ordered to intimidate, for the new agents never spoke to her. She actually became nostalgic for the days when she at least knew the names of the three agents assigned to her: George Langtree, Arabella Madison, and Horace Rendell. George used to share pizza and gossip with Natalie during his surveillance shift, and had even helped rescue her daughter, Callie, from the serial killer Vincent Thresher. George had since quit Corps Security, while Rendell had evidently been killed by Thresher when the murderer kidnapped Callie. That left Madison, catty fashion diva, as the only agent Natalie knew personally.

But there was one advantage to having these nameless rookies following her: they didn't know her tricks as well as the veterans and so were easier to lose when necessary.

Chameleon Man proved no exception. Natalie waited until the theater had lowered the house lights, then took her seat during a scene when the screen went dark to make it difficult for the agent to see where she was. The movie was one of those three-hour-plus epics Hollywood seemed increasingly fond of, and she left to go to the women's restroom twenty minutes into the picture, the canvas bag containing her pantsuit and alternate wig slung over her shoulder.

Satisfied that the agent hadn't followed her into the lobby, Natalie went into one of the stalls in the lavatory and changed into her suit. With no hair of her own, she easily swapped her blond wig for the chestnut brown one. Because her current clients demanded SoulScan readings to prove that her inhabitations were real, she'd kept her head shaved, enabling her employers to attach the machine's electrodes directly to her bare scalp and monitor the souls she summoned. Since she did not want Callie to be ashamed of being a Violet, Natalie no longer hid her violet irises on a daily basis, but today she needed to operate incognito, so she completed the disguise with a pair of contact lenses that turned her eyes a conventional shade of brown.

As scheduled, the car from Daedalus Aeronautics awaited her in the cinema's parking lot—an unmarked black Cadillac. The moment Natalie emerged from the theater, the driver started the engine.

Fifteen minutes later, they arrived at a tower of mirrored glass, home to the high-profile law firm retained by Natalie's client's company. After parking in the underground garage, they took a private, high-speed elevator up to the structure's top floor. At one time, such a ride would have made Natalie sick with fear about what would happen if the carriage suddenly plunged twenty stories. But that wasn't the fear that squeezed her stomach today.

I shouldn't do this, she thought, not for the first time. The North American Afterlife Communications Corps had never forgiven her for quitting the service. *You can forget about getting another job,* Delbert Sinclair, the Director of Corps Security, told her at the time. He had made good on his threat. The Corps blacklisted her from seeking conventional employment, and she found that even temp agencies mysteriously turned her down when, in desperation, she applied for ordinary office jobs. The Corps also did everything in its power to keep her from obtaining freelance Violet work in the private sector, and if the organization discovered that her current job was not only unauthorized but also illegal, she could end up in jail. Or, worse, the Corps could take custody of Callie, forcing the girl to become a new member of the NAACC.

Keeping herself and her daughter out of the Corps extracted an increasingly high price. Personal summoning sessions garnered a few hundred dollars here and there, not enough to feed and house a single mother and child. Natalie had already taken out a second mortgage on the condo as a debt consolidation loan, only to run up new credit-card balances to make ends meet when she couldn't hustle any under-the-table Violet gigs.

She watched the number on the elevator's digital floor counter rise to twenty, wanting to blame someone for her present predicament. Sid Preston, that slimy reporter from the *New York Post,* had promised her six figures for a posthumous interview with the victims in the Hyland murder case. If he'd paid up, she wouldn't have had to bother with the likes of Daedalus Aeronautics. Unfortunately, the journalist wasn't satisfied with the headline-making revelations she'd provided. When she refused to collaborate with him on a tell-all book about the Corps, Preston welched on her. The modest advance he'd given her hadn't lasted long, so she had to scrape up what work she could. The Daedalus offer paid as much as a hundred sessions with little old ladies who wanted to talk to their dead husbands, so she took it, praying that no one from the Corps recognized her in disguise.

Daedalus Aeronautics appreciated her discretion. The aircraft manufacturer, too, could lose a great deal if anyone discovered that it had employed Natalie Lindstrom.

The company driver led Natalie into a large, dim corner office and shut the door behind her. The tinted windows that formed two sides of the room glowed with the sunlit panorama of the city twenty stories below them. Three people sat at an elongated table, silhouetted by the aerial view, while a fourth hastened to greet Natalie.

"Ms. Lindstrom! Arnold Jarvis, Daedalus Aeronautics. We spoke on the phone." The man lifted his hand as if to offer it to her but shied from her touch, choosing to smooth his thinning hair instead. "Um, did you have any...problems?"

"No."

"Great, great." He did not introduce the three people at the table—a blond woman in a shoulder-padded business jacket flanked by two men in dark suits. "Well, we know you're on a tight schedule, and we're all set to go."

"So I see." Natalie circled around to examine the chair he indicated. Positioned opposite the long table, it resembled the chairs found in barbershops, only this one had been adapted for Sweeney Todd. Thick leather belts with metal buckles lolled from the chair's back, armrests, and footplate, ready to lash the writhing occupant to her seat. On a push-cart next to the chair rested an electronic device about the size of a microwave oven, six flat glowing lines tracing across its green monitor screen.

A SoulScan unit.

Jarvis took a coiled cable from the cart, plugged the jack into a port on the SoulScan, and fumbled to untangle the twenty jumbled electrodes at the cable's other end. "If you want to make yourself comfortable..."

Natalie settled herself in the chair and removed the wig from her shaved head. She was anything but comfortable, though, particularly when it became clear that Jarvis had never dealt with either a Violet or a SoulScan before.

"Ah! Sorry." He yanked off the first electrode he'd stuck to her scalp in order to position it more carefully over the tat-tooed node point.

She twitched as the electrode's surgical tape tore at her skin. "Here, let me."

Exhaling gratitude, Jarvis handed her the bundle of elec-trodes. She applied them with the help of a compact mirror from her purse, until her head resembled a bomb wired for detonation. The three backlit figures at the table watched the procedure without comment, even as Jarvis strapped Natalie to the chair with flustered clumsiness.

When he'd finished, Jarvis turned to the SoulScan unit and smoothed his hair again, a puzzled look on his face. The top three lines of the unit's screen now jittered with Natalie's brain waves, while the bottom three remained dormant, awaiting the presence of the summoned soul's consciousness. "Um...the manual said something about a button. Y'know, in case of emergencies."

Natalie extended the index finger of her bound left hand toward the glowing red disc on the SoulScan's control panel. Commonly known as the Panic Button, it could jolt the electromagnetic energy of the inhabiting soul out of her brain with a flood of electric current.

"Only push it if I start to die," Natalie instructed Jarvis.

He bobbed his head, blanching.

"Do you have a touchstone?"

"Huh? Oh...yeah." He dipped his thumb and forefinger into the breast pocket of his dress shirt and pulled out a small plastic pouch. "They used this to identify the body. The National Travel Safety Board crash investigators summoned him with one just like it."

Before she could object, he turned her right hand upward and poured the object onto her palm. Small and hard as a pebble, it glinted with yellow metal, like a nugget of stone laced with gold.

But this gold happened to be a dental filling and the pebble a human molar, its roots broken off and its enamel blackened with soot.

Natalie wanted to drop the thing, to shout that she wasn't ready yet, that she hadn't even started reciting her spectator mantra, but it was too late. Her fist closed on the tooth as if she'd just grabbed a high-tension power line, and the bottom three lines on the SoulScan screen zigzagged into spiky fangs of panic.

The soul was already knocking.

In an instant, Natalie forgot about Jarvis, about the office with its three silent observers, about herself. She now sat at the controls of an airliner, sticky with sweat, her breaths hot and rapid in the plastic cup of the oxygen mask that covered her nose and mouth. Through the dust pelting the windshield before her, she saw the plane's nose dipping as the cloudscape outside shifted to the right.

Next to her, the copilot jabbered distress messages to air traffic control in between long drafts of oxygen from his own mask. From the cabin behind them came the shrieking of men and women, the yowling of a baby.

With her thick, hairy-knuckled hands, Natalie pulled back on the stick, turned the wheel to the left, and pushed down on the left rudder pedal. The plane leveled off, but continued to yaw to the right.

Tail rudder's out, she found herself thinking. *Can I straighten out if I cut thrust in the right wing engines? Wait…I tried that before.*

Natalie separated herself from the dead pilot's desperation long enough to realize what was happening. The pilot was replaying his final struggle in endless variation, confining himself to an eternal flight simulator in which he sought a way to rescue an airliner that had already crashed.

Her objectivity restored, Natalie commenced reciting her spectator mantra:

> *Row, row, row your boat,*
> *Gently down the stream.*
> *Merrily, merrily, merrily, merrily!*
> *Life is but a dream . . .*

The repeated verse enabled her to retain consciousness while the pilot's soul inhabited her and, if necessary, to re-assert control over her body if he refused to leave.

In the meantime, she could share the dead man's thoughts and perceptions. He opened her eyes to discover Jarvis with his palm hovering over the SoulScan's Panic Button, his face more peaked than ever. "Ms. Lindstrom?"

"Lindstrom? My name's Newcomb." The pilot righted her body in the chair, and Natalie groaned with him at the twinge of a pulled muscle in her back.

That's gonna hurt, she thought. The epileptic contortions of inhabitation must have been particularly nasty this time.

"Ah, Captain Newcomb!" Jarvis smiled. "We hoped you could answer a few questions for us."

"Please . . . drop the 'Captain.' Call me Bill." Newcomb looked down at the female body in which he resided, at the leather belts that immobilized his limbs, then at the three figures who watched from the shadows on the other side of the table. "For the love of God, can't you people leave me alone? Haven't I already told you everything I know?"

"That's what we want to find out." In his element now, Jarvis took a clipboard and pen from the pushcart's lower tier and checked off the first of several queries. "Could you describe for us exactly how the accident transpired?"

Natalie could feel Newcomb wither inside her. They'd called him back from the dead only to have him relive the same horror and guilt that tortured him in his personal purgatory.

He drew air into Natalie's lungs as if the room had suddenly become depressurized, and her voice became gravelly with his sadness as he spoke. "As I told you before...we were climbing at an altitude of about eleven thousand feet when we heard a loud *thump* and the whole plane shuddered. I thought something had hit us."

One of the men at the table picked up a sheet of paper and bent toward the blond woman, tapping the page. "Collapse of the rear lounge area."

She nodded.

"When I tried to regain control of the plane," Newcomb continued, "the rudder pedals became stuck in the full left-rudder position."

"And what did you do to try to land the craft safely?" Jarvis asked, making another check mark on his clipboard list.

"Everything." Newcomb let Natalie's head drop back against the chair's headrest. "We radioed Detroit to clear us for a gradual descent and emergency landing. We almost made it, too. If I could have slowed us more after we touched down..." He couldn't bear to finish the thought.

The blond woman consulted one of the papers the man on the left handed her. "Captain Newcomb, do you remember a preflight consultation you had with the maintenance supervisor in charge of inspecting your aircraft?"

"Vaguely." The pilot remained distant, as if longing to disappear back into the void.

"And did the supervisor confer with you about a problem that one of his ground crewmen had securing a cargo compartment door?"

Newcomb sat up. "Door?"

"Yes." The blond woman read from the sheet in front of her. "The investigators have concluded that the cargo door blew off in flight. The rapid depressurization that resulted caused the aft passenger lounge to collapse, thereby severing hydraulic lines to the tail and incapacitating the tail rudder."

The pilot shook Natalie's head. "He told me they *had* secured that door."

"The door itself, yes. But a smaller vent door within the larger door remained open a crack, even when the crewman forced its latch into the locked position."

The vehemence of Newcomb's denial increased, but Natalie could feel his fear tighten around her heart. "The cargo door warning light never came on. I checked it both before and during the flight."

"Nevertheless, the supervisor alerted you to the problem and you agreed to let him sign off on the logbook to avoid delaying the flight. Isn't that correct?"

"Yes." Natalie heard the screams of the passengers echo in Newcomb's memory.

The blond woman folded her hands, a prosecutor's pinpoint gleam in her shaded eyes. "Captain Newcomb, are you

familiar with the term 'pencil whipping'—the deliberate fal-
sification of airline safety inspection reports?"

He sagged forward as far as the leather restraints of the
chair would allow. "Why couldn't you leave me in peace?"

Natalie ached with pity for him. *It's not your fault*, she
told him in the mind they shared. *They're trying to blame
you, but it's their plane that's at fault.*

But she knew Newcomb would not be consoled that easily. Thanks to Daedalus Aeronautics, he now blamed himself
not only for failing to save the plane but also for causing the
accident in the first place.

"I think we've got what we need," the blond woman told
Jarvis.

He glanced from Newcomb's stricken expression to the
SoulScan's Panic Button as if debating what to do. Natalie
knew she had to send the pilot away before Jarvis zapped
both of them.

You did your best to save those people, she reminded
Newcomb, for whatever good it might do. *You're not responsi-
ble for their deaths.*

Then she shifted from her spectator mantra to her protective mantra, the Twenty-third Psalm, and gently nudged
Newcomb's forlorn spirit from her mind:

The Lord is my shepherd; I shall not want...

Natalie regained control almost immediately; the pilot
seemed only too eager to sink back into the Pit and be forgotten. When she opened her eyes again, Jarvis smiled at her
with evident relief.

"Ms. Lindstrom? Excellent work! Now, let's get you out of that chair..."

She barely noticed him as he carelessly ripped the electrodes from her scalp and unfastened her restraints. Instead, she eavesdropped on the three anonymous figures at the table, who ignored her as if she were a computerized presentation screen that had just gone dark.

"You really think this will shield us from liability?" the man on the left asked the blond woman.

"Absolutely. If it goes to court, we'll pin it on maintenance and make it the carrier's problem."

The man on the right, who had so far remained silent, pushed his eyeglasses back up to the bridge of his nose. "What about the vent door latching mechanism? Shouldn't we...?"

"We'll issue a standard service bulletin," the woman replied. "If the airlines want to fix the problem, let 'em. Either way, we should be covered in case of another incident."

"*Incident.*" Was that what they called the killing of more than a hundred people?

If another crash happens, I'll be as much to blame as they are, Natalie thought, and for a moment, she shared the full weight of Newcomb's guilt. But she couldn't tell anyone without exposing herself to prosecution, and Daedalus Aeronautics knew it.

"We can't thank you enough for your assistance." Jarvis helped her to her feet and pressed a folded slip of paper into her hand. "For services rendered."

She didn't look at the paper until she sat in the black Cadillac while the company chauffeur drove her back to the movie theater. A cashier's check, so it couldn't be traced directly to Daedalus Aeronautics or its law firm. Fifteen thousand. Not bad for a day's work. But not enough for selling her soul.

Natalie removed her contacts and changed out of her disguise in the theater restroom and sat through the rest of the movie without really watching it. Immediately afterward, she let Chameleon Man tail her to her bank, where she deposited the check despite a nausea that nearly made her retch. At least she'd be able to cover the checks she'd already written.

Ordinarily, when Natalie had a Violet gig, she left Callie at the day-care center, but this was Tuesday—"Ms. Tabby day"— so she drove directly from the bank to the professional center in Orange. She vainly hoped that, unlike every other Tuesday for the past year, some miraculous progress had been made today, for Ms. Tabby was rapidly becoming a luxury she and Callie could no longer afford.

Except the therapist wasn't a luxury. Natalie was afraid that, without counseling, Callie might end up like Nora Lindstrom, Natalie's late mother. A Violet who once worked for the FBI, Nora had spent the last half of her life in a mental institution, psychologically ravaged by the spirit of Vincent Thresher, whom she had helped to convict and execute. Thresher had since inhabited Callie, filling her with the same horrors that had driven her grandmother insane.

Natalie parked her geriatric Volvo in the professional center's lot and ascended a flight of concrete stairs to the second floor of the complex. Proceeding along the terrace past a dentist's and an accountant's offices, she arrived at a door with a small plaque bearing engraved white words:

Carolyn Steinmetz, PhD
Preadolescent Psychology

The room beyond the door was as unprepossessing as the sign—walls of calming neutral colors with framed prints of fluffy anthropomorphic kittens in pastel clothing. On the waiting room's velour sofa lounged two genuine felines—one a long-haired, blue-eyed Persian, the other a striped tom that provided Ms. Tabby with her nickname. A third cat, a black-and-white one, batted around a velveteen mouse in the corner of the room. The lounge also contained a plethora of games, toys, and storybooks to keep the therapist's patients entertained, which was especially fortunate today, since, in order to make today's Violet gig, Natalie had to drop Callie off at the office almost three hours before her appointment.

Jon, the receptionist, sat at his desk wearing another in his seemingly inexhaustible collection of cartoon-character ties. He smiled at Natalie as she entered. "Callie's still in with the doctor, but they should be done anytime now."

He glanced toward the door into Steinmetz's office, which always remained open. No doubt wary of lawsuits, Ms. Tabby never allowed herself to be alone with her underage patients.

Through the doorway, Natalie could see the psychologist seated on the floor in the center of the room, her legs folded beneath her, her long black hair held up by a cross of intersecting chopsticks. She inclined her head far to the right as she murmured a soft question to Callie, who played listlessly with plastic animals from a Noah's ark set. Refusing to look up, she mumbled some answer that made Dr. Steinmetz nod. The psychologist then noticed that Natalie was watching and led Callie out to greet her mother.

Natalie forced a bright smile as she knelt to receive a perfunctory hug from her daughter. "Hey, baby girl! Did you have fun with Ms. Tabby today?"

"No." Callie stood with her hands in the pockets of her jeans, her violet gaze fixed on the door leading outside. She was only seven, but she had already acquired the prickliness of a teenager. Her mother recognized the attitude for what it was—an armor against fear.

Natalie made an apologetic face to Dr. Steinmetz. "Honey, that's not a nice thing to say—"

"That's all right," the psychologist said, her expression professionally placid. "Callie, would you like to pet Delilah for a minute while I talk to your mom?"

"Okay."

Ordinarily, Callie would have lavished attention on Delilah, her favorite among Ms. Tabby's cats. But today she trudged over, plopped down on the sofa, and stroked the Persian by rote, as if performing a homework assignment.

She's like me, Natalie thought, her smile rapidly losing its wattage. Having been a sullen, frightened child herself, she had been delighted when her daughter seemed to possess a lighthearted, boisterous good humor—the same sort of sunny disposition that had made Natalie fall in love with Callie's father, Dan Atwater.

But that was before Callie had endured the presence of Vincent Thresher.

Dr. Steinmetz motioned for Natalie to enter the office, then shut the door behind them. The office itself resembled a kindergarten playroom, the floor littered with toys, the only furnishings a long table and a few plastic chairs. The psychologist pulled a couple of these out from the table and invited Natalie to sit.

"I'm sorry if Callie was rude," Natalie began, but the psychologist cut her off.

"Not to worry. Actually, the hostility she's displaying is a sign of progress."

"Oh?" Natalie hoped the word didn't sound as sarcastic as it felt. Obviously, Dr. Steinmetz's definition of "progress" differed from hers.

"Yes. The anger is a defensive reaction—a simplification of emotions she can't understand or articulate yet. But she's beginning to remember."

A shiver skittered over Natalie's skin as she recalled the visions of depravity that infested her mind when Thresher had once possessed her: images of the victims whose torsos he'd embroidered with bleeding needlepoint sewn into the living flesh. The thought that he had stained Callie's innocence with such filth made Natalie sick with rage. "What has she told you?" she asked.

Steinmetz never seemed to blink, and the modulated quietness of her voice never changed, giving her the unnerving imperturbability of a grade-school librarian. "It's a bit fragmented. Callie still can't comprehend the psychopathic mind-set to which she was exposed. She only knows that it was *wrong*. And yet the inhabiting soul forced her to see things—to *do* things—that her instinctive morality abhors. Consequently, she feels guilt about actions and thoughts that she experienced but over which she had no control."

Tell me something I don't know, Natalie thought. "What can I do?"

"Encourage her to talk about what's bothering her, even if it means wheedling it out of her. Particularly about these dreams she's been having."

"Nightmares," Natalie corrected her. "And?"

Tiny frown lines appeared at the corners of the psychologist's mouth. "She's also harboring a certain amount of resentment about the loss of her father."

Natalie exhaled. "I know."

"How about you?"

Dr. Steinmetz waited patiently for a reply. Natalie didn't provide one. She didn't like being psychoanalyzed any more than Callie did.

"I'm...not sure we'll be able to make it next week," she said, both to end the discussion and because it was true. "I'll call to reschedule when I can."

But she didn't know if she would. Not with so many other demands on her meager finances. If only she could handle Callie's counseling herself, the same way she'd taken on her daughter's home-schooling and Violet training. That wasn't possible, however. Natalie could hardly help Callie with her problems when she couldn't even solve her own.

* * *

How about you?

The question reverberated in the silent air as Natalie drove Callie back to their condo. She knew her daughter missed Dan. He had died before she was born—slain while trying to save Natalie from the Violet Killer—but Callie's abilities as a Violet enabled her to know her father better than most ordinary children could ever hope to know theirs. For the first six years of her life, she had been able to summon her father's love, attention, and protection whenever she wanted.

Then Dan went to the Place Beyond—a realm from which even Violets could not call souls back.

No matter how many times Natalie repeated Dan's reasons for leaving—that Daddy had moved on to a place where he could be happy, that she and Callie needed to learn how to get along without him—she never managed to justify to her daughter the sudden, gaping void in their lives. In truth, she'd never really satisfied herself with those explanations, either. Natalie had never experienced such loss before, because death had never severed a relationship the way the Place Beyond had cut her off from Dan. Only now did she begin to understand what bereavement meant to ordinary people.

Always paranoid about the safety of her driving, Natalie waited for a red light before chancing a glance toward the rearview mirror. Ever since she'd read an article in the *L.A. Times* about children getting killed by exploding air bags, she'd made Callie sit in the backseat. In the mirror, Natalie saw her daughter staring out the window, her face hidden by a tumble of shoulder-length brown curls. Callie's stuffed bear, Mr. Teddy, sprawled beside her, ignored, its fur nappy with age and hugged thin in places.

"What did you and Ms. Tabby talk about today?" Natalie asked, trying to keep her tone conversational.

"Nothing."

"Oh, come on. You said you liked to visit her."

"Not anymore. She bugs me."

"Honey, that's not nice."

"Well, neither is Ms. Tabby."

"Callie!" Traffic started to move forward again, but Natalie darted a shocked glance at her little girl. "She's only trying to help you."

"Then she should leave me alone."

"That's *enough*." For the first time, Natalie started to empathize with her father for putting up with her own childhood rebelliousness.

"Are you really going out on a *date* tonight?" Callie scrunched her face as if her mother had threatened to serve liver and onions for dinner.

Natalie's mouth wrinkled. Frankly, she didn't feel like dealing with her prospective date, either, but it was probably too late to cancel. "You should give Alan a chance," she said, as much to herself as to her daughter. "He's a nice guy."

"That's what you said about *Phil*." Callie accented the name with disgust.

Natalie pretended not to hear, but the thought of that fiasco made her all the more apprehensive about the evening to come. Like most of the non-Violet guys who'd asked her out, Phil had an ulterior motive. A forty-four-year-old real-estate agent, he'd lost his wife in a car accident the previous year. It soon became clear that he wanted Natalie as a means of maintaining—and consummating—a relationship with the only woman he really loved.

It's not fair she died so young. Natalie's skin crawled as she recalled the sweaty heat of his hand on hers, the thirsting manner in which he moistened his lips. *You…you could give her another chance. We could all be a family together…*

She shook off the memory of Phil and tightened her grip on the Volvo's steering wheel. "Alan's different."

"Maybe." Callie went back to gazing out the window. "But no one's like Daddy."

No, baby girl, no one is, Natalie admitted, but only to herself. She'd tried to stop making that comparison, but every man she met, no matter how appealing, she found lacking in one regard: he wasn't Dan.

That same mixture of disappointment and skepticism hung over her when she got home and found a message from Alan on the answering machine in her kitchen.

"Hi, Nat." He blithely abridged her name, as if he'd known her three years instead of three days. "Just calling to confirm tonight. I can't wait! I thought we could go to this great steakhouse I know—"

"Joy." She hit the SKIP button.

"Ms. Lindstrom, this is Citibank Visa calling," a woman's nasal voice intoned. "We need to speak to you regarding your account—"

"Down, girl. You'll get your pound of flesh."

SKIP.

"Hey, kiddo," the next message began. "How are my two favorite ladies?"

Dad. Natalie grimaced. She'd been so busy, she hadn't called him in more than a month. At one time, that would have been normal; now it was inexcusable.

"Sorry to bother you, honey," Wade Lindstrom continued, his voice hoarse. Despite their reconciliation, he always sounded vaguely ashamed when talking to her. "There's been a little problem, and I thought I should let you know. I'm not at home right now, but you can reach me at..." He gave an unfamiliar number that Natalie scrawled on the pad next to the phone. "Ask the operator for Room 135. Talk to you soon, sweetheart."

The next message—a canned telemarketing pitch from the Corps—inquired whether she had reconsidered enrolling Callie in the Iris Semple Conduit Academy, the government school for Violets, where Natalie had spent her miserable childhood. Natalie barely heard the spiel. She knew her father's capacity for understatement. Wade Lindstrom's "little problem" would be anyone else's dire emergency.

"Wasn't that Grandpa?" Callie peeked into the refrigerator in search of a predinner snack. "Does he want us to visit?"

"I don't think so, honey." Natalie snatched the cordless phone from its cradle and punched in the number she'd transcribed, starting over when her quivering finger hit the wrong button. "Why don't you go upstairs and get ready for the babysitter?"

Callie slammed the fridge door. "I *am* ready."

"Well, I'm not. I'll come get you when I am."

"Can't *I* talk to Grandpa?"

"No. Now go."

She paced the kitchen, drawn-out ring-tones in one ear,

angry girl-steps hammering up the condo's staircase in the other. Natalie was horrified but not surprised when a receptionist for Nashua Memorial Hospital finally picked up. The operator put her through to Room 135, but Natalie had to endure another series of rings before her father answered.

"Yeah?" The dim, out-of-patience tone of an invalid.

The questions stumbled over each other in her haste to get them out. "Dad? Are you okay? What happened?"

"Oh! Hey, kiddo." Wade cleared the fatigue from his throat. "Now, it's nothing you should worry about, honey—"

"*What* is nothing I should worry about? What are you doing in the hospital?"

"I had some minor chest pains," he said, as if talking about a small earthquake or a tiny flood. "But the doc says I'll be fine after the operation."

"*Operation?* What operation?"

"Bypass. I'm supposed to go in tomorrow."

Natalie didn't respond until she thought she could speak without having her voice crack. "It must be pretty serious if they're doing it that soon. What's the prognosis?"

"Good." He cleared his throat again to strengthen his voice. "I'll be up to barbecuing and blackberry-picking before you know it."

He chuckled, but the reference to her daughter's favorite summertime activities only increased Natalie's anxiety. "Callie and I can be there in a few days. We can stay and help out while you recover from surgery."

"Look, I didn't mean to scare you. I'll be fine. That's why I called—to let you know I'm okay."

"Don't be ridiculous. Is Thursday soon enough?"

"Yeah…but don't feel like you have to drop everything on my account. I know you've got your own problems to worry about." The dismissal sounded halfhearted, like a hungry diner who refuses a second helping out of courtesy. "Uh…there was something else I had to tell you, too."

She waited, but he couldn't seem to broach the subject. "Yes?"

"Well, you know, business has been slower than usual…"

"I know." Natalie rolled her eyes. The government still blacklisted her father's climate-control installation and service firm because she had abandoned her post with the Corps.

"…so, to cut costs, we switched to a cheaper health plan a couple years back. Naturally, they buried some clause about 'preexisting conditions' in the fine print, so I'm going to have to pick up the tab for this thing myself."

"Do you have that kind of cash available?"

"Oh…yeah. Little here, little there—I'll scrape it together. I was thinking about selling the infernal business anyway, not that I'll get much for it. And I can always move back into the old house to reduce expenses, since it looks like I'm stuck with the place."

His laugh turned into a cough. The gloom of Natalie's guilt thickened. Her father couldn't sell his house because Vincent Thresher had murdered Wade's second wife there, and no one wanted to purchase a residence where a torture killing had occurred. Even Wade himself hadn't lived there since Sheila Lindstrom's death.

"…but that's all my concern," he went on, as if discussing a backed-up toilet. "Until I get things sorted out, though… the next check may be a little late."

A typical Lindstrom understatement, Natalie thought, her worry compounding tenfold. She knew Wade would sooner survive on dog food than stop sending money to help with Callie, so if his finances were that bleak, it meant he was the one who needed help...except Natalie didn't even have enough cash to cover her own crises, much less anyone else's.

"Don't worry about us, Dad," she said. "Take care of yourself."

"I will, honey. You do the same."

I love you. The words cowered behind Natalie's lips but refused to emerge, for she still felt like she hardly knew her father. "See you Thursday," she said instead.

"Only if you can make it. Thanks for calling, kiddo."

"Anytime."

They said inadequate good-byes and hung up. Without even setting down the phone, Natalie pawed through the local Yellow Pages in search of a travel agent who could book their plane tickets to New Hampshire. She dialed the first number she found, but at the same time the agent answered, the doorbell rang.

"Hold on just a second," she told him, and called up the stairs to her daughter. "Callie, Patti's here!"

She resumed her conversation with the travel agent, but a moment later the doorbell rang again and no one came to answer it. Natalie covered the phone's mouthpiece with her hand and shouted. *"Callie! Get the door!"*

Her daughter tromped down the stairs and yanked open the front door. She barely glanced at the figure on the doorstep before she turned to her mother. "It's not Patti. It's some *guy.*"

Her duty done, Callie stomped back up to her room. Natalie swiveled her head between her disappearing daughter and the nonplussed stranger waiting at the threshold. "Hey! What are you— Look, can I call you back?"

She hung up on the travel agent and went to the door to get rid of the "guy," who most likely wanted to sell her something.

He did not look like the average salesman. Wearing a herringbone tweed suit and white shirt open at the collar, the clean-shaven man stood with his hands behind his back and seemed to have no merchandise or advertising materials to foist on her. His prominent forehead and oval wire-framed glasses gave him a look of scholarly superiority as he flashed a smile. "Natalie Lindstrom, I presume?"

"Yes. Sorry about my daughter." Natalie tossed a wry glance toward the stairs behind her.

"Oh! No problem. She's a cute kid. Look, I have a business proposition I'd like to discuss—"

Ah, here it comes, Natalie thought. "I'm sorry, but you've caught me at a *really* bad time, and I don't think I'd be interested in what you have to sell anyway."

He chuckled. "I'm not selling anything. Permit me to introduce myself..."

He dipped a hand into the inside pocket of his jacket and produced a business card. "Dr. Abel Wilcox, Stanford University. I'd like to recruit your services as a conduit."

3

A Joyless Exercise in Futility

DESPITE HER ANNOYANCE AT THE INTRUSION, NATALIE took the man's card, which repeated his identity and added that he was an "Associate Professor of Archaeology." It also provided phone and fax numbers.

She shook her head and tried to give the card back. "I'm sorry, Dr. Wilcox, but I can't help you. I'm no longer with the N-double-A-C-C, and only Corps Violets are authorized to participate in historical research. You'll have to contact their Archaeology Division."

Wilcox left the card with her. "I'm well aware of the usual protocol, Ms. Lindstrom, but this expedition is a somewhat exceptional case." He looked over his shoulder, then past Natalie into the condo. "Would it be possible for me to come in for a minute?"

"No."

"I see." He smiled again. "As I was about to say...this is a proposal of some urgency. Unless we hurry, we may jeopardize one of the greatest discoveries in history, not to mention the lives of everyone involved."

"And how am I supposed to change that?" Preoccupied

with the problems of her dad and her daughter, Natalie did not want to deal with this conversation.

Wilcox gave a nervous laugh and pressed his hands together. "You force me into a rather embarrassing admission. The people I'm working with…their position is rather *delicate*."

"You mean illegal." Natalie recognized the tenor of this preamble. Arnold Jarvis had employed the same circumspect manner in approaching her for the Daedalus Aeronautics job.

The professor conceded the fact with a bob of his head. "For lack of a better term. But sometimes we have to defy the letter of the law to uphold its spirit."

"Sorry. Not interested." She moved behind the door to slam it.

"Please, Ms. Lindstrom!" He leaned into the door frame in earnest appeal. "You're an artist, aren't you? Could you stand by while someone burnt the *Mona Lisa* or whitewashed the Sistine Chapel?"

She held the door. "How did you know I was an artist?"

"We researched your history with the Corps before selecting you for this opportunity. The fact that you worked for the Archaeology Division and applied for admission to the Art Division weighed heavily in your favor. I saw some of your work and, for what it's worth…I think the N-double-A-C-C made a big mistake assigning you to law enforcement."

"Uh-huh." The memory of past disappointments did not improve Natalie's mood. "So is someone about to burn the *Mona Lisa* or whitewash the Sistine Chapel?"

"In a manner of speaking. Our dig is in Peru, and you may have heard about the systemic corruption in the country's government. If any of these corrupt officials got wind of how valuable our finds are, irreplaceable antiquities might be confiscated and sold or, worse, melted down for their metal before they could ever be cataloged and studied. And there's no telling to what lengths these thieves would go to keep the artifacts for themselves."

"You still haven't answered my first question: What difference would I make?"

"Working with either a Corps conduit or a Peruvian Violet would force us to reveal and perhaps sacrifice a large portion of our find to the Peruvian government. Many of the most precious artifacts might end up in private collections or destroyed. Since you no longer serve the Corps, you could help us get these treasures to legitimate museums for study and preservation before the thieves find out about them."

Natalie groaned and let her head loll against the doorjamb. "Look, it sounds like a worthy cause and all, but I just can't afford to—"

"We're prepared to pay you four hundred thousand dollars."

She glanced up. "Excuse me?"

Wilcox drew a deep breath, as if discussing money made him uncomfortable. "We know how valuable your skills are, and we want to give you adequate compensation. We're offering you a hundred thousand now and three when the job's done."

"Too good to be true, I would say." Despite the queasy feeling the offer gave her, Natalie couldn't help doing the math: pay off the second mortgage, clear out the credit cards, help pay for Dad's surgery, and maybe have enough spare

change left over for Ms. Tabby to treat her daughter's neu-
roses—all without helping corporate criminals get away with
dangerous lies. "Where would I have to go to do this?"

"It's fieldwork in the Andes, I'm afraid. But we'll provide
you with full room and board and as many amenities as we
can. Red-carpet treatment, all the way."

"Even when we get sent to a Peruvian prison?"

The archaeologist laughed. "The expedition's sponsor has
taken every precaution to prevent that possibility. You have
nothing to worry about. And you'll help ensure that some of
the greatest remnants of Incan civilization end up in museums rather than in the hands of fortune hunters."

Natalie sighed, irritated by her own temptation. "When
would I start?"

"As soon as possible, but no later than the end of the
week."

"And how long would the job last?"

"If we're lucky, only a few days. Certainly no more than a
week or two."

Natalie curled her lips over her teeth and bit down on
them to keep from answering too quickly. "I don't know. I'll
need some time to think it over."

Breaking eye contact, she saw Patti Murdoch, the babysitter, coming up the front walk behind Wilcox.

"Hey, Ms. Lindstrom!"

"Hey, Patti. Glad you could make it." Relieved, Natalie dismissed Dr. Wilcox with a flick of the business card she still
held. "I've got your number."

"Of course." The archaeologist raised his hands, backed
away. "Feel free to sleep on it. But please get back to me as

soon as you can. We must act soon if we're going to save these precious relics."

He gallantly offered Patti his place on the doorstep and strode down the front walk to the white Nissan parked at the curb.

The stringy teenager, who'd only recently exchanged the grillwork of her braces for a single-wire retainer, watched him drive away with offhand curiosity. "Who was that?"

Natalie shook her head. "Just some guy."

But she slipped his card into the front pocket of her jeans anyway.

The news from her dad had provided Natalie with the perfect excuse to get out of that night's joyless exercise in futility— also known as her date with Alan. As soon as Wilcox left, she returned to the phone, intending to call Alan and cancel, but she hadn't even finished entering his cell phone number before the doorbell rang again.

"What *else?*" She slammed down the receiver and marched back to the front door. When she yanked it open, Alan grinned at her like a men's fashion advertisement, the sleeves of his dress shirt rolled to the elbows with affected casualness.

"Hey!" His musky cologne preceded him as he entered without waiting to be invited. "Hope you don't mind my getting here a little early. Came straight from work to beat the traffic."

"No…of course not." Natalie tugged at the tail of her baggy pullover. "Hope you don't mind if I take some time to get ready."

"Take as long as you like! I'll get to know the little lady here." He sauntered over to the base of the stairs and squatted at eye level with Callie, whom Patti Murdoch had finally coaxed out of her bedroom. "How's the prettiest girl in the world today?"

Callie didn't answer but glanced at her mother with her brows lowered. "I've got some homework to do."

Patti moved to stop Callie's escape back to her room, but Natalie shook her head.

Alan laughed off the affront. "Smart kid."

"I'll only be a few minutes," Natalie told him, and followed her daughter up the stairs.

In the bathroom, she did a slapdash paint job on her makeup and changed into a knee-length skirt, nylons, and halter top, all the while wondering why she took the trouble. She considered simply telling Alan the truth—that her dad had just suffered a heart attack and she really wasn't in the mood for fun tonight—but somehow the idea of revealing something so personal about her life and having to listen to his trite fabrications of sympathy seemed even more wearisome than going through with the thing.

"You look great!" Alan gushed after she'd given Patti some hasty instructions and accompanied him out of the condo.

"Best I could do on short notice." Anxiety tightened Natalie's midriff as Alan opened the passenger-side door of his cherry-red sports car for her. "Seventies Corvette, isn't it?"

Alan beamed. "Ah! The woman knows a classic when she sees it."

"Oh, yes." Natalie knew it well from some of the automobile crash investigations she'd assisted: fiberglass body, no air bags.

"You like cars?" he asked as they got in.

"No." She strapped herself to the seat with the safety belt and gripped the armrest as if bracing herself for a space shuttle launch.

Natalie had initially resorted to dating to disrupt her recurrent longing for Dan in much the same way she would turn up a radio's volume to drown out her own thoughts. The scheme backfired, however, for she inevitably compared each of her prospective beaus with her dead love.

Dan would have asked me something about myself by now... or at least told a bad joke, she mused as she nodded and feigned murmurs of interest in the anecdote Alan was telling about his work. He'd ordered prime rib for both of them without bothering to find out that she was a health fanatic who favored lean protein and loathed red meat. She left the rare beef, untouched and bleeding, on its platter and continued to nibble at her salad.

Liv, a friend who'd been her hairdresser back when Natalie still had hair, had prodded her into meeting Alan for the first time. *You'll like him,* Liv had promised. *He's cute, and he's my friend Jo's brother, so you know he's not, like, some freak from the Internet or the personals or whatever. And Jo says he's good with her kids. I told him about you, and he says that... you know, that it won't bother him.*

And *it* didn't bother him. On the contrary, Alan seemed

delighted that she was a Violet—and perhaps she should have seen that as a warning sign.

He finished expounding on the office politics at his company, dunked a chunk of beef in the cup of au jus, and forked it into his mouth. "So how's the ghost business going?" he asked while chewing.

"Fine." Natalie's stock answer, even though the work was anything but fine. "It's nice to be self-employed."

Alan chortled, his mouth full, and shook his head. "You're just like me. We waste our talent working for idiots." He leveled his gaze at her. Unlike most people, he didn't avoid looking into her freakish eyes, which she hadn't bothered to hide behind contacts. "C'mon, Natalie. Don't tell me you haven't thought how much money you *could* be making as a conduit."

Natalie remembered Dr. Wilcox's offer, the fee she'd scorned that afternoon. Four hundred thousand.

"I do okay," she said.

"Yeah, and I make a decent living designing computer chips that make my bosses a fortune. If *I* held those patents, I'd be a multimillionaire by now." Alan leaned forward, lowered his voice. "That's why I think we should work together."

Shoulda seen this coming, Natalie thought. "What do you have in mind?" she asked, although she could easily guess.

"Simple. You have access to the greatest minds in history—everyone from Archimedes and da Vinci to Edison and Einstein. I have the technical know-how to make their inventions a reality. We market the results and—poof!—we own the next Microsoft." He mimed a little explosion with his hands and smirked as if he'd performed a magic trick.

Natalie grinned, too, but not for the same reason. Alan

evidently wasn't aware that the NAACC had tried for decades to exploit deceased scientists with only minimal success. The problem was that even the greatest geniuses of the past proved of little use when they'd missed a decade or more of technological advancement. Summoning them for current research was akin to asking an aboriginal medicine man to perform brain surgery.

Natalie decided not to burst Alan's bubble—at least not until she'd toyed with him a bit. For the first time during the meal, she picked up the glass of merlot he'd ordered for her. As a rule, she never drank alcohol—and not simply because she was paranoid about her health. If a Violet lost mental control while intoxicated, she might not be able to defend herself against an unwanted inhabitation. However, Natalie was not above using the drink as a prop. Pretending to sip the wine, she relaxed in her chair and smoothed the sardonic amusement from her voice. "And this...*partnership* of ours. Would it be business or pleasure?"

"Both." He gave her a suggestive look, which he doubtless intended to be charming.

"You do realize that there are risks involved with inhabitation..."

He shrugged off the warning. "No sweat. I've read up on the SoulScan. I can jerry-rig a Panic Button to zap you if a soul starts acting up."

"How thoughtful of you." She weighed the wineglass in her palm, peering into it as if it were a simmering cauldron. "But souls don't always wait to be summoned, you know. Sometimes they knock."

He scooped a spoonful of baked potato from the peel. "Knock?"

"Oh, yeah. That's when—" Natalie let out a mock exclamation of pain and set down her glass, putting a hand to her forehead.

"Natalie? What is it?"

"It's nothing. Happens all the time." She puffed several deep breaths, eyes shut. "I can handle it."

She laid her palms flat on the table, her arms shaking as if she strained to steady herself. An instant later, her right wrist lashed out and knocked over the wineglass. It sloshed merlot on the tabletop, then rolled off to shatter on the floor.

Alan averted his eyes, saw that everyone in the steakhouse was staring at their booth, and looked back at Natalie, more embarrassed than concerned. "Look, if you're sick or something, we can—"

"No, I'm fine." She dry-heaved and let a little spit dribble down her chin. "I...I summoned this ax murderer once, and ever since—"

She wrenched her head sideways, rolled her eyes up beneath her jutting brows. Their waitress approached, accompanied by a busboy with a mop, but the two of them shied back when Natalie gave a glottal hiss.

"Let me IN." Her hand patted the place mat, landed on the steak knife beside her plate, snapped closed on its wooden handle.

Still fluttering her eyelids for effect, Natalie couldn't fully savor the look on Alan's face, but she did enjoy the lovely shades of green and white that blanched his tan skin as he squirmed out of the booth and scuttled away.

The waitress inched forward, asking if she needed an ambulance, but by that time Natalie was too convulsed with laughter to answer.

A true gentleman, Alan not only ran off without paying for their aborted dinner, he also left Natalie without a way to get home. She picked up the tab and was about to call a taxi when inspiration struck.

Bella, she thought with a crooked half-smile, and sauntered out of the restaurant.

Arabella Madison, the last of the original Corps Security agents assigned to shadow Natalie, waited beside her Acura in the parking lot outside. Wearing a black minidress that exposed legs as long as a gazelle's, she looked as if she, not Natalie, had a hot date tonight. The agent was evidently doing calf raises to kill time, balancing on one foot and repeatedly lifting the spike heel of her patent-leather boot from the pavement, but she stopped and grinned as Natalie approached. "I see you already scared off another one. Must be a personal record."

"I'm working on my technique," Natalie replied. "Look, could you be a dear and give me a ride home?"

Madison acted as if she'd just chipped a nail. "You're kidding me, right?"

"Why not? You're going that way anyway, aren't you?" Natalie nodded toward the passing traffic on the street. "Or I could hitchhike, if you prefer."

The agent gave her eyes a Valley Girl roll and unlocked the Acura. "Get in."

"Thanks." Natalie smirked as she plopped into the passenger seat. "Gee, this is almost like Girls' Night Out. Wanna rent a few DVDs and make some popcorn?"

Madison swung in behind the steering wheel. "*Please.* Once I get promoted, I never want to see you again."

"See? We have so much in common. I don't want to see you, either."

"Ha-ha. You should be a comedian. Oh, wait! That's right—you can't *get* a job."

Natalie couldn't dredge up a comeback before they peeled out of the parking lot. The agent sensed that she'd touched an open wound and swiftly started to rub salt into it.

"Employment situation really sucks right now, doesn't it? There is just *nothing* out there. We're so lucky to have a steady paycheck—oops!" Bella put a hand to her cheek in mock distress. "I'm so sorry. How forgetful of me."

Natalie ground her teeth and wondered if she should have hitchhiked instead. "And you have to stab *how* many backs to get this promotion of yours?"

"Hey, at least I'm trying to move up in the world."

"By punishing my family."

"No, Natalie, that's your job—the only one you're good at, as far as I can tell. My job is to make you come to your senses and return to work for the Corps." The agent gave her a sidelong look, and for once she sounded less like a harpy and more like a concerned older sister. "It's time you stopped thinking about yourself and started thinking about your child's future. You might as well accept the fact that the Corps isn't going to let you work for anyone else as long as you live.

That's not my fault—it's just the way things are. The sooner you recognize that, the sooner both of us can move on."

What she said was far worse than her usual snide pleasantries and implied threats. Natalie could parry those with a witty riposte, but serious advice struck straight to her heart, especially since it echoed her own self-recrimination.

The Acura squealed to a stop in front of the condo, and Madison stabbed Natalie with another glare. "Regardless of what you decide, *I* do not intend to spend the rest of my life parked outside your house every night, and I will do whatever it takes to keep that from happening. You can save both of us a lot of grief if you go back to the N-double-A-C-C. Chew on that, won't you?"

"Yes. I will." Natalie knew she was doomed to think about everything the agent had said whether she wanted to or not. "Thanks for the ride, Bella. We should carpool more often."

The sarcasm was toneless and flat. Natalie got out of the Acura and trudged up the front walk to the condo, aware that the home awaiting her would offer no shelter.

"You're back early," Patti Murdoch observed as Natalie stepped through the front door. "How'd the date go?"

"Better than I expected." She didn't smile.

"Oh." The babysitter followed her up the stairs. "I put Callie to bed about an hour ago. I don't know if she's asleep now, though. I think she's having some more of those... dreams."

"Mmm." Natalie stopped outside Callie's bedroom,

inclining her ear to the door. Through it, she could hear her little girl's voice, murmuring with feverish quickness:

> *Now I lay me down to sleep,*
> *I pray the Lord my soul to keep…*

Callie did not continue with the verse "If I should die before I wake…" but instead repeated the first rhyme over and over. It was the new protective mantra she'd practiced recently during the Violet training sessions Natalie gave her. But whom was she trying to keep out? Thresher? Or did Callie simply imagine that the killer was knocking, trying to infest her innocence with his appalling lust?

The child's prayer ended with an abrupt, rattling gurgle, as if from a throat constricted by angry hands. When Callie spoke again, she rasped with adult menace. *"You little minx! Do you know what you've done to me?"*

"I think you'd better go now," Natalie told Patti, handing her the evening's fee. She waited until the babysitter departed before entering the bedroom.

Inside, Callie writhed in her crumpled teddy-bear sheets, spitting curses like cobra venom. Climbing onto the bed, Natalie pushed down the small fists that pummeled her and straddled her daughter.

"Come on, baby girl," she urged. "Fight him."

Her stomach pumping like a blacksmith's bellows, Callie huffed several breaths and shrieked, *"Leave me alone!"*

The baby fat of her cheeks drooped into a jowly, hangdog growl. "Leave you alone?" Her voice dropped to a hiss, mocking itself. "You *killed* me, you little freak!"

Natalie fought to hold Callie still as another eruption of fury racked the girl's body. "The mantra, honey. Say the mantra."

Her daughter's violet eyes popped open, and the face bunched in hatred. "*You.* If it hadn't been for you and your brat, I wouldn't be dead."

The vitriol of the expression reminded Natalie of someone, but she couldn't decide whom. It didn't sound like Thresher. What other soul would hate her and her daughter so much?

"The mantra, Callie." She peered straight into the glaring eyes, trying to speak to the mind behind them. "Say the mantra."

Callie kicked her legs and attempted to twist her wrists from Natalie's grip. Her chest heaved as breath bubbled out of her in drowning gasps. Her face reddened, its expression flickering from angry to fearful, like an optical illusion whose subject changes according to the viewer's perception. Finally, she coughed out a phrase.

"I p-pray the Lord..."

"That's it, honey. What do you pray?"

"...my soul...MY soul...to keep!"

The tension melted from Callie's limbs, and she bawled as if awakened from a nightmare she knew would come again.

Letting go of her wrists, Natalie scooped Callie into a hug. "It's okay, baby girl. He's gone now."

"No, he isn't!" she wailed. "He's *always* here."

Natalie thought of the conversation she'd had with Dr. Steinmetz about Vincent Thresher.

... the inhabiting soul forced her to see things—to do things— that her instinctive morality abhors ...

"Who is it, honey?" she asked. "Is it the bad man we've talked about?"

Callie shook her head, wiping mucus from her face. "Nope. It was the mean man. The one who took me away when I was staying with Aunt Inez and Uncle Paul."

Rendell. Now Natalie knew where she'd seen that expression of festering resentment before. A former associate of Arabella Madison, Corps Security agent Horace Rendell had plotted for years to pry Natalie's daughter away from her in order to obtain the child for the NAACC—and a hefty bonus for himself. He'd finally resorted to kidnapping Callie while she was in the temporary care of Natalie's friend Inez Mendoza and her husband, Paul.

"He says I hurt him." Callie gulped air in between sobs. "That's why he won't leave me alone—*ever*."

You killed me, you little freak! Natalie had heard Rendell rasp with Callie's voice. "How did he say you ... hurt him?"

"He *showed* me how," Callie said. "I stuck a needle into him, and it made him so sick and dizzy that he fell down and went to sleep." She covered her eyes, as if seeing the scene again. "When he fell down, I laughed at him. Except it *wasn't* me! He was mean, but I wouldn't do that to anyone."

"I know, sweetheart." *But Vincent Thresher* would *do that,*

Natalie thought. Thresher loved to stick needles in people and laugh at them as they died. Rendell obviously didn't realize that a killer had inhabited Callie's five-year-old body, so he blamed her for his own murder—and seemed intent on punishing her for it. That was one of the hazards of being a Violet. When people hated you, even death could not end their wrath.

"He made me feel what it was like," Callie sniffled, her words hushed to a whisper. "What it was like to get so sick and…go to sleep like that. And what it was like *after* that." She pressed her face against her mother's shoulder, her tears dampening the bare skin of Natalie's shoulder. "I'd never do that to *anyone*."

"I know you wouldn't, honey." Natalie gently rocked her, brushing the tangled hair from Callie's eyes. "Have you talked to Ms. Tabby about this?"

She felt Callie's cheek wobble against her chest as the girl shook her head.

"I think you should." Natalie clutched her child more tightly, calculating the thousands of dollars Callie's therapy would cost.

For a moment, she considered taking Bella's advice and going back to the Corps. If it had only been her own freedom at stake, she would gladly have sacrificed it. But she knew that the Corps would not relent until they had Callie, too.

Just one big payday, just to give me some time to regroup, Natalie thought, and wondered if she still had that archaeologist's business card in the pocket of her jeans.

4

Travel Plans, Treasure Hunts

DR. WILCOX SEEMED QUITE AMUSED BY THE DISGUISE she wore to their rendezvous the following morning. "I like the hair," he said as they took their coffee out to the café's patio. "Red is a good color for you."

"Thanks." Natalie hoped red was good for her, since her cheeks felt as hot and flushed as boiled lobsters.

She'd put on the coppery wig in order to lose Chameleon Man at the local mall. Before he died, Dan always used to tease a smile out of her by saying that she looked good with whatever color wig she happened to be wearing at the moment. One of the last things he told her before he went to the Place Beyond was that, someday, another man would give her the same compliment. Though she'd been trying to cut down on caffeine, Natalie took a long sip of her latte, hoping it would clear her head of the emotions aroused by the professor's flattery.

"I'm so glad you've chosen to consider our offer, Ms. Lindstrom." Dr. Wilcox sat back, resting the leather elbow patches of his tweed jacket on the arms of his chair. "It's truly a once-in-a-lifetime opportunity."

"Thank you for inviting me, Professor." Relieved that he

wasn't rushing her, Natalie scooted her own chair over to move into the shade of the parasol above their wrought-iron patio table. "I need you to answer a few questions before I can make a commitment."

"Absolutely. I want you to feel completely comfortable with your decision." He cradled a cappuccino in one hand and spooned milky foam into his mouth, dabbing his lips with a napkin when he set the cup down.

Before setting up this meeting, Natalie had done some research on the Internet to make sure Wilcox was legit. She ordered his book about the conquest of the Incas from an online bookseller and found his picture among the staff profiles on the Stanford University Web site. He seemed to have put on a few pounds since that picture was taken, but otherwise looked the same. Natalie had even phoned Stanford's Archaeology Department and asked to speak to Dr. Abel Wilcox, but the department secretary informed her that the professor was on sabbatical for the semester.

Confirming his credentials only partially reassured her, however. "University expeditions don't usually have hundreds of thousands of dollars to throw around," she pointed out.

Wilcox laughed. "Alas, too true!"

"Who's your sponsor?"

"Are you familiar with Azure PLC?"

"No."

"Then perhaps you've heard of Nathan Azure himself..."

Natalie shrugged and shook her head.

Wilcox prompted her, as if unable to believe anyone wouldn't know to whom he referred. "Multimillionaire philanthropist? Heir to the Azure mining empire?"

"Forgive me—I skipped the last issue of *Fortune.*"

He chuckled. "Well, as it happens, Mr. Azure has dedicated his life—and his considerable wealth—to preserving Incan historical artifacts for posterity. We're lucky to have him for a patron."

"No doubt." Natalie swigged some more coffee, discovered that she'd already drained the paper cup. "Who does he want me to summon?"

"Ah! That's the most exciting aspect of this project. You'll enable us to speak directly to one of the most famous explorers in history—the conqueror of Peru himself, Francisco Pizarro."

"I'm honored." Natalie had taken only high-school-level history classes at the Corps School, but what little she recalled about Pizarro made her loath to make his acquaintance. Like Cortés and the other Spanish conquistadors, Pizarro seemed to be a rapacious, genocidal predator intent on stripping the wealth and freedom from any native peoples who crossed his path. Having summoned a few Roman soldiers during her brief stint in the NAACC's Archaeology Division, Natalie knew from experience that there was no glamour in meeting killers from the past. Indeed, nothing dispelled the romance of war faster than to relive its dirty, fetid bestiality through the memories of those whose lives it had claimed.

Still, the work would be no more unpleasant than when she summoned murder victims for the West Coast Crime Division, and the pay was far better—four hundred thousand for a few days of her time. But the size of the fee only increased her unease about accepting it.

If it sounds too good to be true...

"Why do I need to go to Peru?" she asked Wilcox. "Why can't you simply bring the touchstone to me so I can summon Pizarro here?"

The professor leaned over the table as if it were a lectern. "You have to understand—archaeology is an art, not a science. There were no global positioning systems in Pizarro's day. There weren't even any maps for him to follow or to record the location of his cache. He found his way via the landmarks and geographical features around him. In order to relocate the artifacts, he may need to see that region of the Andes again—through you. Therefore, we'll need you to summon him on a day-to-day basis to guide us until we actually pinpoint the treasure's location."

"And how long do you think *that* will take?"

"I'd be surprised if you'll have to remain in camp even a week. With any luck, we'll have you back by Memorial Day. Now, I must tell you, the conditions will be a bit primitive, but you'll have every comfort and convenience we can provide during your stay." He paused, as if anticipating another query. "Um...not to put any pressure on you, but how soon would you be ready to leave?"

Natalie tapped her empty coffee cup on the table, reluctant to give any sign of acceptance.

"Not before next week." She refused to leave without first making sure Dad came through his operation okay. "And, because of the unusual risks involved, I want half a million for my commission."

Wilcox gave a nervous laugh, shaking his head. "Mr. Azure is a generous man, but—"

"Up front."

The professor puckered his lips in sudden displeasure. "I'm afraid that won't be possible. I'm sure you can understand our position. As I said, though, Mr. Azure *has* authorized me to give you a hundred thousand cash advance as a token of good faith."

His expression remained open, like that of a tennis player awaiting a return volley. Natalie balanced the risks and rewards. Even if Azure cheated her the way Sid Preston had, she'd still end up with a hundred grand, which was five times what she'd grossed from her freelance work the whole past year.

"Five hundred thousand—two hundred in advance—or the deal's off," she said, half hoping Wilcox would get exasperated and give up on her.

The professor steepled his hands in front of his face. "I'm sorry. We know you're worth ten times what we can pay you, but four hundred thousand is all our budget will allow."

"Two hundred in advance?"

Wilcox frowned but nodded. "I'll see if we can accommodate you, but I'll need your commitment right away. Are we agreed?"

Natalie drew a deep breath. Another below-board freelance assignment, but at least this one offered more money and a little adventure. *Just one big payday*, she thought—a line that had become another sort of mantra for her lately, one to egg herself on.

"Assuming you keep your end of the deal...then, yes, I'll do it."

"Splendid!" He extended a hand across the table. "Then let me welcome you—"

She didn't move, and Wilcox lowered his arm.

"There's a problem. Corps Security agents are assigned to watch me around the clock. Hence the getup." She indicated her red wig and green contacts. "If I hop a plane to Peru, they're bound to tell their bosses about it. If they discover I'm involved in anything illegal, they could take away my daughter."

"Hmm...I don't blame you for hesitating. I wouldn't want you to do anything that might hurt your family." He pondered for a moment. "These agents, do you think they would respond to some...financial incentive? You know—to report to the Corps that you're safe and sound at home during the whole time you're in Peru?"

Natalie considered Chameleon Man, Arabella Madison, and the graveyard shift operative, whom she'd barely seen. "I know job dissatisfaction is high among them," she said, "and the daytime stooges seem pretty mercenary. You'd have to bribe whatever agents were assigned to me when we left. The graveyard guys work from eleven at night to seven in the morning, so if they didn't see me, they'd probably just assume I was in the house, asleep. You might not have to worry about them. But that leaves Bella."

"Bella?" Wilcox waited for her to elaborate. "A friend of yours?"

"Hardly. Arabella Madison is one of the agents, and she's bucking for a promotion. Turning me in could be the chance she's been waiting for."

Natalie remembered Madison's voice snipping like shears. I *do not intend to spend the rest of my life parked outside your*

*house every night, and I will do whatever it takes to keep that
from happening.*

The archaeologist crooked his mouth in a mischievous
half-grin. "Suppose I told her I only wanted to buy some pri-
vacy while I whisked you off for a romantic getaway?"

Natalie gave a dry laugh. "She'd know you were lying.
You're far too normal, attractive, and intelligent to be interested in me."

"You do yourself an injustice, Ms. Lindstrom. Your unique
gifts aside, anyone would be delighted to have such charming
company."

Natalie's pulse fluttered, whether from excitement or
anxiety she couldn't be sure. "Uh . . . this is strictly a *business* relationship, right?"

The professor raised his hands to halt her train of
thought. "Not to worry. I assure you, I'll arrange private accommodations for you for the duration and will keep our as-
sociation solely a professional one. If you feel that I or anyone
involved in the expedition has mistreated you in any way, you
may withdraw at any time and keep your retainer as a for-
feited deposit."

"Thanks."

An unexpected disappointment tinged her relief. To be
honest, Wilcox *was* more normal, attractive, and intelligent
than any of the men she'd dated since Dan died—the only
one, in fact, who didn't make her want to flee in terror. And
she couldn't help but notice that he didn't wear a wedding
ring.

This is strictly business, Natalie reminded herself as she stood to shake the archaeologist's hand. "I look forward to working with you, Dr. Wilcox."

He rose to accept the gesture. "Please, call me Abe. If you call me Dr. Wilcox, I might mistake you for a student, and we wouldn't want that. And may I call you...?"

She smiled. "Natalie. Yes."

"Well, Natalie, if it would not exceed the bounds of propriety, I'd like to treat you to dinner to celebrate our agreement."

As a Violet, Natalie was accustomed to making other people uncomfortable with her gaze. Now, however, she found the professor's hazel eyes discomfiting, and she dug in her purse for her car keys to avoid looking at them. "Gosh... Callie and I are going to New Hampshire in two days, and I've got so much to do before then. And then I've got to take her to stay with her grandparents up in northern California—"

"Where in northern California? Close to the Bay Area?"

"Sort of. A three-hour drive."

"Perfect! I can pick you up. We'll have to spend the night in Frisco anyway in order to fly out the following morning. If you'd like, I'll take you to my favorite vegetarian restaurant."

No red meat, Natalie thought, impressed. She wondered if Wilcox was really as much of a health nut as she was or whether the Corps dossier he'd read included her eating preferences as well as her interest in art.

"That sounds great... Abe. Assuming you hammer out all the final arrangements—and get those Corps agents off my tail."

"Don't worry about them." He gave a winning smile. "I can be very persuasive."

5
Flying and Other Fears

WHEN BOOKING PLANE TICKETS TO NEW HAMPSHIRE, Natalie made sure that none of the flights happened to be on a Daedalus Aeronautics jet. Despite this precaution, she spent most of the trip braced against the back of her seat, sucking shallow breaths as her old fear of flying reasserted itself. Even the slightest shudder of the plane's fuselage made her wonder if the passenger cabin was about to cave in, and when she closed her eyes, she again felt Captain Newcomb's panic as he fought to bring his aircraft to heel, the clouds drifting past the windshield as the plane veered out of control.

Callie, who'd never been forced to participate in a crash investigation, had no such phobia and insisted on keeping the window shade up so she could see the scenery. "Ooh! Look, Mommy—it's the Grand Canyon!" she bubbled, pointing at the enormous pit 20,000 feet below them.

Natalie dared a quick look out the window but the view made her hyperventilate. "Yes, honey. It's beautiful."

She swiveled her head back toward her right, forgetting that Arabella Madison sat across the aisle from her. The Corps Security agent glanced up from a copy of *Vogue* and gave her an arch, quizzical look, as if to ask whether she'd finally wised up. Whenever Natalie took a trip, the Corps always sent one of her assigned agents to keep her under surveillance until a couple of the regional Security people could cover the other shifts. As luck would have it, she had to travel with Bella dogging her, a constant reminder of their last conversation—about Natalie's selfishness and failure to provide for her family.

Only Callie's excitement made the trip bearable. After visiting her dad in the New Hampshire hospital, they planned to return to California, to Lakeport, where Dan's parents had kindly offered to care for Callie while Natalie went to South America. The prospect of seeing so many grandparents in such a short time had made Callie forget about Vincent Thresher and Horace Rendell for the first time in months. For now, at least, she was Natalie's baby girl again—lighthearted and sweet-natured, just like Dan had been.

The good mood lasted only until they entered Intensive Care Unit #5 at Nashua Memorial and saw Grandpa Wade laid out like a salmon on fishmonger's ice, a tube running from his arm to the IV bag on one side of the bed, wires twining from his heart to the EKG monitor on the other side.

"Hey…kiddo." Unable to lift his head from the pillow when they came in, Wade Lindstrom slurred his greeting. Because his gaze drifted and rolled, Natalie couldn't be sure whether he addressed her or Callie.

"Hi, Dad." She set the spring bouquet she'd brought for him on the shelf beside the IV rack. "How are you feeling?"

"Better." The word dribbled from his mouth like half-chewed food. If his present condition was better, Natalie was glad she hadn't seen him before the operation. His hair, once like spun silver, had tarnished to a yellow-tinged gray the color of smog, and it lay matted and oily from not being washed. Although he'd lost weight, deflated skin had buried the definition of his cheekbones, reducing his face to the consistency of putty.

Nevertheless, he made a limp smile and lifted a quavering hand when he looked at Callie. "How's my...favorite granddaughter?"

Callie stood back from the bed, as if afraid of catching whatever sickness her grandfather had. When Wade called to her, she sought guidance from her mother with a worried look.

"It's okay, honey." Natalie motioned her forward. "Come say hi to Grandpa."

Her daughter shuffled up to peer over the bedrail at Wade. "Sorry you don't feel good, Grandpa."

He maneuvered his hand over the rail, as if positioning the claw in a prize-vending machine, and let it drop onto the crown of Callie's head. The IV tube jiggled as he ruffled her hair. "I'll be fine, honey. After all, I've gotta...be ready for somebody's birthday in a few weeks..."

He smiled again, but his eyelids fluttered shut. Callie took his slackening hand in hers. "Grandpa?"

When he didn't answer, Natalie gently touched his shoulder. "Dad?"

"Huh?" Wade blinked, and his gaze took a moment to find her.

"The operation. How does the doctor think it went?"

"Oh...fine, fine. No problem."

"Then she doesn't think you're in danger of a heart attack?"

"Well...they did a double bypass, and the doc said she'd keep an eye on it. Might have to go back in and do a quad." With his left hand, he made a vague up-and-down motion over his chest. "Told her she shoulda put in a zipper."

He chuckled but Natalie didn't. More surgery would easily add another hundred grand or so to his medical bills. "Where are you going to stay once they release you?" she asked. "Do you need us to help?"

He shook his head. "Nah, nah. I got a room at a convalescent home all lined up. Don't worry about me."

"Is your insurance going to cover that?" Natalie thought of the money Abe—that is to say, Dr. Wilcox—had promised her.

"If it doesn't, I'll just take out a second on the house. Let the bank keep the cursed thing." His laughter exhausted him, and he seemed to drop into sleep.

"Dad?" Natalie bent closer to his ear. "Callie and I have to go away for a while, but we'll be back as soon as we can. You rest up and get better, okay?"

He remained still.

With a jolt of apprehension, Natalie looked at the EKG monitor, but it still registered a slow, steady heartbeat. "I think we'd better let Grandpa rest," she told Callie.

Standing on tiptoes, her daughter laid Wade's slack hand down at his side. "We love you, Grandpa."

The sleeping figure didn't respond, but Callie stepped backward from the bed, as if afraid she might miss his smile if she looked away. Natalie felt a twinge of both guilt and envy at her daughter's automatic, unquestioning affection for Wade. Although his devotion and generosity to Callie had reconciled Natalie to him, she hadn't told her father she loved him since the day he'd left her at the Iris Semple Conduit Academy, better known as the School—the gloomy Victorian mansion where indentured Violets were sent for NAACC training. She had resented the father who'd consigned her to Corps servitude so deeply and for so long that she now became suspicious of her own tenderness toward him. They'd both changed so much in recent years that Natalie felt like a complete stranger to the man with a malfunctioning heart who now lay in this hospital bed.

"See you soon, kiddo."

The sound of Wade's voice, bright with its old vitality, halted Natalie halfway out the door, and she pivoted back toward the bed. Her father remained motionless, an expression of beatific repose on his face, as if arranged by a mortician. Callie, whose hand she held, gave her a quizzical look, apparently oblivious as to why Natalie had jerked her to a stop.

See you soon, kiddo. That was what her father always said on those rare occasions when he came to visit her at the School, just as he was about to leave again. It always meant he wouldn't be back for a long, long time.

Natalie tugged her daughter on out of the room.

"Will Grandpa be okay?" Callie asked, struggling to keep up as her mother walked down the hospital corridor.

"Sure he will, honey," Natalie answered, though she wasn't sure at all.

6

Departure Date

DAN'S DAD COULD HARDLY HAVE PRESENTED A GREATER contrast to Natalie's own father, especially now. Always slender, Wade Lindstrom had thinned to Lincoln-like lankiness in the hospital, and his fair Scandinavian skin had paled to talc whiteness. Ted Atwater seemed to have added a few pounds to his beefy frame since Natalie had seen him last Thanksgiving, and a perennial midwestern ruddiness reddened his complexion.

He looks like he'll live forever, Natalie thought as she watched him and Callie at work on his latest woodcarving.

"Be sure to scrape the excess varnish off on the edge of the can before you use the brush." Grandpa Ted showed Callie how to coat the bristles of the paintbrush and dab the stain into the walnut carving's nooks and crannies. A retired high-school shop teacher, he'd sculpted a whimsical rendering of Dr. Seuss's Horton the Elephant, Callie's favorite storybook character. Like a Violet, Horton could talk to people no one else could see or hear. These tiny people were called Whos, and Callie often used that name to refer to the dead souls that troubled her, such as Vincent Thresher and Horace Rendell.

The "bad Whos" had apparently left Callie alone during the two nights she and Natalie had stayed with Grandpa Ted and Grandma Jean—or perhaps spending time with the family had enabled Callie to forget about the nightly visits from Rendell, at least during daylight hours. Seated with Ted at a patio table in the Atwaters' backyard, Callie painted the wooden elephant with reckless delight, spattering more stain on the spread-out newspapers than she actually got on the figurine.

Stepping up to survey the artwork, Natalie squeezed her daughter's shoulder. "How's it going, baby girl?"

Callie beamed. "Super! Look—I'm doing it all by myself." She slathered some more varnish on Horton's back to demonstrate.

"So I see." Natalie exchanged a wry chuckle with Ted, but frowned inside as she thought of what she was about to do. She didn't want to shatter her little girl's fragile happiness. "Can I talk to Grandpa for a minute?"

"Okay." Callie dunked the brush back in the can.

"Keep up the good work, Sprout," Ted said, using the pet name he'd given Callie when he saw how much she'd grown in the past few months.

Natalie wrinkled her nose at the acrid turpentine smell of the lacquer that clung to Ted as they withdrew from the table. "Is it safe for her to work with that stuff?" she asked.

He smiled away the concern. "Oh, yeah. Plenty of ventilation out here."

They reached the edge of the back lawn, where a man-made channel flowed past the yard toward the green expanse of Clear Lake. Below them, an old motorboat floated beside a graying, weathered dock. Lacking the ease and polish in conversation that Wade Lindstrom had cultivated during his years as a salesman, Ted Atwater shoved his hands in his pockets and idly kicked one of the embankment's wooden pylons with his work boot.

"I guess it's about time for you to head out," he said at last.

"Yeah." Though the late-spring sun was almost uncomfortably warm, Natalie hugged herself as if chilled. "I should only be gone a week or so."

"Take as long as you need."

"I really appreciate your doing this. It's a big favor to ask, and I still feel like I barely know you."

"You're doing us the favor." He squinted back toward Callie with a bittersweet half-smile. "Seeing her is like having a little piece of him back again."

"I know." Natalie glanced from her daughter to the man who would have been her father-in-law. Though Ted's face was plumper than Dan's had been, she could see the family resemblance in the line of the eyebrows, the Atwater nose—the same brows and nose that Callie shared. Likewise, in Jean Atwater's face, Natalie saw the shape of Dan's jaw, the warmth of his smile. Whenever she looked at any of them—Ted, Jean, or Callie—it was like watching Dan inhabit a Violet, molding the conduit's features to match his own.

But Dan would never inhabit anyone again. He had gone to the Place Beyond, and was as lost to Natalie and Callie as he was to his parents.

Dan had not had the opportunity to ask Natalie to marry him. Their entire relationship had lasted less than two weeks, most of which they'd spent either pursuing or evading the Violet Killer. Because Dan had been killed while saving her from the murderer, Natalie had not had the courage to meet his family for almost seven years after his death. She not only hesitated to tell them that she'd conceived a child with Dan out of wedlock, she was afraid they would blame her for costing them a son. Instead, they thanked her for giving them a granddaughter.

Though the Atwaters had welcomed her into their clan, Natalie felt that staying in their house was akin to sleeping on Dan's grave. His spirit may have moved on, but his essence still saturated the place. The living room of the double-wide mobile home was a veritable shrine to the Atwaters' late son. His grade-school science-fair trophy adorned the mantel of the faux fireplace, while framed photos festooned the walls: Dan mugging for the camera in a publicity still as the title role in a high-school production of *The Music Man*, Dan in dress blues as he graduated from the police academy, Dan here, Dan there, Dan everywhere. The crushing weight of his absence made Natalie almost eager to leave for Peru, a place that had never known any trace of Dan Atwater.

"Can I have a few minutes alone with Callie?" she asked Ted. "To say good-bye?"

"Sure. I'll go see if Jean needs some help with lunch." He clomped back toward the house, pausing at the patio table to admonish Callie. "Remember, Sprout—not too much lacquer on the brush."

When he'd gone back inside and shut the sliding glass door behind him, Natalie went over to the table and pulled up a chair next to her daughter's. Energetic a moment ago, Callie's brushstrokes became listless as Natalie sat down.

"You're going away," she said before her mother could speak.

"It's only for a little while. I'll be back soon." With a helpless, drowning feeling, Natalie realized how much she sounded like her own father had when abandoning her at the School.

See you soon, kiddo...

Callie threw down her brush, which bled stain onto the newsprint. "Why do you have to go *now*? Just when we were starting to have fun!"

"You can still have fun with Grandpa and Grandma. And when I get back, we'll take a nice, long vacation and do whatever you want. Okay?"

Callie scrunched her mouth, evidently unsure whether she should trust this promise. "Okay."

Watching doubt contend with hope on her daughter's face was too much like looking in a mirror at her seven-year-old self. *I'm doing this for you,* Natalie thought. *For both of us.*

She averted her eyes toward the half-varnished carving of Horton the Elephant. "You know what to do if the bad Whos come back, don't you?"

"Say the mantra thing." Callie droned the words as if writing them on a chalkboard.

"Right. And if that isn't working?"

"Call Grandma Nora."

"That's right, honey."

No one knows more about fighting the bad Whos, Natalie thought. If Callie summoned her grandmother, Nora could help evict Thresher or Rendell from her brain. Natalie had worried about leaving her daughter with non-Violets like the Atwaters, and it reassured her to think that her mom could protect Callie while she was gone.

The heavy sliding glass door rumbled open again, and Jean Atwater stepped out onto the cement patio, her joints swollen and skewed by rheumatoid arthritis. Despite her pain, she always smiled, as if acutely aware of what a privilege it was to be alive.

"Natalie... there's a young man at the door."

Natalie nudged her daughter. "I've got to go, baby girl. See me off?"

Refusing to look at her, Callie climbed down from her chair and trudged toward the door with rounded shoulders. Natalie drew a long, slow breath and followed her inside.

Standing in the living room with his arms behind his back, Dr. Wilcox broke off his small talk with Ted Atwater to beam at Natalie. "Hey! Hope I haven't kept you waiting."

He gestured to the duffel bag and suitcase that waited by the front door.

She shook her head. "No, you're fine. I always pack a day early."

"Wish I could say the same. I throw a bunch of stuff in a bag at the last minute, then end up a thousand miles from nowhere without any underwear. But I *did* remember to bring this." Wilcox brought his hands from behind him, revealing a stuffed animal with a plump woolen body, long neck, and black sheep snout. He held it out toward Callie. "Say... would you know anyone who'd like to have this?"

Callie sucked on a forefinger in shy skepticism.

Natalie smiled encouragement. "Look, honey! It's one of the llamas we talked about."

"An alpaca, actually," Wilcox said. "Made from actual alpaca wool—the finest in the world, so they say. Feel how soft it is."

When Callie slunk forward to pet the toy, he gently transferred it to her.

She stroked the downy wool, her expression changing from sullen to thoughtful. "I want to see an alpaca. Can I come to Peru with you?"

To his credit, Wilcox did not laugh, but instead knelt beside her. "Maybe when you're a little older. But tell you what—when your mother and I come back, we'll take you to the best zoo we can find so you can see some alpacas *and* some llamas. Deal?"

A smile threatened to break out on Callie's face. "Okay."

Marveling at the exchange, Natalie was startled when Jean Atwater whispered in her ear with gossipy girlishness, "*You didn't tell us he was so handsome.*"

"Yeah." During her previous meetings with the professor, Natalie had been too preoccupied with her concerns to take much notice of his appearance. Now that she considered it, however, she had to admit that he was good-looking in a refined, cerebral way. But Jean implied that Natalie must have more than a business interest in the archaeologist...which she didn't, of course.

"I guess we'd better go," she announced to preempt further speculation about her love life.

Natalie crossed to the front door to collect her bags, but Wilcox got there first.

"Here, let me get these for you." He shouldered the duffel and picked up the suitcase.

Left empty-handed, she kneeled and opened her arms to her daughter. "Do I get a good-bye hug?"

Though Callie still clutched the alpaca, her face turned glum again as she draped her slack arms around Natalie's neck. "I love you, Mommy. Come back soon."

"I will, sweetheart." Natalie squeezed and was relieved when Callie squeezed back. "Love you, too, honey."

Natalie collected farewells from Ted and Jean as they followed her and Wilcox out to the driveway of the Atwaters' mobile home. Two cars loitered at the curb. One was the professor's rented Nissan.

The other was a silver Acura.

Bella must've called every rental place in northern California to find a car like hers, Natalie thought with grim amusement. She wanted to ask Wilcox about Bella, but he was talking to the Atwaters. "It was great meeting you folks. I hope we have more of a chance to talk when we come back…"

She glanced toward the open front door, where Callie stood sucking her forefinger and cradling her new stuffed animal in the crook of one arm. Natalie kept waving and blowing her kisses, but Callie did not smile. The Atwaters bid them bon voyage and went back inside, shutting Callie in the house.

Wilcox popped open the Nissan's trunk, hefted Natalie's bags into it. "I take it your account got the wire transfer?"

"Yeah. Thanks." Natalie had checked her savings balance at a local ATM to make sure the promised advance of two hundred grand had posted. She resisted the temptation to look back toward the house again; if she saw Callie peering out through the window like a stray dog in a shelter, she might not be able to leave. "That was a very sweet thing you did for my daughter, bringing her a present and all."

The professor brushed aside the gratitude. "Actually, I brought the alpaca for you, but when I saw Callie, I figured she needed it more. I know how hard it is for a kid to be separated from her mom."

"Yeah…it's hard, all right. I appreciate your concern." When they got in the car and buckled their seat belts, Natalie finally nodded toward the Acura. "What should we do about her? She's not even supposed to be on yet." The last time Natalie had seen a Corps Security agent working unpaid overtime was when Horace Rendell had plotted to kidnap her daughter.

Wilcox started the Nissan, glancing up with a perplexed expression, as if he didn't know what she was talking about. "Oh! Not to worry—it's taken care of. *Bella* and I have an understanding. Like the local day-shift guy, she'll tell the Corps you're staying with your daughter's grandparents for a while."

"You sure?" In the Nissan's parabolic side mirror, Natalie saw the Acura swing away from the curb to tail them as they drove off. " 'Cause I'm not getting on a plane if she's flying too."

"She's only following us for show, to keep Corps Security off her back. I promise you—if there's any problem, I'll turn this car around and drive you right back to Callie." He reached behind his car seat and grabbed a green bottle from a small ice chest he'd placed there. "Mineral water?"

"Uh…thanks." Natalie accepted the chilled bottle, wet with condensation, smiling at his thoughtfulness, nervous yet excited about her genteel traveling companion and the adventure that lay ahead of them. But many miles passed before she could tear her gaze from the reflection of the car that followed them out of Lakeport and down the highway toward San Francisco.

7

Living the Part

AUGUST TRENT BENT OVER THE BASIN IN THE MEN'S restroom of Chef Champignon—one of San Francisco's best vegetarian restaurants, according to the Zagat guide—and washed away the sweat that had condensed on his brow and upper lip. Dabbing himself dry with a paper towel, he winced at the ghost he saw reflected in the mirror.

It hadn't bothered him to wear another man's face before. As an actor, he was used to changing his hair color and style, covering his features with makeup and latex appliances, even gaining or losing weight when appropriate. Plastic surgery was only a step beyond that and everyone in Hollywood did it anyway, so Trent had let Nathan Azure's surgeons pin back his ears, trim his nose, and sculpt his eyes into their present almond shape before he went to Peru. It had hurt like hell, but if De Niro could pack on a hundred pounds for a role, then he, too, could suffer for his art.

Ever since he'd seen Wilcox murdered in the Andes, however, the archaeologist's visage had begun to feel like a death mask that Trent could not remove. Every time he looked at his reflection, he expected it to spit blood at him, the way the professor had spat on Azure.

Focus, he told himself. *Don't break character.*

Using the yogalike Alexander technique he'd learned as a drama major at UCLA, he straightened his spine, inhaling through his nose, exhaling from his mouth. After he'd centered himself, Trent put on his prescriptionless wire-framed glasses and practiced one of Wilcox's smiles. It struck him as funny that his job was the same as Natalie's, for he, too, had to channel a dead man.

August Trent was his stage name, not his real name. That had been buried a decade ago along with his parents. Later, when Azure gave Trent the million he'd been promised, he would return to Hollywood and change his face again, along with his name. He was thinking about "Lance" something or other but hadn't decided yet.

He'd tried Hollywood before, of course, along with about a billion other wannabes. Relentless hustling and auditioning had garnered him enough walk-ons and extra work to earn him a SAG card, "SAG" in this case standing for "Starving Actor's Gullibility." By the time he was old enough to start lying about his age, he was still waiting tables and spending nights on a friend's sofa.

It was while he worked at Su Casa, a Mexican place on the Santa Monica Promenade, that he finally got "discovered." He was serving lunch to a man he'd never seen in the restaurant before, a bigwig executive type who dyed his hair on top but left a dash of silver at each temple for an air of authority. When Trent handed him his check at the end of the meal, the suit eyed him through sepia-tinted glasses.

"Hey, kid...you're an actor, right?"

"Yes, sir." Pushing thirty, Trent wasn't sure whether to be flattered or insulted to be called "kid," but he had conditioned himself to smile at the condescension of his customers. You never knew who might be a producer or director.

"You interested in some work?" the man asked.

"Always. If the role fits, I'll wear it. What's the project?"

"It's corporate. Nothing glamorous, but it's easy money. I don't have time to go into detail here, but give me a call if you're interested."

He handed Trent a business card with the company logo of Bilderburg Associates and a telephone number on it. The man's name was absent, unless it happened to be Bilderburg. The card had a paper clip on it, and Trent flipped it over to find a folded hundred-dollar bill on the back.

He gave a genuine smile. "Thank you, sir. I look forward to working with you."

Trent was excited. Some of his friends made big bucks doing voice-overs and industrial films. But the job turned out to be a live performance: Trent would "play" a company executive as he went to a bank and set up an account for one of the firm's subsidiaries. "Our staff's time is too valuable to waste on this kind of paper-shuffling formality," the man who hired him said by way of explanation.

Trent doubted that rationale but didn't much care. The gig paid two grand for a single afternoon—in cash, under the table, and wonderfully tax-free. He never found out what the bank account was really for and never saw the man from Bilderburg Associates again.

Yet the man must have given his performance a glowing

review, for Trent soon found himself inundated with offers from an invisible network of string-pullers and mountebanks. One week he posed as the CEO of a dummy corporation designed to hide the parent company's debt from its shareholders. The following week he starred as a cutting-edge biochemist at a venture-capital presentation. The pay and risk increased with each job, as did the adrenaline rush when he carried it off. The improvisation of illegality thrilled him with its high-wire defiance, its dance on the edge of disaster.

Within the past year, that dance had become more precarious than ever as Trent made his debut in corporate espionage. An attempt to steal the latest drug data from a biotech firm had gone awry when his inside man at the company got cold feet and wanted out. Although the guy swore up and down that he wouldn't turn him in, Trent couldn't trust him, so he created "Nick."

Nick was a hard case—a coolheaded, dead-in-the-eyes professional, like Edward Fox in *The Day of the Jackal*. When Trent needed to do a job for which he lacked the stomach, he went into Nick. Nick, not Trent, had killed the potential stool pigeon. Nick, not Trent, had burned the corpse's hands, feet, and face with acid and pulled its teeth with pliers to prevent identification of the victim, then bagged the naked body in a plastic garbage sack and dumped it in a sewer culvert.

After that ordeal, August Trent was only too happy to let Nathan Azure change his face and take him to the remote mountains of a foreign country. But with Azure as his boss, Trent knew that he would soon need Nick again.

Perhaps sooner than he had anticipated.

That was the thought that had nagged him all during the

three-hour drive from Lakeport as he chatted with Natalie and smiled, smiled, smiled. It was the thought that had be-dewed his forehead with sweat during dinner, requiring him to seek out the men's room to refresh himself. A problem had arisen that he had not foreseen and that might prove fatal.

He liked Natalie Lindstrom.

Of the people he had victimized in the past, Trent hon-estly believed that the rubes had only themselves to blame. Rich bastards suckered in by their own greed who could well afford the fleecing he gave them. Not so single-mom Lindstrom, whose financial desperation he had known—and counted on—when he approached her for the Pizarro job.

If only Natalie hadn't looked so normal—so beautiful, in fact—with the long brown hair of her latest wig and the warm cocoa color of the contact lenses she wore. And he was going to spend so much time with her…more than he'd spent with any woman in years. His career had not been con-ducive to relationships of any duration.

He'd managed to keep her talking mostly about herself during the drive to the Bay Area. Although he had re-searched Wilcox thoroughly before taking on the role, Trent wanted to answer as few questions about the archaeologist's background as possible, so he gently pried open Natalie's shell of reserve with casual questions about her art, her fam-ily, her interests. He had perhaps succeeded too much, for the more she prattled about her cute little daughter, the more he dwelled on the fate that awaited her once Azure had finished with her.

Focus.

He smoothed his hair, smiled again at his Wilcox reflection, and left the restroom.

"You okay?" Natalie asked when he returned to their table, which sat beneath a hippie-psychedelic mural of a sunflower. "I was about to send in a search party."

Trent chuckled and patted his stomach. "Still a bit carsick, I'm afraid. How is the portobello?"

"Fabulous!" She forked another piece of roasted mushroom into her mouth. "Best meal I've had in years."

"What did I tell you? I drive all the way from Stanford just to come to this place." He indicated the remains of his ratatouille. "Alas, I'm sorry to report that such vegetarian delights are almost unheard-of in Peru's northern sierra. But we'll keep you fed."

"I'm sure the local food can't be any worse than what I eat every time Callie badgers me into taking her to McDonald's." Natalie took a sip of her mineral water and cupped the glass in her hand. "Um...I'm embarrassed to admit that I haven't had a chance to read your book yet."

"That's okay. No one else has, either."

She giggled as he had hoped, but her expression soon became shadowed with worry. "Can you tell me what to expect from Pizarro? Is he really the genocidal monster I remember from high-school history?"

"Well...I wouldn't invite him to an intimate vegetarian dinner, if that's what you mean." She laughed, and Trent grinned, grateful now that he'd had plenty of time to read about the conquistador during the weeks he'd spent with his face bandaged from surgery. "He was really quite a remarkable man, in many ways. He was the illegitimate child of a

peasant girl and an Extremaduran captain. Legend has it
that his mother abandoned him on the steps of the church
in Trujillo and that his first nursemaid was a sow."

Natalie made a face. "Ugh! Is that true?"

"Maybe not, but an affinity for pigs might explain why
he became a swineherd almost from the age he could walk.
He apparently received no education whatsoever and at the
end of his life could not even sign his name. Needless to say,
this limited his career options, so, like many poor, illiterate
youths of his day, he became a soldier. Unfortunately, his ig-
norance and lack of social standing kept him from being promoted. Ditto for his stint as a sailor.

"About this time, Hernán Cortés had returned from con-
quering the Aztecs in Mexico, bringing back with him an un-
precedented fortune in gold for the Spanish crown. He
became an immediate folk hero, and started a gold rush to
the New World of men seeking instant wealth and fame. You
didn't need book learning or noble birth to be a conquistador. All you needed was absolute immunity to the fear of
death."

Natalie rolled her eyes. "Oh, is *that* all?"

"You see? Amazing, isn't it? Particularly when you consider that Francisco Pizarro didn't set out for South America
until he was past *fifty*." Trent warmed to the story, as if he
really were a history professor. "Now, this was in the sixteenth century, when the average life expectancy was…
what? Forty, maybe? Pizarro was lucky to be drawing breath
at fifty, and here he was venturing into an unknown conti-
nent of malaria-infected mosquitoes and angry natives."

Trent was pleased to see Natalie set down her fork so as not to miss a word of his story.

"If Pizarro hadn't possessed determination and fortitude that exceeded mere greed, his campaign would have ended before it began. He and his small contingent of explorers hadn't even reached Peru when they became trapped on a tiny island off the coast of Colombia. Lashed by storms and forced to live on nothing but the crabs and shellfish they could scrounge from the shore, they starved, shivering from fever and scurvy, for months. When a ship finally arrived from Panama to rescue them, Pizarro faced a mass defection by his demoralized troops, who hadn't received any of the gold or glory they'd been promised.

"Drawing his sword, Pizarro traced a line from east to west in the sand at the feet of his men, then pointed across the line to the south." Trent mimed the action, adopting the conquistador's proud bearing and fierce stare. He'd been waiting to do this monologue for months—a role within a role. " 'Compañeros,' he said, 'on that side are toil, hunger, nakedness, the drenching storm, desertion, and death; on this side, ease and pleasure. There lies Peru and its riches; here, Panama and its poverty. Choose, each man, what best becomes a brave Castilian. For my part, I go to the south.'

"Then he stepped across the line. Only twelve men followed him, but they led the conquest of Peru."

Trent savored the frisson of Natalie's momentary speechlessness. He was in his element, his glory, and he did not want the dinner to end. Particularly not when he thought of what he had to do afterward.

"Wow." Natalie shook her head and applauded. "You almost make me want to get to know this guy."

"That's my job." Trent grinned. "Dessert?"

When they walked back to Trent's rental car after leaving the restaurant, Arabella Madison's Acura crouched in the space next to theirs like a patient Siamese cat.

"She knows something's up," Natalie muttered. "That's why she's here. If she finds out what I'm doing, the Corps will take Callie away from me."

"I would never let that happen. I told you, I've made all the arrangements." Trent reviewed those arrangements in his mind. "She'll be gone by morning."

"And if she's not?"

"Then I take you back to Callie, just as I said."

"You'd better. If you don't, I'm walking." Relaxed and cheerful over dinner, Natalie slipped back into tense despondency as they got in Trent's car. Madison mugged at Natalie through the Acura's driver's side window, waving to her with a big, goofy grin.

Details, details, Trent thought as the agent trailed them to the Winchester Regency Hotel. He'd chosen it specifically because it was located outside the dense center of the city and therefore possessed a dark outdoor parking lot rather than a well-lit underground garage. Parking at the outer perimeter of the crowded lot, he was pleased to see Madison pull into a space not far from theirs.

As Natalie had surmised, Trent found that the Corps Security agent temporarily assigned to the day shift had been easy enough to bribe. As an extra precaution, Trent had recorded the man's acceptance of the payoff on tape in case it became necessary to blackmail him to maintain his silence. But Trent had not approached Arabella Madison with an offer for fear she might blow the whistle on him. Instead, he had made other plans to deal with her. Plans for tonight.

To his relief, Natalie's mood seemed to improve once they entered the hotel and checked in. A smile tinged with melancholy returned to her face.

"You like the place?" he asked when they arrived at the door to her room.

"Hmm? Oh, yeah." She glanced around at the corridor's burgundy carpet, the doors' brass handles. "The last time I stayed in a place like this, I was with…a friend of mine. Brings back old times."

"Enjoy it while it lasts. I'm afraid our Andean accommodations won't be quite so luxurious." He handed her the room's key card. "I'm staying right across the hall. Get a good night's sleep, and I'll meet you downstairs for breakfast at six in the morning."

She wrinkled her nose, laughing. "Ugh! So early. But if you insist, I'll drag myself out of bed." Her expression sobered, but her eyes remained bright with amusement. "Thank you for tonight. It was fun."

"For me, too." The first words he'd said that night as August Trent, not Abel Wilcox. "I hope we have as good a time in Peru."

"I look forward to it. Good night, Dr. Wilcox."

"Please! *Abe.* I'm still on sabbatical."

She smiled. "Right…Abe. Night."

"Good night . . . Natalie."

He gave a small bow and walked away.

Once he heard her enter her room, Trent's loose-limbed nonchalance gave way to a rigid economy of movement. He marched to his own room and locked himself inside. A numbing detachment filled him as he hefted his suitcase onto the bed and opened it. The sight of the reddish brown wig, false mustache, and folded security guard's uniform elicited no emotion, nor did the long hatpin and small glass vial he removed from a hidden pocket in the bag's lining.

Nick thought only of work. Of the job to be done.

He swapped his striped oxford shirt for the gray button-up with the word SECURITY embroidered on the breast pocket. Next, he set aside Wilcox's glasses and applied spirit gum to his upper lip to attach the mustache, which matched the shade of the hairpiece he then put on. A billed cap and a leather bomber jacket completed the outfit.

He checked the costume in the mirror, practiced his voice. "Excuse me, ma'am . . . are you a guest of the hotel?"

Trent lowered the pitch, made the tone more nasal. He was playing Nick playing a security guard. Roles within roles.

With the easy part done, he donned his black leather driving gloves. For an instant, when he opened the vial and dipped the point of the hatpin into the viscous brown sap in the glass tube, Nick disappeared and he became August Trent again, fretful and unsure. His fingers quivered as he rotated the pin to wrap the goo around the pin's tip. Although he could have licked the poison up like honey without any harm, a single pinprick could kill him.

Careful, he thought. *A little dab'll do ya.*

It looked and smelled something like dirty model-airplane glue, and he gently blew on the syrup to dry it. Alberto, one of Azure's Peruvian drug runners, had sold it to him. *Ourari*, he'd called it—a product of the nearby Amazon jungle. Trent had requested it by its more familiar name.

Curare.

Even before returning to the States, Trent knew that his attempt to recruit Natalie might cause him to tangle with Corps Security—armed agents trained in self-defense. His best chance against them was the element of surprise, and for that he needed a weapon that was quick, quiet, and deadly. Although physicians in the U.S. commonly used the substance as a muscle relaxant prior to surgery, sales of medical curare were closely regulated and monitored, and the drug lacked the potency Trent required. He needed the "flying death" that Amazonian tribes used to tip their arrows and blowgun darts, a poison that could drop a wild monkey in twenty seconds.

Nick resumed control as he gripped the blunt head of the seven-inch pin and held its length close against the right sleeve of his jacket. In addition to his costume, he had brought a flashlight and a folded industrial-size plastic trash bag in his suitcase. He shoved the bag in the pocket of his jacket, hooked the flashlight on his belt, and, with calm professionalism, checked the hallway outside his room before strolling out of the hotel and into the dark parking lot.

Although he knew exactly where Arabella Madison had parked, he strutted between each of the intervening rows of cars with an unhurried, flat-footed gait, sweeping the beam of his flashlight back and forth with methodical thoroughness, biding time until he was sure there were no witnesses around. He saw her leaning against the driver's side of her car but let the light brush past her before swinging it back to shine on her face. "Excuse me, ma'am…are you a guest of the hotel?"

Flinching as the beam blinded her, she took one speaker of her iPod headphones out of her ear. "Huh?"

He kept the light in her eyes. "If you're not a guest of the hotel, I'll have to ask you to leave."

Madison pulled the headphones down around her neck with a waspish glare. "Back off, rent-a-cop. I'm a federal agent on surveillance." She lifted aside one lapel of her jacket to reveal her .45 pistol in its holster.

"I'm sorry, ma'am, but unless you can show me some ID…"

"Oh, for Pete's sake!" The agent reached into her inside jacket pocket. "I could have you arrested for obstruction of justice."

Flicking off the flashlight, he raised the hand that held the hatpin, but his resolve wavered. *What would Natalie think?* Trent wondered.

This chick has caused nothing but trouble for Lindstrom and her kid, Nick answered. *You'll be doing them both a favor.*

When Madison flipped open her ID, he jabbed the hatpin into her side.

"OW!" She slapped her hand on the puncture wound, fingers fluttering along the shaft of the pin. "Who the hell do you think—"

The curare cut her off. Madison's eyelids fell and did not open, her facial muscles twitching as if she struggled to blink. One hand flopped toward her gun, then dropped, dangling. Her expression became immobile as the paralysis spread and her head dropped to her chest. Air leaked from her open mouth but she made no sound.

Trent pulled out the pin and sandwiched her slack body between his and the car, restraining her as the neurotoxin took effect. He doffed his cap and tossed it in the car just as a pair of headlights approached. Bear-hugging her to keep her upright, he fondled Arabella Madison as if making out with her, wondering if she was still conscious but unable to react. The curare had evidently already paralyzed the diaphragm muscle that drew air into her lungs, for he felt no breath from her mouth. She might not be dead yet, however, for curare did not affect the heart, and asphyxiation could take up to fifteen minutes.

Trent made sure that he did not touch her lips as he pretended to kiss her, nor did he allow himself to touch any part of her bare skin, for he didn't want to become a touchstone for this woman. In this case, at least, he followed Nathan Azure's example, although he thought his boss took the no-touching thing to a Howard Hughes–like extreme.

When he was again sure that no one was watching, Trent—or, rather, Nick—shoved Arabella Madison bodily back into the car and climbed in next to her, slamming the door closed behind him. Blocking the view from the parking lot, he lifted her legs over the gearshift and folded her body into the floor space below the glove compartment, then spread his black garbage sack over the inert body like a tarp.

He found the Acura's key already in the ignition and drove the car to a run-down strip mall a few miles away. He'd scouted the location the previous day and knew that the shops would be closed at this time of night. Steering the car into the alley behind the mall, he pulled up beside a Dumpster and stopped the engine.

After a quick survey to make sure that no homeless people had camped out in the vicinity, he stretched the garbage bag over Madison's corpse. Moving around to her side of the car, he opened the passenger door and rolled her body out onto the asphalt so he could finish pulling the sack around her. He twisted the mouth of the bag closed, knotted it, then hefted the bundle up to the lip of the Dumpster and tumbled it inside.

The waste container belonged to a Chinese take-out joint, and its contents reeked of rotting chow mein. The bigger the stench, the better as far as Trent was concerned. He climbed inside the half-full Dumpster and piled as much trash as possible over the plastic garbage sack. Someone might eventually find the body, but by then he and Natalie Lindstrom would be in Peru. Of course, there was the problem of the girl, Callie. If the Corps connected Natalie's absence to Madison's murder, they might come for her daughter ... but Trent couldn't worry about that. That wasn't his concern.

The thought of Natalie continued to nag him, however, as he abandoned Arabella Madison's Acura in a grocery store parking lot a couple blocks from the hotel. He'd had a great time with her tonight, and she seemed to like him. He wanted her to like him. Would she feel the same way if she saw him now? he wondered, peeling off his leather gloves before leaving the car. Or would she recoil from the touch of these hands that looked so clean?

But his hands *were* clean, he thought, ditching the gloves and the rest of his security guard disguise in one of the supermarket's outdoor trash cans. That was why he became Nick. Nick had done the job.

Trent strolled back to the hotel, breathing easier, looking forward to a long, hot shower before bed. Looking forward to becoming genial Abe Wilcox again for tomorrow's performance.

8

Landing in Cajamarca

"HOW ARE YOU? *¿CÓMO ESTÁ USTED?*" THE MALE voice on Natalie's CD player enunciated with kindergarten clarity. "I'm fine. *Estoy bien.*"

The pilot of the tiny twin-engine Cessna banked into a turn, the plane hiccupping from wind resistance, and Natalie clapped a hand over her mouth to keep from losing the food she'd managed to eat in the past twenty-four hours. Although she had indeed wanted to brush up on what little Spanish she knew, she'd actually started the language lesson to focus on something besides the kazoo buzz of the propellers.

After the trips to and from New England to visit her father and the flights from San Francisco to L.A. and then to Lima, she had almost become inured to air travel despite her phobia. But the craft Nathan Azure had chartered to take them from Lima to Cajamarca looked like a child's toy compared to the passenger jets they'd been flying, and Natalie almost wished she were on a Daedalus Aeronautics plane instead.

"Where do you come from? *¿De donde es usted?* I'm from the United States. *Yo soy de los Estados Unidos.*"

The Spanish teacher's measured phrases droned on in her headset, but Natalie scarcely listened.

Seated across from her, Abe smiled sympathetically and tapped one ear to signal that he wanted to say something. She nudged aside one of her headphone speakers.

"I know how you feel! These trips always make me ill." He patted his midsection, shouting to be heard over the engine's whine. "But don't worry! We'll be there soon. You might want to take out those contacts before we land, though. The lower air pressure at this altitude can change the curvature of your corneas and make the lenses uncomfortable."

She nodded and put her colored lenses in the storage case in her purse. Although she appreciated the professor's tip, it only increased her anxiety about arriving, particularly since everyone who saw her would know she was a Violet.

At last, the tiny Cessna screeched to a landing on an airstrip in Cajamarca, a city in northern Peru. Natalie imagined falling to her knees and kissing the ground in gratitude, but the expected relief failed to materialize. It was late autumn here in the southern hemisphere, and the waning day was overcast and cold as she descended the plane's fold-down steps. Natalie set her luggage on the tarmac beside her and took several deep breaths in a vain attempt to restore her equilibrium. At nine thousand feet above sea level, the oxygen-deprived air made her feel as if she'd arrived on the moon without a spacesuit.

In some ways, she might as well have.

The international airport in Lima had comforted Natalie

with its cosmopolitan familiarity. The inevitable McDonald's franchise greeted her as she entered the terminal, and the Peruvians she passed wore jeans, tank tops, and fashionable blouses. She even saw one little girl in a Mickey Mouse T-shirt. If it wasn't for the shops selling miniature Peruvian flags and Incan souvenirs imported from China, the terminal would have been indistinguishable from the airports in any other big city.

Natalie found no outlets for multinational retailers at the airfield in Cajamarca, however, only a small control tower and terminal building in the middle of an arid sheet of asphalt. Instead of the glass-plated skyscrapers that bejeweled Lima's downtown, she saw only a small mosaic of flat whitewashed buildings with tiled roofs. Beyond the town rose the foothills of the Andes, where she and Abe would be heading tomorrow. The darkening clouds overhead turned the mottled green brush of the mountains black.

The few local people in Natalie's view all seemed to be wearing wide-brimmed hats: the men in fedoras, the women in a distinctive hat with a high, cylindrical, flat-topped peak. Bareheaded but for her brown wig, Natalie felt acutely conspicuous, afraid that she might be violating some sartorial taboo. Although, as a Violet, she was accustomed to being an outsider, she couldn't remember ever feeling so alien before.

Natalie shivered and zipped up the front of her down jacket. Abe had cautioned her to bring cold-weather attire.

The archaeologist ducked through the Cessna's low door and descended to the runway, shaking the kinks out of his long legs. "Well, what do you think?"

Natalie brushed windblown strands of hair from her eyes. "Not much to it."

"More to it than you might imagine. Charming town, really. I'll have to show you around a bit before we leave tomorrow. But right now I'm starved. How about you?"

"As soon as my stomach lands, I will be."

"A good hot meal will take care of that." He signalled a Peruvian man advancing toward them with his back hunched against the wind. "Honorato!"

The man kept his head tilted forward as he approached and bent to pick up Abe's knapsack, his expression nearly invisible in the shadow cast by the brim of his fedora. Like many descendants of the Incas, he possessed vaguely Mongolian features, with sienna-tinted skin, almond eyes, and full, broad cheeks.

When he stooped to collect Natalie's suitcase and duffel bag, she grabbed the handles before he could. "It's all right. I can take them."

For the first time, he met her gaze, and his eyes widened. Natalie had grown used to such gawking since she stopped wearing colored contacts to cover her violet irises while in public.

"Nonsense! You're the honored guest. Let me carry those for you." Abe beckoned, grinning, until she relinquished the bags with a smile. *"¡Vámanos!"*

As Honorato and the professor led Natalie out through the terminal to the parking lot in front of the airport, the Peruvian flicked surreptitious glances back at her as if to make sure she hadn't vanished in a puff of smoke. A brand-new Range Rover awaited them, spotless but for a few mud spatters on its fenders. In a city where battered pickup trucks and decades-old buses predominated, the SUV stuck out like a stretch limo. Nathan Azure must have imported it just for this expedition.

The light-headedness that had assailed Natalie when she got off the plane grew more disorienting, making her unsteady on her feet. She puffed deep breaths to counteract the sensation, yet still felt winded. By the time she plopped into the Range Rover's backseat, the tipsiness imploded into migraine pounding, starburst shimmers obscuring her vision. Natalie ground the heels of her palms against her temples to massage away the pain.

Abe occupied the seat beside her. "Headache?"

She nodded.

"Me, too. That's *soroche*—altitude sickness. With any luck, you'll be gone before you even have a chance to get acclimatized." Pulling a plastic sandwich bag from his side coat pocket, he took out what seemed to be a dead leaf and fed it into his mouth as if it were a stick of chewing gum. The leaf crunched between his teeth until his saliva moistened it to softness. "Forgive me. I would offer you some, but I'm afraid they're rather an acquired taste. When we get to the restaurant, though, I'll give you something better than aspirin."

Natalie would have asked him what on earth he was eating but the headache wrung all energy for conversation from her. They rode in silence as Honorato drove them from the airport to the Plaza de Armas, the large square in the center of the city. Twilight deepened to night outside the car, and the whites of Honorato's eyes shone like crescent moons in the rearview mirror every time he glanced at Natalie's reflection. Self-conscious, she dug in her purse for her contacts, then remembered the professor's warning about the low air pressure.

The café where they ate dinner cheered Natalie a bit with its warm lighting and folksy ambience, its walls festooned with the colorful geometry of Andean blankets, hand-knitted tapestries of abstract birds and llamas. However, she couldn't help but feel the stares of the locals as she accompanied Abe into the restaurant, and regretted the lack of her contacts more than ever.

"*Bruja,*" she heard one of the women whisper to her companion.

Natalie waited until she and Abe reached their table before inclining her mouth to his ear. "What's a *bruja?*"

He chuckled. "A witch. Or, more accurately, a sorcerer. But don't worry—*brujos* and *brujas* are popular here. They heal people, bless crops, and such."

"Oh."

The scrutiny she received made Natalie doubt whether *brujas* were really as popular as the professor seemed to think. Although her Spanish was sketchy at best, she attempted to eavesdrop on the conversation of the men ogling her from the next table. At first, she figured they must be speaking too fast for her slow comprehension. Then she realized that the words sounded all wrong, closer to some Polynesian or Asian tongue than anything originating from Europe.

"What language are they speaking?" she asked Abe, who was perusing the menu.

He listened for a moment. "Quechua. Language of the Incas."

"Of course. You quoted some of it in your book." Natalie resisted the temptation to glance at the men for fear of making eye contact with them. "Can you tell what they're saying?"

He let out a little laugh of embarrassment. "I'm afraid you've found me out! I'm not fluent—just another book-learned, ivory-tower academic." He cupped a hand around his mouth in a mock whisper. *"Don't tell the tenure committee."*

He winked and she giggled, but laughing made her head throb harder so she turned her attention to the menu. After asking Abe to translate the descriptions of several dishes, she settled on a potato and vegetable soup, figuring that was all her queasy stomach could manage. The professor ordered the same. *"Y mate de coca, por favor,"* he told the woman serving them, adding, to Natalie, "This'll fix you right up."

Unsure what he'd requested, Natalie guessed that the server would bring her either a Coke or a hot chocolate. Instead, the woman returned with the soup and a cup of steaming greenish tea. Natalie sniffed it with suspicion, took a tiny test sip on her tongue. The warm liquid was very sweet with a slight, but not unpleasant, medicinal taste, like a flavored cough drop. She swallowed a couple gulps of the stuff and found that it seemed to shrink her swollen brain and to lift her haze of fatigue.

Abe's eyes sparkled. "Better?"

"Yeah. It helps." Natalie peered down into the cup, discovered she'd already downed half the concoction. "What's in it?"

"Coca leaves." He pulled the plastic bag of leaves from his pocket with a grin.

She nearly spat a mouthful of tea into her soup. "You gave me *cocaine*?"

Abe held up his hand to placate her. "Don't worry. It's perfectly safe. And the best cure for *soroche* there is."

"Are you nuts? You want to get us arrested?" Natalie glanced around the restaurant, scanning for anyone in uniform.

He shrugged. "It's legal. Everyone uses coca here."

"And what if I get addicted?"

"It's harmless, I promise you. It's not refined. Those lattes you drink are more addictive."

"If you say so." But Natalie set the cup down and didn't pick it up again. Although she was tempted to drink the dregs to ease her headache, she knew it would be just her luck to drop dead of a tea overdose on her first day in Peru.

They finished their meal and headed for the door, but the woman who had referred to Natalie as a *bruja* accosted her on the way out. Dressed in a striped poncho and an ankle-length orange dress, the woman held out the peaked, wide-brimmed hat she'd been wearing and motioned for Natalie to take it.

Abe beamed as if he'd just solved a puzzle. "Ah! She sees that you aren't wearing a hat and wants you to have hers. That's Peruvian hospitality for you."

Natalie gaped at the offering in awkward astonishment for a moment, wondering if the woman was a peddler. She'd exchanged some of her dollars for nuevos soles at the airport in Lima, and she dug some of the colorful paper currency out of her handbag and offered it to the woman. But the latter ignored the money and used her calloused fingers to close Natalie's hands on the gift.

Still uncertain whether she was doing the proper thing, Natalie bowed her head. *"Gracias."*

The woman smiled and nodded her approval before returning to her companion.

"What was that all about?" Natalie asked Abe when they left the café and returned to the Range Rover.

He shrugged. "Probably an attempt to buy your favor. Everyone here knows it's best to stay on the good side of a *bruja.*"

Honorato, who had evidently stayed in the car while they ate dinner, chauffeured them to their hostel a few miles outside town.

"It's worth the trip," Abe said. "I've stayed there a couple of times already. The place has some unique amenities—ah! There! You see?"

In the darkness outside the SUV's window, Natalie could make out a small group of buildings clustered around what seemed to be a set of public swimming pools of various sizes. A layer of wispy mist roiled up from the waters.

"What is it?" she asked.

"The Bānos del Inca. Natural hot springs. They say Atahualpa was bathing here when he first heard that the Spaniards were coming—strange men with white skin who ate gold."

Natalie gave him a quizzical look. *"Ate* gold?"

"Yes. The conquistadors had such an insatiable appetite for it, demanded so much of it, that the Incas assumed the white men needed it for sustenance." The archaeologist gave an ironic smile. "Not so far from the truth, actually."

Their hostel was located about a block away from the Baños del Inca, but it piped mineral water from the hot springs directly into the baths of each guest room.

"You'll see. Your headache will vanish like magic," Abe told Natalie as he checked in. He tossed her the key to her room. "Enjoy! See you at six tomorrow."

She gave him a weary salute and went to see if these mineral baths were as great as the professor boasted they were. At present, she had to admit that nothing sounded as appealing as lounging in hot water for an hour or so.

The baths must have been the hostel's principal attraction, for the guest room's deep, tile-lined tub was positioned right beside the bed rather than in the tiny spartan bathroom. Natalie dropped her bags on the bed and turned the tub's hot-water tap on full. Mineral-rich steam wafted up into her face, smelling faintly like burnt matches.

While the tub filled, Natalie undressed and removed her wig, peeling the double-sided tape from her bare scalp as if it were dead skin. She still fretted over what effect drinking that coca tea had on her; the throbbing in her temples had subsided, to be replaced by an anesthetic fuzziness that seemed to spread to her fingers and toes.

When the water level was still about a foot below the tub's rim, she shut off the tap, tested the temperature with her foot, and added enough cold water to make the scalding bath tolerable. Needles of heat pricked her skin as she stepped into the tub and eased down onto the bath's inner ledge. Grateful for the drowsy numbness that enveloped her, Natalie rested the nape of her neck against the tub's rim and shut her eyes.

The stinging prickle in her extremities intensified. She dropped into a half-doze, her eyelids pulsing with the rapid movement of the corneas beneath them.

She sat up in the tub, saw the murky outline of her nude legs in the water below. But when she stood, the body that emerged from the bath was a man's, pale, skinny and flat-chested, the black hair on the arms and torso swept downward by the water that streamed off the skin...

Natalie snapped awake and discovered that she was, indeed, standing up in the tub, only now the body was her own, its flesh speckled with goose pimples. A strong sense of déjà vu seized her. Although she had never seen this room before tonight, the dream she'd just had convinced her she'd been here before, as if in a past life.

She gasped with the realization.

Someone was knocking.

I should have known better, Natalie thought. Hotel rooms could be powerful touchstones for past guests who had since died. If she hadn't been so tired, she would have remembered to use her protective mantra earlier. As it was, she'd let her guard down, and this soul had taken control of her body long enough to make her stand up.

Fists clenched at her sides, Natalie closed her eyes and recited the Twenty-third Psalm in her mind.

The Lord is my Shepherd...

Unlike most of the random souls that attempted to inhabit her, this one fought her effort to exile it. It clamped onto her consciousness like a ravening hound, and the soul's visual sense-memory that had begun while she was dozing continued.

She climbed, dripping, from the tub, and tied a bath towel around her waist. Leaving a trail of foot-shaped puddles on the floor, she shuffled over to the room's dresser, where she saw a man's blurred reflection—her reflection—in the mirror. Her eyes refused to focus, so she pawed the top of the dresser until her touch located a pair of spectacles, which she fumbled to put on.

The face sharpened in the mirror, and Dr. Abel Wilcox stared back at her...

Natalie nearly forgot what verse of the psalm to say next. She must have been mistaken. The man in the mirror couldn't be Abe. Abe wasn't dead.

> *He maketh me to lie down in green pastures;*
> *He restoreth my soul...*

The knocking spirit did not yield, but its strength ebbed. At last, as if it would rather self-destruct than depart, it exploded from Natalie's mind, leaving a final image seared into her memory: a man's face, but not Abe's. This man was blond, with a cold handsomeness, his jaw narrowing down to a pointed chin like the beak of some predatory bird. An incandescent hatred accompanied the man's visage, so that Natalie's whole body shook with sympathetic rage at the sight of him.

A frantic knocking—real knocking, on her hostel room's

door—jolted Natalie back to self-awareness. With the rapping growing ever more rapid, she clambered out of the bath, much like the man in her vision had, and snatched up a bath towel as she scampered for the door.

"Hold your horses!" she shouted at the visitor, wrapping the towel around her torso for as much modesty as she could manage. She unlocked the door but stood behind it, leaning her face into the crack she opened. "Yes?"

Seeing Abe so soon after the unsettling reverie made her jump. He seemed equally startled to see her, and Natalie recalled that he'd never seen her without a wig before. He flinched back, but quickly recovered.

"Oh! Natalie."

"You were expecting the pope, maybe?" Natalie shivered, water trickling down her half-naked body to pool at her feet.

"Look, I'm sorry to bother you, but we'll have to switch rooms."

"Why on earth—"

Abe put a hand to his forehead. "This is so embarrassing."

"It certainly is."

"When I finally noticed what your room number was…" He shook his head with a nervous laugh. "I had this room before, see. And there were *fleas* in the bed! They practically ate me alive. I told the manager, but I don't know if he ever did anything about it. Anyway, I checked the bed in my room tonight and it's clean, so I'd feel better if you took that one."

"Uh, sure, I guess." Natalie always had trouble shifting from the pressing concerns of the dead to the petty complaints of the living. "But won't that leave you with the fleas?"

"Pah!" Abe grinned. "They won't kill me."

＊ ＊ ＊

Though the professor's courteous gesture seemed unnecessary, Natalie dressed, gathered her things, and traded rooms with him for the night. This time, however, she initiated her protective mantra right away. And although she didn't know when she might enjoy the comfort of a hot bath again, she never set foot in the new room's tub.

9

The Ransom Room

BY THE FOLLOWING MORNING, NATALIE WAS READY TO dismiss the prior night's experience as a dream. She was sure that *someone* had knocked, but the part about seeing Abe naked in the mirror must have come from her imagination, a product of an oxygen-deprived brain and coca-laced tea. She'd been with the archaeologist almost continuously for the past three days—and had to admit that she found him attractive. Still, she couldn't believe she'd already started fantasizing about him.

Natalie found it harder to explain the image of the blond man, whom she did not recognize, but maybe she'd seen him on TV or in some magazine. Drugs could dredge all kinds of things out of your subconscious, after all.

Gray and glowering the day before, the sky had cleared to a cloudless iceberg blue. Natalie hunched inside her down jacket to ward off the chill breeze as she waited for Abe along the curb outside the hostel's entrance.

At the appointed time, the Range Rover drove up and the professor got out on the passenger side, then offered Natalie his seat. "I need to make a few arrangements here," he explained, "so why don't you go on into town and grab some breakfast at the café, and I'll catch up with you later."

She agreed, although she felt a bit intimidated at riding alone with Honorato. Yesterday he could hardly keep his gaze from straying toward her; today he apparently made a point of *not* looking at her.

Natalie's limited command of Spanish made her timid about talking to the locals. Nevertheless, she figured anything would be better than the oppressive silence that filled the car as they left the hostel.

"Me llamo Natalie." She tapped her chest, as if there might be some confusion about whose name she'd said. Then she gestured to him with a smile a bit too wide. *"Honorato?"*

He darted a glance at her, his expression one of annoyance or pity or both. *"Sí."*

"Sí," she repeated. Her smile shrinking, she strained to think of something else to say, but only came up with phrases from her language CD: *¿Como está usted? ¡Muy bien!*

She let the conversation die, and didn't even muster the courage to bid Honorato *adios* when he dropped her off at the Plaza de Armas.

In the bright light of the sun now rising above the Andes, Cajamarca's central square became picturesque. Topiary llamas populated its English-style garden, and paved paths like wagon-wheel spokes led to the tiered water fountain at the garden's heart. Like the fountain, the baroque facade of the cathedral that bordered the plaza had been sculpted from local volcanic rock. Filigreed with dense

Old World designs of grapes and leaves, the church's unfinished towers ended abruptly, as if some vengeful Incan deity had decapitated their belfries.

The city's charm lifted Natalie's mood considerably. Her headache had diminished to a subdued smarting behind her eyes, and the sun gilded her face with warmth as she admired the scenery.

As good as the sunlight felt, Natalie knew the UV rays would roast her before long in this thin air. Although she'd already slathered her skin with SPF 50 sunblock, she was grateful to wear the hat the woman had given her the previous night. It looked like an upside-down toadstool on her head, but at least its brim shaded her face. Since she couldn't wear her colored contacts, she hid her eyes behind sunglasses, but everyone she passed still gaped at her, for her T-shirt, jeans, and Doc Marten boots all branded her as an American tourist.

When she got to the café, Natalie ordered breakfast as well as she could with her fragmented Spanish. She ended up with a couple of runny fried eggs and two sweet triangular biscuits, but she was famished and ate every last scrap, mopping up the yolk with scraps of the bread. Instinct told her to eat as much as possible now, since she had no idea what kind of food she'd be served at the archaeological dig up in the Andes.

To entertain herself while she munched, Natalie dug Abe's book, *Conqueror and Conquered: Pizarro and Peru*, out of her canvas tote bag and propped it open on the table in front of her. With everything that had been going on, she had only managed to skim the first section, which detailed

Francisco Pizarro's rise from illiterate pig farmer to discoverer of Peru, and the initial contact the Spaniards made with Atahualpa, the Inca, or king, of the native people.

She skipped ahead to Pizarro's first face-to-face encounter with Atahualpa—the fateful meeting that took place right outside the restaurant window, where the fountain now burbled in the formal gardens of the Plaza de Armas. The conquistador had sent an intermediary to tell the Inca that he "loved him dearly" and to invite him to Cajamarca for a diplomatic parlay. Atahualpa accepted and came to the city with more than five thousand men, intending to awe the invaders with his wealth, pomp, and power.

Hundreds of servants in red livery preceded the imperial train, singing songs of victory and sweeping the ground with palm leaves so that not even a pebble would profane the feet of the nobility. Slaves wearing white carried golden vases and hammers of silver and copper. Pendulous gold charms distended the earlobes of the elite royal bodyguards, who were attired in blue. Finally, at the center of the entourage, the Inca himself rode in on a palanquin fluttering with parrot feathers—a platform supported by long poles carried on the shoulders of prominent dignitaries. Seated on an immense throne of pure gold, the monarch wore the *borla,* a ritual red circlet, as well as a headdress of colored plumes that fanned out from his crown like a peacock's tail. Around his neck glittered a collar of brilliant emeralds. His face rigid with regal indifference, he projected the unyielding ascendance of the Andes, the eternal supremacy of the sun.

The Inca's glory would be short-lived. He had paraded into an ambush.

Pizarro and a hundred and fifty of his fellow conquistadors had hidden themselves in the abandoned buildings surrounding the plaza, cannons aimed at the courtyard, cavalry ready to charge. They sent a hapless priest, Vicente de Valverde, to confront Atahualpa alone. He exhorted the Peruvian monarch to submit to the rule of King Charles V of Spain and abandon his pagan sun worship in favor of Christianity. When the Inca rejected this plea by casting the priest's Bible to the ground, Pizarro waved a white scarf to signal his troops.

Spanish horsemen and foot soldiers surged from their hiding places, lances pointed and swords flashing, as artillery hailed cannonballs upon the crowd of unsuspecting Peruvians, fogging the courtyard with smoke. Armed only with maces, slings, and bags of stone, Atahualpa's warriors found that their blows glanced off the Spaniards' armor, while the conquistadors easily hacked a path through the throng. Terror-struck, the Peruvians stampeded over the bodies of both the dead and the living, suffocating their own countrymen in their panic to retreat.

Meanwhile, Pizarro himself sustained the Spaniards' only injury of the day—a small cut he received from one of his own frenzied warriors as he charged the Inca's palanquin. A painting in the book depicted how Pizarro seized Atahualpa by the ankle and yanked him from the throne as if punishing an insolent child.

"I can save you the trouble of reading that."

Natalie glanced up from the picture to see Abe standing

beside the table with his hands in his pockets. She set the book aside. "Sorry. Didn't mean to ignore you."

He grinned. "No apologies necessary. I'm flattered you were so interested."

"I thought I should know more about this guy who's going to be in my body. Would you like to join me?" She indicated her empty breakfast plate.

"Already ate. Look, we have a couple hours till we hit the road. Let me give you a little tour." He tossed a couple of rumpled bills on the table to pay for her meal and led her out into the sunlit square.

Natalie wanted to tell him that she was perfectly content to read about the genocide of the Incan people without visiting the actual ground where they were butchered. She had shunned the pleasant gardens of the Plaza de Armas as if skirting a graveyard, afraid of being assaulted by a thousand slaughtered souls all knocking at once. But Abe shifted into lecture mode before she could object.

"In order to properly appreciate the significance of the artifacts we're seeking, you need to understand who the Incas were, what they accomplished..."

The equatorial sunshine had turned hot, and Natalie took off her down jacket. To her relief, the professor turned away from the gardens and guided her a few blocks down one of the avenues perpendicular to the plaza.

"To our modern sensibilities," Abe continued, "Inca society seems rigid—a totalitarian regime. But to the people of the culture, it was the natural order of things. The Inca was divine, the son of Inti, the sun god." Natalie almost bumped into him as he stopped to gesture dramatically. "No one was permitted to look at the Inca directly, and when his most powerful nobles came to an audience with him, they stripped off their sandals and carried a sack of earth on their backs as a sign of subjugation to the monarch. Any items touched or worn by the Inca—utensils of gold, velvety capes fashioned from the skins of bats—were destroyed when he had finished with them to prevent them from being desecrated by profane hands."

"No laundry or dishwashing," Natalie deadpanned. "It's good to be the king."

The professor chuckled and walked on. "It was a benign dictatorship, as far as dictatorships go. Though the Inca technically owned all the land in the empire, each family received an acreage, or *topo*, to farm for its own benefit. Instead of levying a tax, the system required that, in addition to raising their own crops, the people all had to work for the state between the ages of twenty-five and fifty. After fifty, you became a ward of the state. The Inca nation kept large granaries to dispense food to the needy during famine years, so as long as you pulled your weight, the empire would take care of all your basic needs. Think of it! For centuries, the Incas maintained a moneyless economic system virtually without deprivation—no hunger and no homelessness. Beats the heck out of Social Security, eh?"

"You forgot the part about 'no freedom.'" Natalie was an embittered expert in compulsory government service.

"Hey...you can't miss what you've never had. There was no upward mobility in the system. You were either a noble or a priest or a farmer, and whatever you were your children would be, too."

"I know how that goes." She thought of how the Corps had tried to railroad Callie into its membership just as it had railroaded her. "So if this place was such a utopia, how come it only took a few hundred Spanish guys to overthrow it?"

"Ah! Quite right. If twelve million Peruvians ganged up on the conquistadors, even their armor, horses, and artillery wouldn't have saved them.

"But Pizarro lucked out in that he arrived at a time of upheaval in the kingdom. The previous Inca, Huayna Capac, had died only a few years earlier, and he made the classic King Lear mistake of dividing the empire between his heirs. To Atahualpa, he bequeathed the northern portion. With its capital at Quito, Atahualpa's birthplace, the region included much of modern-day Ecuador and Colombia. To Huáscar, Atahualpa's half-brother, he left the southern portion with its capital at Cuzco, encompassing most of what is now Peru.

"Needless to say, a bloody war of succession soon flared up, a war that the brilliant and ambitious Atahualpa started and won. Forces loyal to him had defeated his rival's troops and captured Huáscar in Cuzco, but Atahualpa did not have time to consolidate power before he learned of the strange white-skinned, bearded warriors who had invaded his realm. He worried that these men might be the descendants of Viracocha, the white-skinned deity who had created humans from stone and brought them to life. Perhaps Viracocha had sent them to punish him for usurping his brother's throne.

"Pizarro quickly ascertained the political situation and exploited it. He made overtures to both Atahualpa and Huáscar's loyalists, knowing that neither side would want the

Spaniards to join the enemy in their civil war. And once he'd lured Atahualpa into his trap, Pizarro held him captive, using the Peruvians' reverence for the Inca to subdue them...which brings us here."

Crossing a smaller courtyard, Abe and Natalie arrived at a long, low structure wholly different from the Spanish colonial architecture that dominated the rest of the city. Stones of various sizes had been shaved to form enormous irregular bricks that fit together precisely to create what looked like an ancient bomb shelter.

"No mortar. See?" Abe pointed to the airless cracks between the stones. "And yet, it's withstood hundreds of earthquakes. Incredible, isn't it?"

Natalie regarded the Incan construction with both amazement and unease, wondering if she'd be any safer here than in the Plaza de Armas. "What is this place?"

"Before Pizarro, it was part of one of Atahualpa's palaces. Now it's known as the Ransom Room."

The name startled her. "The what?"

He grinned. "Come take a look."

Abe paid their entrance fee to the uniformed guard and conducted her through the open, flat-topped arch of one of the building's doorways. The temperature cooled considerably as they stepped out of the sun into the dim stone room, and Natalie put her jacket back on. Roughly seventeen feet wide by twenty-two feet long, it was empty except for a couple of other tourists, who gawked at the masonry and read the multilingual explanatory plaques mounted on the wall. The barrenness of the place added to its aura of desolation.

Natalie shrugged off the chill that rippled up her back. "Not much to see."

"It's not what *is* here—it's what *was* here that makes the room special," Abe explained. "After taking Atahualpa alive, Pizarro imprisoned him here, because he knew the Peruvians would do anything to rescue their king."

He crossed to the rear wall and called attention to a painted red line about six feet above the floor, as if blood had flooded the room and left a high-water mark. "In exchange for his life, the Inca promised to thrice fill this cell to the height of a man with his tribute: once with gold and twice with silver." Abe's voice turned husky, as if he could see the hoard piled on the vacant stone floor around him. "And if you think their masonry is impressive, wait until you see their metalwork. That's what *you* can help us find."

Natalie grimaced. "If Atahualpa made good on his part of the bargain, what happened to him?"

"Pizarro trumped up some charges of treason against him and condemned him to be burned at the stake. To get a more lenient sentence, Atahualpa agreed to convert to Christianity. The Spaniards added insult to injury by christening him 'Francisco' before they garroted him to death." He shook his head.

Natalie frowned and headed back toward the entrance. "As I said... not much to see."

But that wasn't entirely true. A painting by one of Cajamarca's most celebrated artists had been mounted on the wall by the door, and although Natalie had passed it with barely a glance on the way in, it now made her pause before passing through the archway.

On the left side of the picture, Francisco Pizarro gleamed in silver armor, his eyes blue, his beard white. Red stained both Pizarro's furious countenance and the blade of his sword. An ironic cross topped the weapon's hilt.

Atahualpa peered out of the right corner of the painting with stoic resignation yet inextinguishable dignity. Rendered in calm earth tones, the Inca's proud Asian features reminded Natalie of Honorato's.

Abe noted how her gaze lingered on Atahualpa. "Tragic, isn't it? He really was an extraordinary man. After only two weeks of captivity, he could speak Spanish and learned to play chess and cards."

"If he was so smart, why did he let himself get taken to the cleaners?" Natalie asked.

"There's a lot of speculation about that," the professor conceded. "Some historians believe Atahualpa suggested the whole ransom idea simply to buy himself more time to regroup his generals for another attack on the Spanish. Because the Inca had promised to have gold brought from every corner of the empire, Pizarro allowed him to send and receive messages from his local officials." Abe paused with dramatic gravity. "He used one such communiqué to have his captive brother Huáscar drowned in the Andamarca River to keep him from becoming an ally of the Spaniards."

Natalie rolled her eyes. "Great. Does this story *have* a good guy?"

The archaeologist let out a laugh. "You've got a point. In terms of Machiavellian tactics, Atahualpa and Pizarro had a good deal in common."

She shifted her attention back to the crimson avarice in

Pizarro's expression. This was the man they expected her to allow into her head, inundating her mind with memories of treachery, extortion, betrayal. She dreaded his presence almost as much as that of Vincent Thresher.

"I...I've got to go—" Natalie tore her gaze from the painting and lurched away from Abe. Afraid that Pizarro or Atahualpa or both might start knocking, she hurried out of the Ransom Room into the sunny courtyard, gulping lungfuls of the warm outside air as she babbled under her breath: *"The Lord is my shepherd; I shall not want..."*

When Natalie had recovered her composure, Abe offered to show her some of the city's other sights, but she declined.

"I need to call some people," she said, an excuse that happened to be true.

The professor nodded. "Best to do it here. There aren't any phones where we're going."

Trying not to dwell on the implications of being cut off from all communication with the outside world, Natalie asked Abe to wait in the square for her while she sought a pay phone to call Callie. When she finally located one, she squandered about ten minutes trying to figure out how to use her credit card to pay for the international connection—listening repeatedly to recorded instructions in Spanish she couldn't quite translate—then gave up. Dashing into a nearby store, she cashed in about twenty dollars' worth of her Peruvian money for coins to feed as needed into the pay phone's slot.

"Hello?" Ted Atwater said when she finally got through.

A digital counter on the phone started ticking down the amount of credit she had left.

"Hi, Ted. It's Natalie."

A pause followed, the delayed response of a satellite relay. "Oh, hi! How's the trip going?"

"So far, so good." Alarmed at how fast the first handful of coins ran out, she fed in the rest. "Look, I'm kind of in a hurry. Can I say hi to Callie?"

"Sure, let me get her."

She waited, irritated that she should have to pay the phone company so much for silence.

"Mommy?" Callie answered at last.

Natalie beamed. "Hey, baby girl! How are you?"

"Okay, I guess." Perhaps it was the time delay, but Callie's reply struck Natalie as flat, almost robotic. "You sound funny. Where are you?"

"In Peru, down in South America. Remember? I showed you where it was on the map."

"Yeah. Have you seen any alpacas yet?"

"Only the one Professor Wilcox gave you." Natalie laughed. "I miss you, honey. I wish you were here."

"I don't." The satellite transmission couldn't dull the edge of her daughter's resentment. "I wish *you* were *here*."

"I will be, baby girl. Soon. And I'll bring you back some souvenirs. Would you like that?"

"I guess."

"Have you ... had any problems with the bad Whos?"

A longer pause. "Some."

"Did you have to call Grandma Nora?"

"Uh-huh."

"Well, keep practicing your mantra the way I showed you. And be good for Grandpa Ted and Grandma Jean, okay?" Natalie rushed the words as she watched the liquid-crystal display counting down the last of her money. It was like talking into a time bomb. "I love you, sweetheart."

Another maddening pause, this one seeming to stretch even longer. "I love you, too, Mom—"

The counter ticked down to all zeroes, and the connection ended in an abrupt dial tone.

Natalie slammed down the receiver and went to get more change.

This time she called the hospital in Nashua. The operator put her on hold, and Natalie fretted that her credit would dwindle to nothing before she was connected to Wade's room. *I love you, Dad,* she rehearsed in her head while she waited. *I love you, Dad.*

A female voice answered. "Room 135. May I help you?"

"Yes. May I speak to Mr. Lindstrom? I'm his daughter."

"I'm sorry, he's resting now. Can I take a message?"

I love you, Dad. "Just 'get well soon,' I guess."

"Can you call back in a couple hours? He'll probably be awake by then."

Natalie glanced at the Andes Mountains that loomed behind her. "No. I don't think that will be possible."

10

The Camp in the Clouds

ABE HAD NEVER SAID ANYTHING ABOUT RIDING horses—Natalie was sure of that. If he had, she doubted that *any* amount of money could have persuaded her to climb on the back of an animal that might, at any moment, buck her off its back and then stamp her head to a pulp with metal-shod hooves.

"I'm afraid they're the only way to get where we're going," the professor replied when she complained. He patted the side of his black-and-white mount, which snorted and shook its leather reins. "But, really, you don't need to worry. They're trained, and tame as anything. You'll be perfectly safe. Honorato will make sure of that."

He gestured to Natalie and said something to the Peruvian in Spanish, and Honorato gave her a confident nod.

Natalie clicked her teeth together as she gazed back down the rutted dirt road they'd taken to get here. They'd driven a few hours from Cajamarca to this tiny scattering of stone huts between the towns of Celendin and Chachapoyas. In the process, they'd penetrated the cloud layer, rising from nine thousand to more than thirteen thousand feet above sea level. No trees grew at this altitude, only dry-looking grass and scrub brush. Natalie's headache had come roaring back like a famished tiger, and she was tempted to hitchhike back down that road rather than follow Abe and Honorato even farther into the stratosphere.

To her right, the man from whom Abe had rented the horses was already covering the Range Rover with a waterproof tarp. The professor had evidently paid him for the privilege of parking the SUV beside his Hobbit-size house. Seeing the car disappear beneath its plastic shroud killed Natalie's hope of turning back.

"Okay," she grumbled. "How do I do this?"

They loaded their gear into packs on the three horses and let Natalie take the smallest of them, a patient gray mare barely bigger than a pony. It failed to make things much easier. With Abe instructing her, Natalie attempted several times to put her foot in the left stirrup, lift herself into the saddle, and swing her right leg over to the other stirrup. But the stirrup wobbled under her weight, she slipped against the side of the horse, and the mare huffed and shimmied away. Each time Natalie lost her nerve and jumped back to the ground.

Finally, while Abe held the mare's reins and calmed the animal, Honorato grabbed Natalie around the waist and lifted her onto the saddle. Once she was straddling the horse's back, the Peruvian put her feet in the stirrups, pushed her knees into position against the horse's side, and placed the reins in her hands. He then tied a rope from the mare's bridle to his brown gelding's saddle, forming a small horse train.

Spurring his own horse, Abe took the lead and Honorato

clopped behind him. The rope became taut, and the mare began to plod forward. Natalie's stomach squirmed like a beached jellyfish as she bobbed with the movement of the horse's powerful flanks. Her knees felt each swell of the mare's breathing.

Natalie couldn't help but wonder if Dan could see her from his vantage point in the Place Beyond. If so, he must be having a good laugh at her expense, given how much he'd had to cajole her just to get her to ride a fiberglass carousel horse. Terrified of losing her balance, Natalie gripped the pommel as well as the reins, wishing that this mare also possessed a brass pole she could hang on to.

They ascended the mountain ridge above them with painstaking slowness, the steep path barely wide enough to accommodate the horses. No one had either the breath or the inclination to speak. Natalie stared at the back of Honorato's seesawing head to keep from looking down at the edge of the trail, where the grassy slope slanted down to a plunging chasm between the mountains. The horses picked their steps with care, Natalie's pulse stuttering every time her mare's hooves slipped on the loose gravel and dirt. In a few places, the trail grew so rocky and treacherous that the skittish animals stopped entirely, requiring Honorato and Abe to whip their flanks to urge them upward again.

If going uphill frayed Natalie's nerves, going downhill shredded them. As they crested the ridge and descended the other side, she slid forward in the saddle, which shifted from grinding her tailbone to chafing her crotch. Natalie now had no choice but to gape at the panorama that filled her view: green peaks floating on the puffed mist of clouds. The forward pull of gravity created a constant sensation of falling, and the horses hunched back on their hindquarters to keep momentum from accelerating them into a rolling tumble. Whenever she started to hyperventilate in panic, however, Abe would flash Natalie a reassuring smile over his shoulder, calming her enough to keep her conscious and alert.

Natalie's terror turned into tedium as they plodded for mile upon mile, and, to occupy her mind, she listed everything she could do with the money she'd get for suffering through this. First and foremost, she and Callie would take a long, long vacation, stay in comfortable, modern hotels, and refuse to enter any building constructed before 1960.

It was nearly sunset when the ground leveled off into a raked shelf overlooking the valley that divided the peak from its neighbors. A small village of flimsy-looking tents occupied the incline, their canvas walls shuddering in the breeze. The scale of the surrounding mountain range made the camp resemble a flea circus, with tiny specks flitting between the structures like mites.

As the horses approached the encampment, the mites enlarged into men, all engaged in some form of manual labor: a few digging in roped-off pits, others sifting through buckets of soil. The lazy carelessness with which they toiled reminded Natalie of a few of the highway construction workers she'd seen, who did as little as possible while trying to appear busy until quitting time. When she trotted into the village behind Abe and Honorato, they each stopped what they were doing and stared at her. Natalie felt like Lady Godiva riding nude into Coventry. Not only was she a *bruja* here, she seemed to be the only woman at all.

She wasn't the only one to notice the sudden quiet. The moment the sounds of activity in the camp ceased, a pale blond man in a navy blazer and blindingly white pants and shoes emerged from the largest tent and awaited them at the center of the camp with the composure of a host attending to his dinner guests.

"You've got here at last, then," he murmured to Abe in an officious English accent as the professor halted and dismounted in front of him. "I was about to send Romoldo to hunt you down."

Stiff from the ride, the archaeologist limped over to him and strained to smile. "Sorry to keep you waiting, Mr. Azure. But you know you can always rely on me."

Natalie's inner thighs were so sore that she could barely straighten her legs to support herself as Honorato lifted her off the mare. It hurt to move, yet she had only a moment to regain her balance before Abe led her over to the blond man while Honorato unloaded the horses.

"Natalie, may I present our patron, Nathan Azure?"

"Happy to meet you, sir." She put out her hand and, for the first time, looked into Azure's eyes. A reflexive repulsion made her pull her arm back. This was the blond man she'd seen in her vision in the bath at the Cajamarca hostel. The hatred attached to the memory flooded her with irrational loathing for Azure, a man she'd never met.

He did not seem offended by her reluctance to shake his hand. Indeed, he kept his own hands clasped in front of him, his leather driving gloves making it look as if he'd just climbed from behind the wheel of a Jaguar. He acknowledged her with a martinet bow.

"Ms. Lindstrom—the pleasure is mine." But Azure looked more cross than pleased. His left cheek twitched, and he brushed it with his gloved hand as if shooing a mosquito. "We hope to make your stay as pleasant as possible. I'll have one of the men prepare your supper directly."

"Uh…thanks." During the journey over the mountain, Natalie's mind had been so filled with fear of imminent disaster that it crowded out the concept of hunger. Now that Azure mentioned food, she realized that, yes, she *was* starving, but was almost too exhausted to eat.

"While you're waiting to dine, I thought you might want to learn a bit more about why you're here. If you'll be so kind as to follow me…" Although Natalie wasn't really in the mood for another history lecture, she accompanied Azure into the large tent nearby.

To Natalie's surprise, Abe did not go with her as she dipped under the tent's low-hanging opening and entered the dark interior. The dim light of dusk shone through the canvas like an X-ray, revealing the skeletal structure of tent poles but leaving the shelter's contents in shadow.

"I hear your family's in the mining business," Natalie said, hoping to cover her previous rudeness. "I'd think you'd have easier ways to find gold than this."

"We mine borax," Azure informed her dryly. "Keeping the world's toilets sanitized for your protection."

The tycoon moved around behind a small table to loom above the tent's only light source, a small halogen lamp that he'd turned upward to illuminate his face from below, as if he were a vaudeville magician before the footlights. He had placed an object on the table, but in the darkness Natalie could only make out the vague shape of a human face with oversize ears and a broad chin. The fact that she could see neither its eyes nor its expression gave her the unsettling impression that a third person was silently witnessing their conversation.

Azure peered at her over the lamp. "I don't know how much the good Dr. Wilcox has told you about Pizarro and the Inca…"

"We got to the part where Pizarro killed Atahualpa after shaking him down for everything he had," Natalie summarized.

"Splendid! Then you know what a vast quantity of wealth we're concerned with here: nearly eighty-eight cubic meters of gold, and twice that again in silver. But not merely gold and silver. Artworks of transcendent beauty and inestimable value, irreplaceable relics of a civilization and culture as advanced and refined as any spawned in Europe. Treasures such as this one."

He swiveled the lamp's bulb downward to illuminate the object on the table. Placed upright on a wire rack, the face of wrought gold irradiated the tent's interior with its opulence. The visage glowed with a fluid sheen as if still molten, its flat-mouthed inscrutability suggesting the restrained ferocity of a volcanic deity. Inlays of polished turquoise ornamented the arc of its headdress and its large circular ears, while the stylized Asian eyes glowered with indigo discs of lapis lazuli.

Natalie forgot her hunger and fatigue. Before this, the most gold she'd ever seen firsthand was in the band around her father's finger.

Her mouth dry, she raised her hand toward the shine of the mask's burnished surface. "May I...?"

"I would rather you didn't, actually."

Natalie drew back, abashed.

Like a museum docent, Azure waited for her full attention before continuing. "The conquistadors disdained such masterpieces as pagan idolatry and thought nothing of forcing the native goldsmiths to melt down their own art into ingots for shipment to Spain. Icons from the Temple of the Sun ended up gilding the altars of Catholic churches. Pizarro pillaged Peru so thoroughly that only a handful of preconquest gold relics remain. I paid more than a million pounds for this burial mask at Sotheby's."

I could retire on that, Natalie thought, coveting the metal with her eyes since she could not touch it. "What makes you think the Spaniards left any of these things lying around?"

"Because Pizarro's greed was insatiable, and his treachery knew no limits—even when it came to stealing from his own men." Azure picked up a thick tome that lay on the table beside the mask and opened it to a bookmarked page, citing the text as if quoting Scripture. "In return for the patronage of Charles the Fifth, the conquistadors customarily paid twenty percent of their spoils of war to the King—the 'royal fifth,' as it was called.

"But when he divided Atahualpa's ransom, Pizarro set aside more than three-fourths of the treasure for Charles, a huge tribute, ostensibly to curry favor with His Majesty. The amount was so vast that neither the King nor the conquistadors would have been the wiser if Pizarro had skimmed the cream of the hoard and hidden it for himself."

"Maybe he did," Natalie said. "And maybe he spent it."

Nathan Azure set aside the book, shaking his head. "Pizarro could only have concealed the treasure in this area before continuing his conquest of the south. And he never returned to the northern sierra during his lifetime, because his former comrades murdered him in Lima in 1541. I'm certain his cache is still here. And, with your help, he'll tell us where it is."

I can't guarantee that, she wanted to say but didn't. "And what happens to these artifacts if we find them?"

"*When* we find them, I will ensure they are properly preserved for posterity." He stepped from behind the table. "It's not about money, Ms. Lindstrom. Precious metals were sacred to the Incas: gold was the sweat of the sun; silver, the tears of the moon. Turning their idols to bullion was sacrilege. If any of their works survive, we must rescue them." His gaze gravitated toward the mask. "I understand you fancy yourself an artist. Could you stand by and watch a masterpiece like this be lost forever?"

Natalie considered the golden face with its indigo eyes; it was fearsome yet also awe-inspiring. "No," she answered at last.

"Then we'll begin first thing tomorrow, once you've had a chance to refresh yourself. I imagine your supper's nearly ready now. I'm sure Dr. Wilcox will be happy to show you to your quarters." He swept aside the tent door's flap for her.

"Yeah. See you tomorrow." Grateful to be dismissed, Natalie ducked through the opening to the camp outside to find the professor.

* * *

His breath growing heavier, Nathan Azure waited until the Lindstrom woman was gone, until he and the burial mask were alone together. Then he unfastened the strap of his right driving glove and removed it so he could stroke the skin of the face with his bare fingers.

Gold. No other substance on earth felt like it—slick as frozen honey, yet with an organic suppleness that baser metals lacked. The Incas were quite right to worship it as the divine essence of the gods.

Nathan Azure had risked everything to obtain it.

Even now he felt the same chill of desire as he did as a boy of seven, when he goggled through bulletproof glass at one of the gleaming figurines in the British Museum's Egyptology exhibit, cold sweat soaking into his Eton school uniform. That day Nathan determined that he should be the next Howard Carter, that he would not let anyone or anything stop him from unearthing the most stunning treasure in human history.

It's rubbish, lad, his father had said of his ambition to be an archaeologist. *We make more money from washing powder than you'll ever dig out of the ground.*

Nathan did not object when Father forced him to major in finance at Cambridge, although he continued to study ancient cultures and languages on his own. When he graduated with distinction, he took his place on the board of Azure PLC, as any dutiful son would have. Within ten years he'd accumulated enough influence to force his father and all three of his siblings out of the company.

With no one left to object, he was free to use the profits from all that washing powder to pursue his true passion. The fortunes of ancient kings and lost civilizations proved more elusive than he anticipated, however. He funded a series of fruitless digs in Africa and Southeast Asia, squandered millions on ventures to locate sunken ships in the Caribbean and the South Pacific. He personally oversaw the last of the scuba expeditions, sending his divers down in relentless round-the-clock searches, keeping them underwater to the limits of their air supplies.

Two of them died, and one was now crippled by the bends.

Each failure only fired Nathan's determination to validate himself to his father, his family, the world. But his enemies were circling around him. The Azure PLC board members had grown impatient with his inattention to the company and its falling revenues, and his sister Jane had conspired with a rival firm to mount a takeover offer.

Nathan Azure would not let them keep him from fulfilling his destiny, however. He had leveraged his remaining shares in the company to finance this Peruvian expedition. He *knew* Francisco Pizarro had hidden a cache of priceless gold artifacts somewhere in these godforsaken mountains, and he would find it. Natalie Lindstrom would make sure of that.

Azure's cheek spasmed, and he scrubbed it with his gloved left hand, cursing Wilcox again. The thought of being a touchstone for that sanctimonious scholar's soul galled him, particularly when he'd gone to such great lengths to ensure that neither he nor any of his men ever touched the professor with their bare hands. Now, because of the dead man's spittle, Lindstrom could use Azure himself to summon Wilcox...if she ever touched him. He would make sure she didn't, at least for as long as he needed her.

To calm himself, Nathan Azure once more caressed the burnished gold of the mask with his naked fingertips. He *would* succeed this time because he had sacrificed too much to fail. He had no other choice.

Neither did the Violet.

11

Settling In

WHEN NATALIE EMERGED FROM AZURE'S TENT, SHE SAW that the mountains to the west of the camp had swallowed the sun. Her remaining energy waned in tandem with the ember-orange cast of the sky.

"Natalie! Over here." Abe stood outside one of the camp's smaller tents and waved to her, his white shirt ghostly in the dusk. Legs aching, she trudged the twenty-odd paces to where he waited, and he pulled aside the flap of the entrance with a flourish. "Welcome home."

I wish, Natalie thought. "I'd love to have dinner with you," she told the professor, "but I'm barely maintaining consciousness at the moment."

He gave a sympathetic nod. "Understood. Get some rest, and I'll see you in the morning."

"Thanks." She entered her new lodging and, to keep from collapsing into sleep, started unpacking her luggage, which had been left on the floor.

Working by the light of a hissing propane lantern that dangled from the tent's framework, she laid out her tooth-brush, toothpaste, and other toiletry items, then dug out the few other nonclothing items she'd brought for her brief stay:

her CD player, Abe's book on Pizarro and a paperback novel, a fresh sketchpad, and a set of pastel chalks with which she hoped to draw some of the Peruvian sights, time permitting. These items she placed on the tiny worktable by the entrance.

Aside from the table, a cot, and a director's chair, the only other furnishing was a large water keg on a stand and a toilet seat with legs that sat in the far corner, a roll of toilet paper on top of its closed lid. Natalie had been constipated all day, and she groaned as she saw the black plastic trash bag that hung below the seat's oval.

"What have I got myself into, baby girl?" she said with a sigh to the framed photo of Callie she took from her bags.

"It is better than what we have," a deep, accented voice said from behind her. "At least yours is private, yes?"

She started, ashamed that someone had caught her sneering at the makeshift potty. Her surprise only increased when she saw Honorato standing inside the door holding a tray of food. *You speak English!* she almost shrieked but stopped herself. She'd already acted the dumb American around Honorato enough.

"*¡Hola!* I didn't see you there." She laid the photo on the table and put out her hand. "Thanks for all your help today."

"*De nada.*" He set the tray beside the picture and shook her hand. Like everyone else in camp, he wore thick leather gloves. He nodded toward Callie. "Your little girl?"

"Yes." She smiled, relieved to be able to talk about home. "It's from her birthday party last year."

The photo showed Callie grinning over her Horton the

Elephant cake, a big lump of stolen frosting on her finger. Natalie handed it to Honorato, who bobbed his head in appreciation.

"Very pretty. My wife would be very jealous." He handed the picture back. "We have four boys, but she keeps trying, yes?"

Natalie laughed. "Be careful what you wish for! One girl can be as much trouble as four boys." She propped the photo on the table. "This one will kill me if I'm not back by her birthday in June."

Honorato did not smile. "The girl—she is with her father, yes?"

At the thought of Dan, Natalie's levity fluttered away. "No. He's dead."

Honorato's somber face grew a bit longer. "I am very sorry."

Natalie surveyed her dinner, which smelled strongly of chili, and wondered if she would be able to eat any of it. "You speak wonderful English," she said, conscious of how Honorato stared at her. "Where did you learn it?"

"Wyoming. I herd sheep there six years to make money to go to university in Ayacucho, yes?" He raised six fingers for emphasis. "Then I waste ten years reading Marx and Mao and fighting for the people, only to see Fujimori and his thieves ruin us. Now I want only to make money and move my family to U.S."

Natalie didn't know much about Peruvian politics, but she remembered seeing something in the *L.A. Times* about President Fujimori being driven into exile to escape prosecution for corruption charges. "I know what you mean. I came here to make money for my family, too."

Honorato evaluated her for a moment and lowered his voice. "You want to go home for the birthday of your little girl, yes?"

"Yes…"

"Then do not give the big *gringo* what he wants until he gives you money and takes you back to U.S. You understand, yes?"

The urgency with which he delivered this common-sense advice made Natalie wonder if she really did understand, but she nodded.

Honorato did not seem satisfied with the response. "Remember what I tell you," he said. "You do not want to be like *el profesor.*"

He didn't explain what he meant by this, although Natalie guessed that he was warning her not to become indentured to Azure the way Abe had.

Honorato's expression relaxed to its usual solemnity. "I hope you like the food. I cook it for you."

"*Gracias.* I'm sure I will." She pulled the director's chair up to the table and sat down.

Honorato moved to leave but paused halfway through the tent's door. "And do not tell the *gringos* that I speak English. They give me too much work already, yes?"

Natalie chuckled. "Yes."

The Peruvian left, and Natalie began eating the dinner on the tray. The food was simple but good—a spicy stew of chicken, corn, potatoes, and carrots—but the fork became heavier and heavier in her hand with each bite she took.

Ordinarily a fanatic about oral hygiene, she skipped brushing her teeth and saved her remaining strength to use the homemade toilet.

Without taking off her clothes, her wig, or even her boots, Natalie shut off the tent's lantern and lay on the cot in the darkness, pulling its thick gray blanket up to her chin. Her eyes closed automatically, and she remembered neither falling asleep nor any of the dreams she might have had that night.

12

A Drink with the *Marqués*

THE FOLLOWING MORNING, RAIN SPATTERED THE tent's canvas roof like the impatient drumming of a thousand fingers. Natalie became conscious of the sound but felt no urge to move or even to open her eyes. She lay there for a long time, vainly hoping that she might wake up and find herself back with Callie at the Atwaters' house in Lakeport.

"You must eat quickly," Honorato's voice said, rousting her out of her half-doze. "The big *gringo* wants you now."

Moaning, Natalie rolled onto her side, feeling stale in the dirty clothes from the day before. "He doesn't waste any time, does he?"

Standing next to the worktable, Honorato struck a match and lit the lantern. "That is the problem. He thinks he has wasted too much time already."

As he turned the valve on the propane tank, yellow light revealed that he had already replaced last night's dinner tray with a plate of scrambled eggs and toast. Pushing aside the flap to exit the tent, he gestured to the downpour outside. "If you hurry, you can take a nice shower now, yes?"

He abandoned Natalie to sulk over her breakfast. She scratched her arms and found them speckled with flea bites.

So much for Abe's attempt to protect her from Peruvian parasites. Ghosts or not, she already found herself missing the hot tubs of the Baños del Inca.

Though Natalie didn't shower al fresco as Honorato suggested, she did change her clothes and brush her teeth, which made her feel somewhat better. She became especially glad for the Peruvian hat the woman had given her in Cajamarca, for its bell shape and broad, drooping brim kept most of the rain off her as Abe escorted her to the smallest tent in the camp, which had been set up as an interrogation room for her summoning sessions. Nathan Azure had to stoop to keep from brushing the canvas ceiling as he stood to welcome her inside.

"Ms. Lindstrom! Good morning. I trust you slept better than I did." He indicated the vacant director's chair opposite him at a table draped with white linen. "Let's get started, shall we?"

"Sorry if I kept you waiting," Natalie said, taking her seat. Behind her, she heard Abe zip up the tent entrance as if sealing a body bag.

Azure waved off the apology with one gloved hand. "Not at all. Forgive me for disturbing you so early, but I felt that the sooner we got started, the sooner you could get home to that charming daughter of yours."

"Yes. Thanks."

The lantern that hung above the table revealed a large oblong object covered with a satin cloth. The hidden item was probably the touchstone Azure wanted her to use, and the sight of it aroused the customary anxiety Natalie felt prior to an inhabitation. But what she didn't see bothered her even more.

There was no SoulScan unit.

Natalie had already taken the hat and wig from her head before she noticed the machine's absence. Her apprehension growing, she inventoried the tent's contents with another glance.

Azure arched his eyebrows. "Something wrong?"

"Don't you want... verification?" She tapped her scalp, calling attention to its tattooed node points.

"That won't be necessary." The tycoon relaxed into the sling of his chair's canvas back. "I have complete trust in you."

Natalie fidgeted with the wig in her lap. As much as she detested the SoulScan—hated the barnacle adherence of its electrodes to her skull—she now longed for it like a child pining for her security blanket. She remembered the scarlet cruelty of Francisco Pizarro's face in the Ransom Room painting, imagined that bestial nature subjugating her mind with its violence. Natalie knew from experience that, although the nerve-searing discharge from the SoulScan's Panic Button was painful, it was better than being the slave of another soul's psychosis.

You could *fake it*, a voice inside her suggested. *Simply use your protective mantra, then pretend that you failed to summon the Spanish creep. Azure won't know the difference; he'll just get mad and send you home, getting you out of this mess.*

Across from her, Nathan Azure drew the cloth from the object on the table, exposing a rusty breastplate etched with a faded family crest. He nudged it toward her. "This should suffice, I think."

The temptation to abort the summoning without telling Azure nearly overwhelmed Natalie in that moment. She hardly cared whether she enraged the millionaire or lost the money he'd promised her as long as she could return to her safe, comfortable condo with Callie.

But her own unwillingness to admit that she'd made a mistake—that she'd put herself and her family through this whole experience for nothing—egged her on. She could handle Pizarro. He was merely another sociopath, and she'd dealt with his type before. In the Corps Crime Division, he would have been just another day at the office. She couldn't wimp out now, not when Callie needed therapy and her dad had inadequate health insurance.

As she spiraled her consciousness into the circular holding pattern of the spectator mantra, Natalie laid her palm over the cuirass's engraved crest.

Row, row, row your boat,
Gently down the stream.
Merrily, merrily, merrily, merrily!
Life is but—

She hiccoughed, lungs collapsing as if punctured by the intersecting swords in a magician's box. She had encountered souls before who relived their deaths when summoned, but never had she endured more than one death simultaneously. Now she felt herself stabbed, shot, lanced, strangled, bludgeoned, and exploded all at once. The sensations of hundreds of men and women, captured in their final moment of mutilation, fused in Natalie's mind into a single excruciating fugue of annihilation.

Francisco Pizarro suffered the memories of far more murders than his own.

The flimsy director's chair wobbled as Natalie doubled up, her mantra forgotten, her thoughts smothered by an avalanche of agony. White to black, her perceptions flared to supernova brightness, then winked out completely.

Nathan Azure regarded the comatose form of Natalie Lindstrom with folded hands, unsure how long this inhabitation was supposed to take. After several minutes, he rose to examine the Violet's body, which had sprawled forward to form an awkward bridge between the chair and the table. His perpetual frown deepened with concern—not for the Violet herself, but for the catastrophic effect her premature demise might have on the expedition's success.

Azure reached tentatively toward Lindstrom's delicate neck, hoping he could detect a pulse in her carotid artery without having to remove his glove. The body spared him the trauma of touching it by snapping upright.

Lindstrom's violet eyes seemed to have receded into her skull, and she scanned the tent's interior with the fierce, futile wariness of a dying panther. *"¿Qué nuevo infierno es esto?"* she rasped.

What new hell is this?

Nathan Azure's face relaxed into an expression of gloating confidence. He retook his seat and addressed the Violet in the lisping Castilian Spanish of Francisco Pizarro's native Extremadura. "Welcome, *Marqués.*"

The honorific was Pizarro's title at the time of his assassination, and he responded to it now, turning Lindstrom's eyes toward Azure with a glare both baleful and intrigued. "You seem to know me, *señor.* Should I know you?"

"Know that I am a friend," Azure replied. "And an admirer."

"I was killed by friends and admirers." The conquistador looked down at the skinny femininity of the Violet's body. "And this—this is the witch you use to raise me from the Pit?"

"You might call her that."

Pizarro showed no surprise. "I know about witches. In my youth, during the Inquisition, I heard them speaking with the voices of the dead. I saw such witches burned at the stake, but I suppose there is not wood enough in the world to rid us of all the devil's servants. Why have you brought me here?"

"To share a drink with you." Azure retrieved the two gold goblets and the bottle of expensive Spanish wine he'd hidden beneath the linen-draped table. Nudging aside the cuirass, he uncorked the bottle and poured them each a cup of wine. "I think you will appreciate this vintage," he remarked, lifting his own goblet in a toast. "In your honor, *Marqués.*"

But the conquistador did not drink with him. He stared not at the goblet set before him but at the breastplate that bore the engraved seal of the King's favor. "You are not the first. Others have used their witches to call the great Pizarro from his grave to tell his story. Everyone wants to hear how a swineherd outwitted a king, eh?" He tapped a finger on the insignia of the Andes, the mountains he had claimed for Spain.

"Outwitted *two* kings. Atahualpa...and Charles the Fifth." Azure took another sip of wine, but did not blink as he eyed Pizarro's expression over the rim of his goblet.

The old warrior squared Lindstrom's shoulders into a posture of military pride. "I was a loyal servant of the Spanish crown."

"Yes, and such loyalty must be rewarded. Why should the King mind if his royal fifth was not as large when it reached Spain as when you collected it from your men?"

"What are you saying, *señor*?" Pizarro sounded as if he were offended, but the way he cocked Lindstrom's head suggested curiosity, even amusement.

"I am saying that *you*, Francisco Pizarro, conquered Peru, and therefore deserved a larger share of Atahualpa's ransom than any of your compatriots...or even King Charles himself. Is that not so, *Marqués*?"

The conquistador spat air, laughter for a man who never laughed. "If so, what of it? All the gold in Creation cannot help me now."

"It could return the glory that belongs to your name. The world has largely forgotten you, *Marqués*. But when they see again the fruits of your victory, everyone will again hail the courage and cunning of Pizarro."

"Hail me, will they?" He leaned forward, and the expression on Lindstrom's livid, bald visage fossilized into a death's-head. "All my life I fought for the honor of God and Spain. With my two hands alone, I killed hundreds of heathens. I filled the coffers of the Holy Roman Empire and delivered thousands of souls to the Church. And what was my reward? I was cut navel to neck by men I treated like brothers, and in death, the God I served sends the spirits of the cursed Inca savages to sting me like a swarm of bees. Atahualpa himself delights in sharing with me how the kiss of the garrote felt on his neck." He pinched a hand around Lindstrom's trachea for emphasis. "The only rest I have is when a fool like you pulls me from the well of Hades to tell my tales. Now I ask you, *señor*...what possible good could your glory do me?"

Azure's left cheek twitched as he put down his wine. "If the gold will do you no good, then there is no harm in revealing where you hid it."

Pizarro snorted again. "No, if I indeed hid such gold, as you say."

Azure slammed his fist on the table, rattling the goblets. "I *know* you left a fortune in these mountains, you miserable pig farmer! Now tell me where it is!"

At that, Francisco Pizarro grinned—a smile as unnatural and misbegotten as a mastiff born with three heads. "I like you, *señor*. We are alike, you and me. Perhaps I shall help you find my gold...if I remember where it is."

The Englishman's face turned cold. "How could you not remember where it is?"

The conquistador shrugged, tapped Lindstrom's temple. "After a few centuries, the memories they fade, do they not? But do not fear! Maybe tomorrow I remember, maybe the next day. It is only a matter of time, eh, *señor*?"

Known for his temperance in life, Pizarro lifted his goblet in a mock toast to Nathan Azure, then drained the wine in a single guzzle.

The head rush jolted Natalie out of the stunned semiconsciousness into which she'd fallen when Pizarro inhabited her. She could feel the raw burning at the back of her throat, the prickling that needled her face and her inner ears. Since she never drank alcohol, she did not recognize these symptoms. She only knew they meant she was in greater danger than ever.

Row, row, row your boat, she recited. *Gently down the…*

But wait—that wasn't the right one. She wanted her *protective* mantra, the one that would purge Pizarro from her brain.

The Lord is my shepherd; I shall not want.

He leadeth me beside the still… no, that came later.

He restoreth my soul came next… or did it?

Whether it was the initial fuzziness of intoxication or simply her own panic, Natalie grew increasingly flustered as she struggled to assemble the phrases of a psalm she'd repeated countless times since childhood. The dim sense of her body began to recede from her again, and she would have welcomed the electroshock of a Panic Button or even a lightning bolt to clear her head.

She forced herself to pause and concentrate.

The Lord is my shepherd; I shall not want.
He maketh me to lie down in green pastures…

As her consciousness supplanted Pizarro's inside her head, Natalie caught flickers of his thoughts, as if she were gazing through a train window into the passenger cars of a locomotive headed in the opposite direction. Weird totems of men with flat, tombstone-shaped bodies and shieldlike heads perched in the mouth of a cave, desiccated human faces like shrunken-apple sculptures, sun-bleached skulls—

Her body's perceptions slammed her back into consciousness with the suddenness of a swinging door, and the visions ended. Her stomach churned with nausea as overlapping images of Nathan Azure vibrated before her.

"Ms. Lindstrom?" the twin Azures said in tandem. "Is that you? What did you see in his mind?"

I'm fine, thank you, she thought, and squinted until the twins became a single, stereoscopic Azure. When her view of the tent stopped quivering, she saw the bottle and goblets sitting before her. "You gave him *this*?" she snapped, indicating the wine.

He seemed genuinely perplexed by the question. "Yes. I thought it might get him to talk. What of it?"

"You could have killed me, that's what!" She sprang to her feet, snatched up her wig and hat. "A Violet has to maintain absolute mental control during an inhabitation. If I got drunk, I might not be able to retake control of my body in time."

Azure blocked her exit from the tent. "I—I'm terribly sorry. Horribly careless of me, and it shan't happen again. But no harm done, eh? Now, what did you see in his thoughts?"

Pincerlike pain pressed at Natalie's temples. She wanted

only to go back to sleep, and to appease Azure, she almost blurted descriptions of the nonsensical pictures of slant-browed icons and mummified faces that flitted through Pizarro's memory. But then Azure's face trembled like the lid of a pot about to boil over, and Natalie recalled the stern advice Honorato had offered her.

Do not give the big gringo *what he wants until he gives you money and takes you back to U.S.*

"What was Pizarro thinking?" Azure asked again.

"I don't know," she told him. "It was all in Spanish."

The tycoon's breath hissed out like escaping steam. "Then we shall try again later."

He stepped aside and Natalie hurried to leave, but the door's zipper got stuck halfway up. She crawled through the low opening into the fusillade of rain outside and ran back to her own tent.

When she was gone, Nathan Azure swept his arm across the table, flinging the goblets and wine against the tent wall in an explosion of red.

13

The Spaniard's Stalemate

A TEETOTALER, NATALIE HAD NO TOLERANCE FOR
wine, and alcohol only compounded the effects of her altitude sickness. She spent the rest of the day on her cot, although the relentless grindstone of her headache kept her
from sleeping until late in the evening.

Nathan Azure gave her no such respite the following day.
He insisted she summon Francisco Pizarro both in the morning and in the afternoon. The day after that, he demanded
three sessions, to no avail. By the end of the week, Natalie
spent the majority of her waking hours inhabited by the conquistador, and she began to have the eerie, detached feeling
of being a guest in her own body—a silent observer, powerless to stop the dead Spaniard who commandeered her flesh.
Yet Azure still learned nothing about the location of Pizarro's
gold.

Not that he had any difficulty in getting Pizarro to talk.
The old warrior seemed only too happy to ramble about
his past triumphs while Azure simmered in exasperation.
Pizarro especially delighted in tantalizing the Englishman
with tales of the fabulous wealth he'd accumulated in his
campaigns.

"The Temple of the Sun in Cuzco—you should have seen it, *señor!*" he rhapsodized. "The mummies of the Incas, each one seated in its own throne. The gold on every wall, so much it would blind you. We pried the metal from the stone, took it all.

"When we divided the spoils, my men became so rich they wagered fortunes on a single roll of the dice. There was a cavalier, Leguizano, who lost a plate like this"—Pizarro spread Natalie's arms wide—"with the face of the pagans' sun god on it. After that, the men would challenge each other to 'gamble the sun before sunrise.'" He made a sound that might have been a chuckle. "A pity you cannot join them in a game of *dobladilla* today, eh, *señor?*"

At other times, the Spaniard would taunt Azure with references to the hidden hoard itself. "I chose a group of savages to help me move the gold," he reminisced over a meal the tycoon had ordered for him. "As you might imagine, I could not employ any of my conquistadors without offering them a share of the treasure. Twenty savages and ten mules I needed to carry my wealth into the wilderness. One of the pagans suggested the location—a place that no native would disturb and no white man would find. When we returned, I had him and all the others executed to protect the secret." Pizarro then stabbed a fork into a piece of potato and lifted it from the stew. "I must say, of all the foods we discovered in Pirú, I enjoy these homely vegetables the most." And he popped it in Natalie's mouth, smacking her lips as he ate, while across the table from him Nathan Azure brooded in livid silence, his face purple, his lips white.

After each of these fruitless conversations, Azure grilled

Natalie at length about what she'd gleaned from Pizarro's mind during the inhabitation. "Nothing I could understand," she told him each time. He pressed her to repeat the Spanish words she'd heard in the conquistador's thoughts, but she merely mumbled some mispronounced gibberish that wasn't Spanish or any intelligible human tongue. Driven to distraction, Azure threatened to strap her in a chair and school her in Spanish himself.

But Natalie knew the conquistador did not string Azure along for amusement but rather as a pathetic deferment of damnation. Never had she felt a soul that so yearned for peace—for nonexistence, if necessary—yet his victims would not let him go and the Place Beyond wouldn't have him. Every time she pulled him from limbo, she glimpsed the memories inflicted upon Pizarro by the Incas he'd slaughtered. For every notch he'd marked on his sword's hilt, he suffered the pain of the same blade a thousandfold. Worse still, he was forced to view his own rabid countenance from the victim's perspective, feeling how he had hacked their limbs and cleft their entrails. Having been subjected to the sense-memories of dozens of murder victims in brief but awful inhabitations, Natalie shuddered to imagine what it would be like to endure such torment for centuries without respite—and know that you alone had caused the agony.

The unkindest cut of all for Pizarro, though, was the recollection of his own assassination. *Death to the tyrant!* shouted his former comrades in arms, now turned conspirators determined to wrest control of the country from him. Ten against one, they stormed him in his palace bedchamber, not even permitting him to fasten his cuirass before attacking. His swordsmanship was still keen, however, and the traitors called for ten more of their confederates to overwhelm him. At last, one of the mongrels slashed his neck, and Francisco barely had time to gasp his last confession before his throat filled with blood. Natalie shared his bitterness as he recalled how, in lieu of the last rites, he had moistened his fingers with his own blood to draw a cross on the floor beside him. With his remaining strength, he kissed the symbol—his final act of devotion to the God whom he believed he had served with unswerving righteousness. A God who now seemed to have consigned him to an endless Purgatory of remonstrance and regret.

Forced to empathize with the ancient warrior, Natalie could almost pity him. In Abe's book, she had read that, by the age of sixty-six, the old veteran had wearied of battle and tried to reinvent himself as a statesman and patron of public works. He was known to play tennis with his servants and once leapt into a river to save an Inca native from drowning. He founded great cities in the lands he had conquered: Trujillo, named after the village of his ignoble birth, and his crowning achievement, *la Ciudad de los Reyes*—the City of Kings, which was now the Peruvian capital, Lima.

Having never formed emotional attachments to other human beings, Pizarro made construction the monomaniacal passion of his later years, as if to compensate for a life of destruction with an equal fanaticism for creation. Even now, during the hours he idled in Natalie's mind, his only happy thoughts were not of people but of buildings—his miradors, his churches, and his splendid governor's palace, its patio lined with orange trees. How crestfallen would he be, Natalie wondered, if he learned that every single one of these edifices had fallen prey to time, earthquakes, or modernity?

May dissolved into June, but Natalie could not say precisely when, for she lost track of time in the dreary sameness of the days. Session after session, Pizarro's crushing ennui wore down her spirits, as if she were forced to share the psyche of a suicide. Ground between the conquistador's despair and Azure's volcanic temper, she would have sunk into depression herself if it weren't for Abe. His visits were the high point—and, often, the only bright spots—of her days.

Usually, Azure would finally relent and let her go around four in the afternoon, and Abe would take her for a walk back along the trail they'd ridden on horseback. They dawdled long enough to enjoy the roseate hues of sunset in the Andes, which bathed the western faces of the mountains in orange while draping the eastern slopes in a purple penumbra. Since she had already learned more than she ever wanted to know about Pizarro, Abe spun gentle tales of Inca mythology to divert her before they headed back to eat dinner together in her tent.

"Manco Capac was the first Inca," he told her on an outing toward the end of her second week in camp. "They say he and his wife, Mama Ocllo, climbed from the waters of Lake Titicaca. Before them, the people lived like animals, but Manco Capac taught the men to till the soil and to build shelters, while Mama Ocllo taught the women to weave and cook and raise children."

Natalie gave a wry smirk. "How very gender-appropriate.

You suppose if Mama came back today, she'd teach us astrophysics and open-heart surgery?"

Abe laughed. "I have no doubt."

Standing a few feet from the slope's drop-off, she surveyed the canine teeth of peaks aligned before her and inhaled the cold breeze that gusted up the mountainside. She had stayed at that elevation long enough for her *soroche* headaches to vanish, and the air's thinness now felt heady, clean, and bracing. "So how about you, Abe?" she asked idly. "You ever consider settling down with a Mama of your own? Maybe having a kid?"

She cocked her head to study his reaction to the last question.

He didn't miss a beat. "Only if the kid was as bright as Callie. And only if the Mama was as charming as you."

Natalie crossed her arms, gasping in mock astonishment. "*Dr. Wilcox!* Are you sure you should be addressing a coworker that way? She might think you had more than business on your mind."

"Oh, you needn't worry about that, Ms. Lindstrom. My brain can't handle anything past the sixteenth century."

"What a shame." Their smiles both faded, and Natalie looked out at the panorama again to keep her gaze from lingering on him. "What *do* you plan to do when the expedition's over?"

Wilcox shrugged. "Catalog and report the discovery. Write a book about it. Make sure the artifacts end up in the right museums. Bore my students with 'What I Did During My Sabbatical' stories." He grinned. "Maybe ask out this coworker I've had my eye on…when we're finished with business."

Natalie winced, thinking how Abe's career plans might hinge on the information she was keeping from Azure—the weird images she'd seen in Pizarro's memories. "Suppose we don't find the treasure. What then?"

"Well…I could still ask out that coworker I mentioned."

"I'm sure she'd like that…when you're finished with business." A warmth filled her cheeks that even the wind couldn't chill.

He stepped within a foot of her, but she resisted the impulse to draw back. Then he put out a hand to touch her temple. "Natalie, I—"

It was too much. She took his hand in both of hers and pulled it from her face, yet did not let go of it. *"Not yet,"* she said.

Abe's mouth twitched, but he smiled and nodded.

She squeezed his hand and released it. They walked back to camp in silence, the distance between them smaller than it had been when they left.

Not yet. The words gave hope to the man once known as August Trent.

He had now discarded that name as he had the fantasy of returning to Hollywood for a triumphant comeback. Instead, a new pipe dream occupied his mind during the long hours of idleness and isolation in the camp when he did not have Natalie to talk to. He'd grown accustomed to the face he saw in the mirror as he shaved every morning, answered only to the name of the dead man he resembled. Why, he thought, couldn't he simply *be* Dr. Abel Wilcox, amiable professor of archaeology? That was the man Natalie liked anyway, not the failed actor he'd never let her see. He could shuck his past—as Trent, as Nick—like a shriveled snakeskin, to be reborn with a life that was better than any he'd ever had.

Of course, he couldn't go back to teach at Stanford. Too many people who might spot his imposture—who might hear the difference in his voice, catch the significant lapses in his knowledge and memory. But suppose he resigned from the university and remained here in Peru, where people accepted him as Abel Wilcox as long as he had the passport to prove it? Would anyone ever be the wiser? More important... would Natalie want to stay with him?

He contrived elaborate visions of how he would realize this fantasy. With the money Azure would give him, he could buy a splendid hacienda in the countryside on the outskirts of Lima where he and Natalie could live. They could send the girl, Callie, to the finest private schools, and together, as a family, they would travel the globe, no longer having to sully their hands and souls with the awful compromises required of those who toil for a living.

The awareness that his dream was doomed only increased the fervor with which he tried to preserve it, like a child who frantically props up a sand castle even as the incoming tide erodes its foundation. Once Azure had located the treasure, Trent told himself, he could intercede with the tycoon on Natalie's behalf. After all, she wouldn't dare report

Azure to the authorities if she was married to his chief accomplice, would she?

Playing such puppet shows in his mind brought a smile to his lips—a smile for himself, not for an audience.

When he was not visiting Natalie or imagining his new life with her, Trent continued to spend most of his time researching his role, rereading some of Wilcox's books for the third and fourth times, committing facts and stories to memory with which to regale Natalie at their next meeting. He became so engrossed while poring over one such tome during a meeting in Azure's tent that he missed what his agitated boss was telling him.

"She's holding out on us."

Trent kept his fingertip on the page so as not to lose his place. "Hmm?"

"The Violet. She knows perfectly well where Pizarro put his gold." The tic in Azure's cheek had become chronic, and he'd rubbed it red.

Trent shook his head. "No way. I know Natalie—she's trying her best."

The tycoon glowered at him. *"Natalie?"*

"Yes…Ms. Lindstrom." He glanced back at the text to break eye contact. "It's that cursed Spaniard that's holding out on you."

"Perhaps. Or maybe *Natalie* fancies she can find the treasure by herself."

"Don't be absurd! Even if she found it, what would she do? She couldn't even move it."

"There are any number of people who would pay a great deal for such information."

Trent sighed. "Look, if you want, I can go offer her more money and see what she tells us."

"No. I want you to cut her food allowance to bread and water. See if hunger makes her any more forthcoming." His hands a blur, Azure snatched the book from Trent's hands, ripped a fistful of pages from it, and flung the torn remains on the floor. "And if you ignore me again, I'll do the same to you. Do you understand?"

Trent dared only a fleeting glance at the eviscerated volume before he nodded, his smile broad but shaky.

14

Hunger Pangs

BY THE TIME HONORATO BROUGHT BREAKFAST TO her tent the next morning, Natalie had already been up for more than an hour, sitting on her cot with her sketchbook and chalks. Since she'd packed only two books in her luggage, she had little else with which to occupy herself during the hours that Francisco Pizarro wasn't lazing in her brain like an engorged tapeworm.

Fortunately, she did not lack for subjects to draw. Pictures already filled half the pages of the tablet: rough portraits of Azure, Abe, and Honorato, along with a few crude land-scapes of the surrounding mountains. But she devoted by far the most paper and effort to depicting the macabre images she'd glimpsed in Pizarro's thoughts. Jawless human skulls staked atop wooden posts. Human bodies with crumbling papyrus skin, shriveled into fetal positions as if cowering from the afterlife. And her current drawing—a cave's mouth filled with the jagged teeth of those monstrous icons, white and weathered as driftwood, their owllike faces inscrutable yet somehow malefic.

Natalie had once hoped her passion for drawing and painting would become her career, allowing her to serve as the conduit for such past masters as Botticelli and Monet. Heck, she would have settled for Jackson Pollock or Andy Warhol. The NAACC's art division rejected her, however, and the only art she did while employed in the Crime Division was sketches of murder suspects. Since leaving the Corps, her drawing skills had become nothing more than a hobby, albeit one that comforted her in times of stress.

Yet Natalie drew these pictures not for comfort but for a more practical reason—to get her out of Peru and away from Nathan Azure.

Over the past two weeks, he had gone from unnerving to unbalanced as Pizarro gleefully frustrated him. Natalie ended one inhabitation session abruptly when Azure became so enraged by the *Marqués* that he seized her shirt collar and swung his arm back as if to belt her across the face. When he saw that she had exiled Pizarro with her protective mantra, the tycoon let go of her but never apologized. Since then she'd worried more and more about what he might do to her while acting out his rage against the conquistador.

Natalie's chalk strokes grew more furious, highlighting the aquiline nose on one totem's face as she debated what to do. These images meant nothing to her, but maybe they would appease Azure. Would they reveal the treasure's location, as he demanded, and if so, would he provide her with safe-conduct back to the States? Or would he keep her captive here until he got his leather-gloved mitts on the loot itself? How long would that be? Weeks? Months? Or longer? And how long would Abe's bribes keep Bella and the other Corps thugs from ratting on her and taking Callie away?

Do not give the big gringo *what he wants until he gives you money and takes you back to U.S.,* Honorato had counseled her. But *how* could she make Azure let her go unless she gave him what he wanted?

As if the memory of his advice were his cue to enter, Honorato unzipped her tent door and shuffled in with her breakfast tray.

Natalie slapped her sketchbook shut. "*¡Hola!* Umm…*el desayuno es tarde. ¡Tengo hambre!* Or, wait…how would I say *I'm starving?*"

Over the past week, Honorato had patiently indulged her clumsy attempts to practice Spanish, correcting her mistakes and slowly repeating his responses as many times as it took her to understand what he said. Today he set the tray on the table without looking at her and mumbled "*Lo siento*" followed by a bunch of words she couldn't make out.

"I'm sorry, I didn't catch that. What did you say?"

Honorato kept his head tilted forward so that the brim of his fedora hid his eyes. "The supplies, they are low, yes? This is all I can give you now. I am sorry."

She would have said *de nada*, but he did not wait for her to excuse him. Only when he left did she discover what he was apologizing for. Her breakfast consisted of a cup of tepid water and a small stale roll.

"Only the best," Natalie muttered. She tore off a tiny piece of the stiff bread and chewed it back into dough in the hope that eating slowly might make the meal seem more substantial.

It didn't. A half hour later, her stomach gurgled like a car engine sucking sludge from the fuel system.

To her surprise, Abe did not come to collect her for the usual morning inhabitation session with Azure. She did not see him until almost noon, when he personally delivered lunch to her tent.

Another stale roll and cup of water sat on the tray he carried.

Abe hung his head, as abashed as Honorato had been. "This is all I could sneak in for now. I'll try to get more later." He pulled a foil-wrapped energy bar out of his pocket and offered it to her. When she didn't take it, he tossed it on the cot. "I can't tell you how sorry I am about this inconvenience, Natalie—"

"What's going on, Abe?" She snatched up the roll. "I can't live on this."

He set down the tray, his movements as slow as if he, too, were weak with hunger. "We've hit a tight spot in our financing. Mr. Azure has been spending nearly thirty thousand pounds a day on this expedition, and one of our suppliers has held up a shipment pending approval of a new credit line. Therefore, we've had to institute some rationing."

"Oh, really?" Natalie cast a withering look at the professor. "And how soon will this rationing end?"

"Well, we could get credit now if we had ... collateral."

"You mean Pizarro's gold."

"That would help, yes."

"*Ugh!* What do you people expect of me?" The throb of a hunger headache made it difficult to think. Her first instinct was to tear into the roll with her teeth, yet she forced herself instead to hurl it against the tent wall.

"*Please,* Natalie." Abe clasped her hand and gently pulled her over to sit down on the cot, a new urgency in his tone. "Azure's out of control, and things are desperate. If there's *anything* you can tell us … even something that doesn't seem important…"

His pet-store-puppy eyes pleaded with her from behind their oval glass windows.

She shook her head. "Abe, I need to get out of here. I need to get home. If the Corps comes after Callie while I'm gone…"

"I know." He put his face in his hands, his features shadowed with a chiaroscuro of guilt. "This is all my fault. I should never have brought you here."

Without any fuel to feed it, Natalie's anger burnt itself out. She touched his shoulder. "I don't blame you. You couldn't have known. It's that maniac you work for."

"I know, and I won't let him do this to you. If only we had some … bargaining chip to hold over him."

"If you back me up, maybe we can both get out of here. Together." She stared at him until he met her gaze and gave a weary nod. "Now take me to Azure."

As she asked, Abe took her out of the encampment to a precipice where their mountain commanded an Olympian view of its neighbors. After the recent rains, the sky above had become a cloudless blue, but cobwebs of mist still floated in the dell below. Against the backdrop of dusty brown peaks, the spotless figure of Nathan Azure gleamed as white as an albatross. He stood a few feet from the cliff's edge with a golf

driver, and as Natalie approached him, he smacked a golf
ball up and out into the void of the valley.

Thok!

Azure shook his head as the ball arced into the mist and
disappeared. "Still slicing a bit to the right, I think."

He teed up another ball.

Abe remained at a discreet distance while Natalie came
abreast of the tycoon, fuming. "What kind of game are you
playing?"

"Golf, actually. Marvelous fun—you should try it some-
time." He swung the driver and sent the second ball soaring
into oblivion.

Thok!

"Don't get cute with me. What's the deal with the food?"

Azure leaned on the club in debonair insouciance, as if it
were a cane. "Oh? Do you have a complaint regarding our
amenities?"

"You could say that. Starvation is not conducive to pro-
ductivity."

"On the contrary, I find that hunger often sharpens the
mind. Very motivational."

His audacity left her speechless for a moment. "How the
hell do you expect me to keep summoning your stupid
Spaniard when I can't even maintain consciousness?"

"Perhaps we wouldn't have to trouble ourselves with
the dear *Marqués* if you could be a bit more helpful in our
endeavors." He stooped to balance another white ball on
the tee.

Natalie's vision shimmered with the pulse of blood

behind her eyes. "I can't tell you anything because I don't *know* anything."

"Come, now! I'm sure if you try a bit harder, something will come to you."

Natalie sliced the air with her hand. "That's it! Say good-bye to your Violet—*and* your archaeologist."

"Oh?" He cast an amused look at Abe, who bowed his head in silence. "Eloping, are we? You make a charming couple."

"Perhaps I didn't make myself clear," Natalie said, sarcastically overenunciating each word. "You can take your money and shove it. Abe and I are leaving."

"Be my guest. Lima is about four hundred miles *that* way, I believe." He lifted the golf club until it pointed due south.

Outrage sprung the mousetrap tension in Natalie's body. Without making a conscious decision to do so, she hauled back and slapped Azure's left cheek as hard as she could.

Too late, Abe sprang forward to stop her. "Natalie—*no!*"

The instant her palm made contact with his skin, a whipcrack of electric discharge vibrated her bones, as if she'd touched a high-voltage power line. A ghost-image embossed itself upon the scene in front of her: Azure, his face haughtily indifferent, extended a gun toward her, its shots riddling her chest. She lifted her head to glare at him, the oval glasses askew on her nose, and hacked up enough blood to spit her dying condemnation at his face...

The momentum of her hand broke the connection. Her eyes and mouth gaping, Natalie staggered, nearly fell.

Azure stumbled backward, dropping the golf club to shield his cheek with his gloved hands as if struck with leprosy. *"Get her away from me! Get her away!"*

Abe pushed Natalie back as if breaking up a fight, but she kept staring at the shrieking tycoon. The soul that had clenched her mind a moment earlier left a residue of hatred that hardened her face into ice. Azure seemed to recognize the expression, for he retreated a few more steps, his shouts becoming more frenzied. "Don't let her touch me! It's *him*."

Abe gently steered her away from him. "Come on, Natalie."

In a stupor of shock, she turned to peer at his face. She remembered seeing that same visage in the mirror of the Cajamarca hostel room, remembered peering through those same oval glasses at Azure, the man who shot her to death.

But that was impossible. Abe could not have been the soul who knocked. Abe was alive.

No, she thought. *It can't be . . .*

The fearful sidelong glance Abe gave her did not reassure her, however. He seemed more afraid of her than of Azure.

"Are you . . . okay?" he asked in a tone of ambiguous concern.

That depends. Are you dead?

"Yeah. I'm fine." She walked back to camp beside him, corking the horror in her heart to keep it from pouring out onto her face. *Maybe it wasn't him*, she told herself. *I need to be sure.*

All the Peruvian workers stopped their pretense of work to stare at her, until the only sound was the spirited voice of pop singer Anita Santivañez fluttering from a battery-powered boom box. Honorato had introduced Natalie to Santivañez's music. She sought his face in the crowd and spotted a worker wearing a fedora like Honorato's, but he turned away when she looked at him.

A man with a wispy beard and a face like chiseled hickory waited at the door of her tent. As they approached, he grinned, baring teeth stained green from chewing coca leaves.

Abe frowned and attempted to shoo the man away as if he were a stray dog. *"¡Ai, Romoldo! ¡Vaya!"*

Romoldo came forward instead, and the professor interposed himself before the Peruvian reached Natalie. Abe opened the tent door for her and shepherded her inside.

"Look, stay here until I take care of this, okay?" he said in a low voice while keeping his eye on Romoldo. "I'll see about getting you some food."

"Yeah. How about an intimate vegetarian dinner?" Natalie did not smile as she said it.

Abe couldn't look at her as he zipped her inside. Still visible through the canvas wall, the professor's silhouette hurried off, but Romoldo's outline remained as he stood sentry outside.

Abe did not return with food that night, nor did anyone else. Her stomach cramped with hunger, Natalie wolfed down the nutrition bar Abe had left. It didn't begin to fill the vacuum within her, so she fell to her hands and knees and searched the floor of her tent until she found the roll she'd thrown aside that afternoon. Its crust had become as stiff as cardboard, its heart as dry as paper, and it smelled of incipient mold, yet she gorged herself on it, nearly choking on the half-chewed mouthfuls she tried to swallow.

The act of eating expended as much energy as it gave her. She curled up under the covers of her cot afterward and soon dropped into sleep.

15

Dr. Wilcox, I Presume

WHEN NO BREAKFAST ARRIVED IN THE MORNING, Natalie pawed through her handbag until she unearthed a rumpled pack of peanuts from one of the half-dozen plane flights she'd taken...was it only three weeks ago? It seemed like months since she'd hugged Callie good-bye.

Natalie forced herself to eat the peanuts one at a time, rolling them around on her tongue until they became soft and tasteless before chewing and swallowing them. Ever a finicky, health-conscious eater, she now craved all the empty calories she'd always denied herself: pizza dripping with stringy melted mozzarella; hamburgers—heck, make it *cheese*burgers—gushing pink juices and slathered with Thousand Island dressing; french fries saturated with salt and moist grease. Fat, carbs, sodium, cholesterol, triglycerides—bring 'em on! At least she'd live to regret the indulgence in her old age.

A confirmed junk-food fanatic, Dan would have had a chuckle or two at her newfound jones for McDonald's...until he saw how her shrinking skin had already begun to cling to the ridges of her ribs.

But she couldn't allow herself to think about Dan, Callie, home, or food, lest she waste more time with wistful yearn-ing. Sucking on another peanut, she dumped the contents of her toiletries bag out onto the cot to see what she could use to attempt an escape from Camp Azure. She'd deliberately packed as little as she could, figuring she'd only be gone a few days, and the resources at her disposal were pitifully innocuous: small bottles of shampoo and skin moisturizer, an eyeliner pencil, a lipstick, a compact, a handful of tampons, a roll of double-sided tape to attach her wig, a can of shaving cream and a couple of twin-blade disposable razors for when her rechargeable Lady Remington ran out of juice. About the most dangerous item in her possession was a pair of nail clippers, which she'd had to pack in her luggage so airport security wouldn't confiscate them. Natalie guessed that you *might* be able to kill someone by puncturing his carotid artery with the clippers' pointed nail file, provided that you could get the file within an inch of the person's throat.

That prospect seemed unlikely considering she was going up against twenty-odd men the size of Romoldo. And even if she managed to escape, what could she do? Hike back to Cajamarca on foot over the Andes, alone, with no food or water? She'd be dead within a day or two.

Her captors must have felt secure in such advantages, for they were cavalier and careless about guarding her. She'd seen a silhouette that she assumed was Romoldo's through the tent wall that morning, but he wandered off after a couple of hours. Since then she'd been able to unzip the door and stick her head outside without attracting more than an offhand glance from the Peruvians. The men now lazed and joked with each other in small groups, their work forgotten.

Natalie flicked the nail clippers open, made a practice jab

with the file, then rolled her eyes and tossed the clippers back with the rest of the useless junk scattered on the cot. She took her drawing tablet from underneath her pillow and flipped through the pictures she'd drawn from the fragmented images in Pizarro's mind. They made no sense to her, and she didn't give a damn about the stupid treasure anyway. Why not simply give the pictures to Azure and say, "Here, knock yourself out"?

Because he'd kill you, that's why, she thought. *He's only keeping you alive because he thinks you know where the gold is.*

You do not want to be like el profesor, Honorato had warned her. Did he mean Abe? Or had Azure killed the real Abel Wilcox? Was that who had knocked in the bath at Cajamarca and then again when she slapped Azure's cheek? And if the real Wilcox was dead, who was...Abe?

She couldn't believe it. He could not be an impostor. Not the man who had walked with her in the sunset, the man who had given her daughter a stuffed alpaca. She had looked in his eyes and seen real caring there, the first she'd seen in any man since Dan. How could he have faked that?

Eager to prove her suspicions groundless, Natalie grabbed her copy of the professor's book and flipped it open to the back cover flap to scrutinize the black-and-white author's photo. Now she studied it with a portraitist's eye for detail, and the sickened feeling in her gut made her forget about hunger for the moment. Was the shape of this man's ears just the tiniest bit different from those of the man who brought her to Peru? Weren't the cheeks a bit more hollow, the eyes a bit wider?

She could have answered these questions if only she

could summon the soul once more. For better or worse, it hadn't inhabited her long enough to make her body a touchstone, and there was no way Azure would let her touch his bare skin again. Everyone else in camp wore gloves, including the man calling himself Abel Wilcox. No doubt they had disposed of all the late archaeologist's belongings as well, in anticipation of her arrival...

Except his passport.

Inhaling sharply, Natalie remembered that Abe had no trouble getting through passport control either when leaving the U.S. or upon entering Peru. Passports, she knew, had even more counterfeit-prevention gimmicks than currency or checks, and to take a chance on a forgery would be to risk detection and disaster. A phony Dr. Wilcox would have been far safer using the real professor's passport.

So Abe—or whoever he was—must still have it somewhere. If she could get hold of it and summon the real Dr. Wilcox, at least she would know the truth. She could find out more about her captors...including, she hoped, how to get away from them.

Relieved to be taking action, however pointless, Natalie took out her chalk set and made a hasty sketch of a small, squarish Incan structure, concocting the imaginary building from the patterns of cut stones she'd seen in the Ransom Room and from photos in Wilcox's book. She filled in the background with nondescript Andean peaks to make Nathan Azure wonder where in the Peruvian mountains this fictional treasure-house might be.

To this drawing she added some of the pictures of corpses and skulls she'd already done, ripping each of them from her tablet as she selected them. She did not include any depictions of the strange sentinel icons or the cave where they roosted. Natalie didn't want to give Azure so much information that he might deem her no longer useful to him; she only wanted to tantalize him enough to buy some time and food for herself...and to create an opportunity to search for Wilcox's passport.

She hid the sketchbook underneath her cot's mattress and gathered up the stack of drawings she'd torn from the tablet. Stepping outside, she scanned the camp for "Abe." *Please be in your tent,* she thought when she didn't see him.

Laughing crudely with one of his countrymen, Romoldo stiffened and stepped toward her as she came out.

"Wilcox," Natalie demanded. *"¿Dónde está el profesor?"*

Romoldo frowned but jerked his head to the left, commanding her to follow him.

When he left her at the professor's door, Natalie wondered about tent etiquette, since she couldn't knock on canvas and there didn't seem to be a bell to ring. Finally, she simply raised her voice, trying to sound bright and cheerful. "Abe? You in there?"

Footsteps scuffled toward the door, and the man who claimed to be Abel Wilcox pushed aside the tent flap. His smile lacked its usual confidence. "Natalie! Look, I'm sorry I haven't been able to get you anything to eat. Azure's locked down the supplies until further notice, and the men have been watching me like hawks."

"I understand," she said, although she didn't. "Maybe I can help both of us. I thought over what you said about Pizarro's memories. About things that might not seem important at first, and, well…" She waved the fistful of folded drawings she held. "Here's what I came up with, for what it's worth."

He brightened as if receiving a last-minute reprieve from the governor. "That's wonderful! Let's have a look…"

Emerging from the tent, he took the pages from her and shuffled through them. The more pictures he viewed, the more his pace slowed, the longer his attention lingered on each one. His face glowed with relief. "Natalie—this is fantastic! This is sure to get you a good meal. Wait here!"

His head bent over the sketch of the Incan building Natalie had fabricated, he moved off in the direction of Azure's tent. One of the Peruvians stood guard outside, probably to prevent Natalie from gaining access to the tycoon's sanctuary, but a nod from the professor made him open the door.

Once Abe was out of view, Natalie satisfied herself that none of the workmen showed any interest in her. She then slipped through the unzipped slit of the archaeologist's tent entrance, praying that Azure and the phony archaeologist would pore over her forged drawings long enough for her to locate the real Wilcox's passport.

Natalie nearly groaned aloud when she saw the tent's interior: it looked like a bomb had gone off. The cot and the floor lay buried beneath layers of scattered clothing, scholarly journals and historical texts, scraps of food, and the shed foil skins of energy bars. How was she supposed to find anything in this rag heap?

She scanned the surface of the mess, hoping that the passport might be sitting on one of the scattered shirts like a castaway on a life raft. Hesitant to disturb anything, she lifted one corner of a book at her foot, but let it drop back. Drawing a long breath to stave off her growing sense of futility, Natalie forced herself to concentrate. What had "Abe" worn the day they passed through airport security? The tweed jacket with the leather patches on the elbows, wasn't it? The passport might still be in the coat's inside pocket.

In the far left corner of the tent, near the base of his garbage-bag toilet, one tweed sleeve thrust out of the surrounding flotsam. Natalie tiptoed over the intervening mess, cringing whenever some buried object crunched beneath her foot, and raised the jacket up from the floor by its arm.

Remembering how the dead man's soul had knocked immediately when she struck Azure's face, Natalie recited her protective mantra as a precaution. She couldn't take the chance that the real Wilcox might inhabit her before she was ready to speak with him... in private. Her pulse quickened as she reached into the coat's inside breast pocket and felt the passport's faux leather cover.

The Twenty-third Psalm still unspooling in her mind, she stuck the passport underneath the waistband of her jeans, hiding it beneath the tail of her T-shirt, and replaced the tweed jacket in the same position in which she'd found it. Hopping back over the detritus, Natalie made it to the tent's entrance just as "Abe" pulled the door flap aside.

He looked askance at her. "Can I help you with something?"

Now it was her turn to give a shaky smile. "Sorry, but I had to get out of the sun. My skin'll get burned to a crisp in this thin air. Hope you don't mind."

"Uh, no... of course not. I just hate for you to see what a

lousy housekeeper I am." With a nervous laugh, he swept aside the tent flap for her, his eyes moving as if inventorying every dirty sock and candy wrapper.

When they emerged, Natalie gave him an expectant look. "Well?"

"These look promising, but we need some more specifics." He led her back to her tent, indicating that she would resume her house arrest. "Keep trying, and we'll set up another session with Pizarro if necessary. In the meantime, you impressed Azure enough to win yourself a hot meal."

"That's something, at any rate." Natalie pulled down her shirttail to make sure it didn't ride up. Beneath it, the sweat on her midriff stuck to the passport's slick cover, and an itchy, pricking sensation spread from her stomach to her entire body.

Thou preparest a table before me in the presence of mine enemies, Natalie continued in her head, praying she could keep the knocking soul at bay until she was alone.

"Um…you want to go for a walk later?"

"Not today, Abe. Now that I've made a breakthrough, I want to see what else I can come up with. Thanks anyway, though."

She stepped through the tent entrance and zipped it shut behind her. When she was sure Abe had gone, she removed the passport from her jeans and hid it underneath the cot's mattress.

The smell of food made Natalie salivate even before she saw what it was. Honorato must have left the meal on the table for her: a plate of chicken in yellowish gravy with a sliced hard-boiled egg on top. Didn't short-order cooks call that a "mother and child reunion"? The name struck her as ironic, since she had no idea when she'd see Callie again.

Natalie devoured every scrap of the meal—skin, fat, yolk, and all—in less than ten minutes. A green apple sat on the tray as well, but she restrained the urge to gobble it immediately. Instead, she hid it deep beneath the clothes in her suitcase. She sensed that she would need to save as much food as possible. As much as she could carry.

She didn't dare retrieve the passport until late that night, when the entire camp was dark. Even then, she left her propane lantern unlit. Although she had never in her life summoned a soul without some sort of light on—the thought of doing so still terrified her—it seemed far less risky than alerting Azure and his goons to the forbidden séance she was about to conduct. In this case, the dead didn't scare her nearly as much as the living.

Natalie lay on the cot, still fully dressed, and pulled the covers to her chin. Her lips silently shaped the words of her spectator mantra as she took the passport from underneath the mattress. If anyone did happen to look in on her, he might mistake the contortions of her inhabitation for the tossing and turning of a nightmare.

Row, row, row your boat,
Gently down the stream . . .

The passport's cover bowed and crumpled as her hands curled around it and snapped closed like railcar hitches. The itchy numbness of inhabitation spread over her skin, followed by a hot-faced breathlessness. Choking with a rage that wasn't hers, she rolled over with such force that she rattled the springs of the rickety cot, nearly tipping it over.

Images of Nathan Azure looped through her head, accompanied by the endless chant *bastard bastard bastard bastard*. The refrain of loathing caught Natalie in its thought spiral, but she measured out her breaths and resumed her own mantra, determined not to surrender control of her body.

> *Merrily, merrily, merrily, merrily!*
> *Life is but a dream.*

The spitting rant in her head ceased, yet she could feel the soul stewing inside her, like a mumbling drunk in the back corner of a bar. *Who are you?* it snipped. *Are you dead? Are we still in hell?*

"No. My name's Natalie. And we're in Peru." She whispered aloud out of habit, although she could have spoken to the soul with her thoughts alone.

The soul's tone slowed with understanding. *You're the Violet, aren't you? The one Azure talked about.*

"Oh my God. You *are* Abel Wilcox, aren't you?" She put her hands to her mouth, thinking *Abe*.

Are you working for Azure?

"I was. Until I found out he killed you."

Then you know.

"I know the man who told me he's Dr. Abel Wilcox isn't. Who is he?"

A bit player named Trent. I don't know if that's his last or first name, but if I ever see him again, I'll peel his face from his skull for daring to pass himself off as me.

"It was Azure who shot you, though. Correct?"

Yes. Why did you bring me back? Did he put you up to it?

"No. I wanted to learn the truth, because I'm afraid he'll kill me, too."

He will, as soon as he gets his lily-white hands on Pizarro's gold. Since you're still alive, I can only assume he hasn't succeeded yet.

"Not yet. Can you help me get away from him?"

How am I supposed to help you? I'm dead, as you may have noticed.

"You know Azure and . . . Trent better than I do. More important, you know Peru. I can barely speak Spanish."

Wilcox's spirit became quiet and still within her, and Natalie suspected that he had rejected her plea and was trying to retreat into the void.

I'm sorry you got mixed up in this, he said at last. *Tell me everything that's happened since Azure first contacted you.*

As quickly as she could, she related how Trent had used Wilcox's identity and reputation to lure her to Peru and the camp in the Andes. She did not, however, mention their mutual attraction. She also described how Pizarro had turned coy and cagey when summoned and how Azure had punished her for not providing clues to the fabled treasure.

Wilcox interrupted her when she mentioned the sketches of Pizarro's thoughts, his anger abruptly forgotten in an agitation of curiosity. *These drawings—do you still have them? Can I see them?*

"Now?" she complained. "The light—they might see it."

If they do, I'm sure you can think of an excuse. Please, it's important.

Cursing under her breath, Natalie clambered out from under the covers and patted the tent floor beside the cot, where she kept a box of wooden matches. When she found it, she struck a match and took her sketchbook out from under the cot's mattress. Huddled on the floor, she held the wavering flame over the tablet and hastily flipped through the pages, allowing Wilcox to see them through her eyes. As soon as she came to the picture of the cave with the stoic idols in its mouth, Natalie felt her pulse quicken with the dead archaeologist's excitement.

Chachapoyas, he thought. Natalie recognized the word as the name of a nearby town she'd seen on a map.

The match threatened to burn her fingers and she waved it out. "Is that good enough for you?" she muttered in the sudden darkness.

Yes . . . I'll help you, Wilcox mused. *And maybe you can help me, too.*

"Help you *what?*"

Keep Nathan Azure's filthy mitts off Pizarro's treasure. Will you?

Natalie tensed. She knew well how dangerous it was to cut a deal with dead people who have a personal agenda. A Violet named Lyman Pearsall had made such a bargain with Vincent Thresher and ended up becoming the serial killer's puppet, allowing the executed murderer to use his body to commit further atrocities.

"I'll do what I can," she vowed, hoping that Wilcox didn't demand specifics.

It's a deal, then. The words closed the negotiation like a briefcase snapping shut. *Now, first things first. We'll need some supplies…*

Natalie crawled back beneath the covers of her cot. She did not sleep, however, but instead mumbled in an apparent delirium until just before dawn.

16
Natalie and the Professor

"YESSSSSSS. VERY INTERESTING—*VERY* INTERESTING." The man Natalie now knew as Trent peered through his Dr. Wilcox glasses at the latest sketches she'd drawn. "I think Mr. Azure will be most pleased. Want to celebrate with a hearty breakfast together?"

"I'd appreciate the food, but I think I'll eat alone this morning." Natalie wiped crumbs of sleep dust from her eyes. "I worked overtime on those, so I'd like to rest today."

This statement was partly true. She'd stayed up most of the night plotting with the real Dr. Wilcox, and the professor had given her tips on some convincing details she could incorporate in her phony drawings to keep Azure occupied while she made her escape.

"Oh...fine." Trent folded the sketchbook sheets in half. "Dinner, maybe?"

She smiled. "Maybe not."

He raised his hands. "Hey, no obligation. Enjoy the rest—you've earned it." He headed off toward Azure's tent.

"Go to hell, Abe—you've earned it," she murmured, but only when he was out of earshot.

✳ ✳ ✳

Honorato delivered her lunch that day. He still seemed reluctant to speak to Natalie or even to look at her, as if refusing attention to a stray dog for fear it might try to follow him home.

"Could you bring me a poncho like one of those I see the men wearing?" She tried to make the request sound like an afterthought. "I've been a little cold the past few nights."

"I will do what I can," Honorato said, head bowed as he set down her tray and departed.

Oh, well, it was worth a try, Natalie thought, gobbling the food he'd left her. She needed to proceed with the escape plan with or without Honorato's help, and there were a lot of preparations to make.

She saved the apple that came with lunch, adding it to the one she'd hidden last night and the two triangular rolls she'd kept from breakfast. These she put into her duffel bag. At Dr. Wilcox's insistence, she also tore all the pictures of the macabre, glowering totems out of her sketchbook and added them to the bag, along with a few bare necessities like a toothbrush, toothpaste, toilet paper, credit cards, money, passport…and her photo of Callie, which she zipped inside the duffel's outer pocket for safekeeping.

The remainder of her work had to wait until nightfall, so Natalie spent the next few hours drawing some additional red-herring treasure clues. Her time was well spent, for Trent came back to visit her later that afternoon. Nathan Azure had found her most recent sketches promising, he said, but he needed more specifics.

"Try these." She smiled and handed him her latest nonsense doodles.

To Natalie's surprise, Honorato brought her the poncho she'd asked for along with her dinner. It looked much like those she'd seen all the men wearing, for years of dust had dulled the bright red, orange, and gold of its stripes and zigzags and stiffened the coarse wool of its weave.

"My *mamá* made it for me." Honorato handed it to her, his eyes bright with unspoken meaning as he looked Natalie full in the face. "I hope it warms you as it has warmed me, yes?"

Natalie fancied she could feel Honorato's mother knocking as she took the heirloom in her hands, but perhaps that was only the guilt that swelled in her stomach. She shook her head and moved to hand the garment back to him. "I can't—"

He lifted a hand. "No. Keep it. Please."

The finality in his voice unnerved her. Did he suspect what she intended to do? Did he know that he would never again see the poncho his mother had woven for him?

If so, Honorato gave no indication that he would stop her. Nevertheless, even when she was alone again, Natalie lingered too long over her dinner, afraid to commence the most dangerous phase of her plan.

You're dead if you stay, she thought, to whip herself into action. *At least this way, you have a chance.*

Taking long, slow breaths to focus her attention, she used her nail clippers to snip the plastic safety guard off one of her disposable razors, exposing the paper-thin edge of the first of the twin blades. She then got on her hands and knees in the tent's far left corner and chewed at the canvas with the clippers' jaws until she'd opened a small hole in the fabric. Sliding one end of the razor's head into the hole, Natalie sawed the canvas with the blade, leaving a long, frayed slit in the tent wall. She made a lateral slit perpendicular to the top of the first one and a parallel vertical cut, so that a square of canvas flapped onto the ground behind the tent, creating a ragged hole just big enough for her to crawl through. Cold air oozed from the rip, as if the blackness of the night outside bled through the wound.

Natalie shivered and shoved her suitcase up in front of the hole in case anyone looked in on her before she was ready to leave. Already wearing her black jeans and Doc Marten boots, she changed from a white T-shirt to a black one. She bunched up some of her other clothes into a humanoid shape underneath her cot's blanket, then took off her wig and draped it over the sweatshirt she'd shaped into a head on her pillow.

When her decoy was in place, Natalie crushed some of the black chalk from her drawing set onto her dinner tray and rubbed the pulverized powder onto her face, scalp, and forearms to darken her pale skin.

She sighed, contemplating her chimney-sweep complexion in her compact's mirror. "Time for the main feature."

She dropped the nail clippers, razor, and box of matches into her duffel, slung its handle over her right shoulder, and extinguished the tent's propane lantern. After moving the suitcase aside long enough for her to crawl outside, she tried as best she could to pull the bag back in place to cover the hole.

A blast of frigid mountain wind buffeted her as she crouched behind the tent, out of view of the camp's main corridor. The cliff's edge lay a few feet beyond her, almost invisible in the night's opacity. Her teeth chattering, Natalie pressed on the spot where she kept the passport tucked beneath the waist of her jeans, its cover against her skin.

Don't wimp out on me now, Wilcox, she thought as she recited her spectator mantra.

The professor answered the summons with perky briskness, as if taking a business call. *So far, so good, I see,* he said upon settling inside her head.

"Says you. I'm freezing out here," she hissed. "Now, where do I find the supply tent?"

I'm not sure. From what you've told me, it sounds like they've moved the camp since killing me.

"Great."

The tent should be easy to recognize, though, since it's the only one they bother to guard around the clock. Otherwise, the men would steal stuff to sell on the black market.

"No honor among thieves, eh? Okay, I think I know where that is."

Natalie recalled seeing a bored Peruvian posted in front of the tent adjacent to the large mess tent where the workers ate their meals. She started making her way toward it, slinking from the shadows of one structure to another. Although she'd waited until most of the men had confined themselves to quarters before venturing out, she kept to the cliff side of the camp, since all the tent entrances faced away from the precipice. She hunkered down and skulked beneath each net window, paused to reconnoiter at every alley between shelters.

When she reached the rear of the supply tent, Natalie peered around its corner toward the front, where she could see the guard's left side limned by the light of his propane lantern. He paced in and out of view, either to relieve his tedium or to keep himself awake.

Natalie withdrew behind the rear wall and took the nail clippers and razor from her bag. Working as best she could in the ambient light from a clouded moon, she pinched a bit of the wall's canvas in the clippers' jaws and gnawed a hole large enough for the razor's head. Repeating the process she'd performed in her own tent, she sliced out an opening large enough for her to crawl through, forcing herself to cut slowly so she made no audible ripping sounds.

As soon as she'd peeled the tongue of canvas outward, Natalie risked striking a match to check if her way into the tent was clear. Hiding the flare of dull yellow light with her free hand, she discovered that beyond the hole lay a wooden shelf lined with gallon jugs of water.

What luck! Wilcox exclaimed with irritating cheer. *We'll need one of those.*

Swell, Natalie thought. She extinguished the match, pulled out the plastic jugs, and set them aside until she had cleared a path into the tent. Flattening herself as much as possible to squeeze between the wooden shelves, she slithered through the opening and ended up belly-down in darkness on the supply tent's tarp floor.

Once inside, she lit another match and got to her feet.

Stacks of boxes, towers of wooden crates, and shelf units laden with packaged foods and other necessities surrounded her.

Look for flashlights, Wilcox said. *I know they keep them in here somewhere.*

Natalie cupped a hand around the match flame and swept it along the shelves. Just before the heat forced her to wave the match out, she found a box of orange plastic flashlights. She grabbed one and thumbed its switch back and forth but remained in darkness.

You've got *to be kidding*, she thought, now too afraid to speak aloud. Striking another match, she found a box of alkaline batteries farther along the same shelf. Natalie wasn't about to fumble in the dark to install the batteries now, so she threw a few packs of the C cells in her bag along with the flashlight and kept lighting matches.

There! Wilcox said. *Three shelves down, all the way to the right. Take as many as you can.*

Natalie directed her gaze where he'd indicated and found a carton half-full of the energy bars whose wrappers littered Trent's floor. *These?* she asked with distaste.

Yes! They're lightweight, high-calorie, and vitamin fortified.

She groaned but scooped handfuls of the glorified candy bars into her bag. *What else?* she asked, looking around for real food.

Bottom shelf on the left. Take as many tanks as your bag can hold.

Natalie crouched and saw that next to the jugs of water sat row upon row of sausage-shaped propane cylinders like the one that fueled the lantern in her tent. *Yum. Do I eat them with ketchup?*

Look, you asked for my help. I'm telling you—we need those tanks.

Natalie didn't have time to argue, so she stuck four of the metal cylinders in her duffel, about as much weight as she wanted to carry over a mountain.

Behind her, Natalie heard voices conversing in Spanish outside the supply tent's entrance.

He's coming in, Wilcox informed her as he listened to the man who spoke to the guard. *Time to go.*

Flustered by the sudden urgency, Natalie threw down her latest match and dropped to her knees beside the pale square of moonlight that illuminated the hole she'd cut in the tent's rear wall. As she stuffed the duffel through the opening, the dragonfly buzz of an opening zipper came from the front of the tent.

Natalie banged her head when she wriggled between the shelves, but she clamped her jaw on the cry of pain. Once outside, she jackknifed to her feet, snatched up the bag, and started to run.

The water! Wilcox reminded her. *We need the water!*

Growling, Natalie pivoted and doubled back a few steps, shooting her arm out to hook the handle of one of the gallon jugs that still sat in the dust behind the supply tent. Dim light now shafted from the hole, and staccato Spanish peppered the air. Natalie couldn't understand the words but suspected they were the sort not included in her CD lessons.

As she straightened, the counterweight of the water jug nearly tipped her over. In the second she took to regain her balance, the oval blot of a man's head jutted out through the hole and swiveled toward her. Natalie broke into a sprint, pursued by unintelligible curses.

She didn't dare to glance back until she'd reached her own tent. Before she could move aside the suitcase to crawl through the hole, however, she heard the ratcheting hiss of someone unzipping her own tent's flap.

Natalie jerked back from the hole, peered at an angle through the narrow gap above the bag that hid the opening. She saw a flashlight beam sweep the tent's interior until it fell upon the cot. The searchlight circle lingered on the body she'd fashioned on the bed, on the tangled hair of the wig that covered the lump of the decoy's head.

Natalie held her breath.

Then the light withdrew and the tent door zipped shut.

What do we do now? she asked Wilcox, afraid to exhale.

Finish packing, he replied as if reading the next item on a checklist.

What if those guys wake up everyone in camp?

They won't. They'll be too busy covering up the supply-tent break-in because they'll get blamed if Azure finds out about it.

This theory didn't reassure Natalie much, but since she didn't have any better options, she reentered the tent to prepare for the journey ahead. Wary of lighting her lantern, she fumbled in the dark until she managed to get a pair of batteries into the flashlight she'd stolen. She pulled the cot's blanket over her to hide the light as she combed out her wig and wove its locks into a long, swinging braid like those worn by some of the women she'd seen in Cajamarca. She then darkened the wig's brown hair by sprinkling it with some of the black dust she'd ground from her chalk.

Not to rush you, Wilcox gently admonished her, *but if we don't leave at least three hours before dawn, we might as well throw ourselves at Azure's feet and beg for mercy.*

"I *know,* I *know.*" Natalie tucked one hem of the cot's blanket under the waist of her jeans. She arranged the rough gray cloth around her legs until it formed a floor-length skirt. Not as colorful or attractive as the ones she'd seen on the Peruvian women, but it might fool people from a distance, especially if they thought she was a poor farmer. There wasn't much she could do about her Doc Martens; she didn't have a pair of sandals with her, and she wasn't about to walk down a mountain barefoot.

She fattened her torso by putting on her down jacket, even though she worried that it might be too heavy for hiking. *In the Andes, it's better to be too hot than too cold,* Wilcox cautioned her when she asked him about it. *The autumn's pretty temperate this close to the equator, but it still gets chilly at night.*

With the lower part of her costume complete, Natalie hitched the handle of her duffel bag onto her right shoulder, then covered her upper body with Honorato's enormous poncho, which drooped past her hips. Last of all, she taped her restyled wig to her scalp and topped it with the broad-brimmed hat she'd been given in Cajamarca.

Natalie frowned as she checked her reflection in the compact mirror, twining the tail of her braid around one finger. The hair was okay, but her blackface complexion wouldn't fool anyone. And then, of course, there were her eyes. Without her brown contact lenses, the irises stood out starkly in her face. Oh, well. She'd simply have to keep anyone from getting a good look at her.

Time to go, Wilcox said.

"Yeah. Time to go."

Natalie shoved the compact into her jacket pocket and got on her hands and knees beside the hole in the tent's wall. Like a mouse in a granary that has overeaten and can't get out, she discovered that the costume and duffel made her too big to fit through the opening. Grunting with exasperation, she pawed through her bag until she found the razor so she could widen the rip in the canvas.

At last, Natalie squirmed, grublike, out into the predawn chill. She held the jug of water in one hand, the flashlight in the other, but she kept the light off as she skirted the perimeter of the sleeping camp. To avoid passing anywhere near the supply tent, she headed in a southerly direction, which brought her to the spot where she, Trent, and Honorato had first entered the tent village on horseback. From there, she intended to retrace the trail they'd ridden to get there, taking her back to Celendin. At a discreet distance from the camp, she would switch on the flashlight and continue walking south.

No, Wilcox said, vetoing her plan. *They'll expect you to go that way. It's the first place they'll hunt for us.*

Natalie stopped, surveyed the terrain. With only a clouded moon to brighten the night, one direction was indistinguishable from another. The black outlines of the mountains nearly disappeared against the dark field of the sky. "Okay, bwana. Which way *should* we go?"

North, toward Chachapoyas. They won't think you'll dare

to go that way because you don't know the country. If necessary, we can loop back south later, when we're sure they're no longer following us.

"Yeah. And we could also walk right off a cliff if we're not careful."

Then we'll have to be careful, won't we?

Natalie rolled her eyes, wondering if this Wilcox was really any better than the last one. Angling the flashlight beam toward the ground at her feet, she trudged in the wake of its drifting spot, stepping only where it showed solid ground ahead of her. The hem of her improvised skirt got in her way, further slowing her progress, and the water jug weighed on her hand like lead ballast.

Before long, she became winded in the thin air, yet when she paused to catch her breath, she found that the camp was still visible, barely fifty yards behind her. She could just make out the beacon of the supply-tent guard's lantern amid the huddle of dark shelters.

Great. Not having slept since the previous night, she already verged on exhaustion, and the trip had barely started.

Keep moving, Natalie, Wilcox urged. *We've got a lot of miles to cover before dawn.*

"Easy for you to say." She swapped the water jug and flashlight to opposite hands, inhaled several drags of the cold air, and marched forward.

After crossing the plateau where she'd slapped Nathan Azure on the cheek, she picked her way over rocks and gravel as she clung to the curve of the mountain's summit. The next time she glanced back, the camp had disappeared from view.

17

A Long Night's Journey into Day

BEFORE SHE CAME TO THIS MOUNTAINTOP, NATALIE had imagined that the Andes would be thick with Amazonian jungle, canopied by dense rain forest, or lush with verdant trees and vegetation, like the photos she'd seen of the peaks surrounding Machu Picchu. But here in northern Peru, little grew above the timberline except scrub brush and spiky *ichu* grass, which smelled rather like damp straw after the recent rains. Although she was glad she didn't have to chop a path with a machete through miles of hanging vines, the scenery grew as dreary and monotonous as Arctic tundra, especially since she saw only the three-foot circle of ground illuminated by her flashlight.

Natalie soon lost all sense of time. She expended her nervous energy traversing the uneven ground, until the drudgery of planting each step seemed to drag on for minutes. Yet she also sensed that the precious hours before sunrise were slipping away from her, that at any moment she'd hear the snort of horses and turn to see Azure and Romoldo grinning at her from their saddles.

The water jug turned from a nuisance into a menace. It was too big to fit in her duffel bag, but carrying it strained the biceps in both of her arms until they screamed from the ache. Far past the end of her patience, Natalie started to guzzle the water simply to lighten the load.

Not so fast, Wilcox cautioned her. *That water may have to last us for days.*

"Couldn't we get some more from one of those rivers down below?" she suggested.

Not unless you've got some iodine tablets handy to purify it.

She snarled but capped the jug and staggered onward. Her cumbersome disguise forced her to waddle, penguinlike, over the sloping terrain, and holding both the jug and flashlight made it difficult to use her hands for balance. Trying to answer nature's call outdoors while in her getup actually made her nostalgic for the trash-bag potty.

Only a year ago, Natalie could have summoned Dan to help her cope with a crisis like this. Not that he knew any more than she did about Peru or Spanish or surviving in the wilderness, but at least he could have cheered her on, roused her from despair with a corny joke...told her he loved her.

Anyone ever tell you you look good with that braid?

A smile faltered on her lips, sank into a grimace. The realization that she would never again speak to Dan in this life still surprised her with its sudden pain. Every time she thought she was finally rid of it, something would touch it, jabbing its splintered point into her heart.

Instead of Dan, she had to settle for the constant company of Abel Wilcox. He was the closest thing to a native guide she had, and the dangers of these mountains made her afraid to be without his knowledge even for a minute. Yet he was also a constant reminder of how she'd been duped.

She had to give credit to Abe—that is to say, Trent. The more she got to know the real archaeologist, the more she saw that Trent had Wilcox *down*.

"So how—did you—get roped into this?" Natalie puffed, climbing over an outcropping of rock. She hoped talking would at least pass the time.

Azure convinced me Pizarro's treasure really existed, the professor confessed. *It was like being told I could check out books from the Library of Alexandria. I couldn't resist.*

"But surely you could see what kind of person he was." Natalie didn't bother to disguise the skepticism in her tone. "You had to know he'd want to keep it all for himself."

No, I didn't. I believed that he wanted the same thing I did— to see these priceless pieces of history studied and preserved for humanity.

"Uh-huh. That's what he told me, too."

But he had the knowledge, the passion! You see, in order to properly appreciate the significance of the artifacts we were seeking—

"—you need to understand who the Incas were, what they accomplished...yes, I've heard this lecture."

Trent. He said the name as if through clenched teeth. *I guess now we can add plagiarism to his rap sheet.*

"It was a good lecture," Natalie said to console him. "If it means anything, I really liked your book—"

She stepped on a patch of loose gravel, and her feet slid out from under her. Her hands still clamped on the flashlight and jug handle, she started skidding down the incline on her back.

The jiggling circle of illumination cast by the flashlight

196 ○ **Stephen Woodworth**

did not extend as she accelerated down the slope. Instead, she sped toward a jagged line that separated dusty earth from black uncertainty.

A ledge.

Unable to draw enough breath to shriek, Natalie flattened her arms against the ground and dug her heels into the dirt. Her skirt pulled loose from her jeans and Honorato's poncho scooped up soil, increasing the drag. The soles of her Doc Martens plowed small furrows, pushing up a tiny dune as they crunched to a stop an inch from the precipice. Grit whispered off the ledge and into the vacuum below.

Natalie sprawled there, panting, unwilling to move lest she slip into the darkness that leered at her in the flashlight's beam.

Careful. Wilcox's advice was well meant, but entirely unnecessary.

Natalie nudged herself back from the edge, her heels bulldozing another trickle of dust into the void. When she'd put a couple of feet between her and empty space, she jammed the flashlight into the loose dirt and wedged the water jug between a couple of rocks. Fear subsided, leaving sucking tide pools of fury at her own helplessness, at the comical absurdity of her predicament. The silly costume, the cliff-hanging brush with disaster—it could have been a scene from a Harold Lloyd movie.

Grunting with determination, Natalie yanked the blanket from her waist and flung it higher up the slope, not really caring whether she ever saw it again. She then removed the leather belt from her jeans, looped it through the handle of the water jug, and notched the buckle to create a strap that she hooked over her shoulder.

With the water jug now slung against her side, she snatched up the flashlight, flopped over onto her belly, and clawed her way back up the incline in a geckolike crawl. When she made it to firmer terra, Natalie managed to relocate the blanket, which she folded and flung over her shoulder.

You should put that back on, Wilcox chided her. *What if someone sees you?*

"No one's going to see me before dawn, and in the meantime I'll move faster without it." With one hand free and her legs unrestricted, she improved both the speed and control of her stride. She could have moved even faster by lightening the load that chafed her shoulders.

"Why on earth did you want this stupid propane, anyway?" Natalie imagined the joy she'd feel as she pitched those clattering metal canisters into the chasm beneath her.

Self-defense. The professor did not elaborate.

"What am I supposed to do? Clock Azure over the head with them?"

Although she had some doubts about the professor's master plan, Natalie had to hand it to him for discovering the trail over the mountain to its northern face. If, that is, one could actually call it a trail, since it was little more than a shallow shelf barely wide enough for a mule. Foot traffic had stamped it clear of vegetation, while weather had beveled it smooth, eroding it to rubble in some places.

Her muscles jellied by fatigue and her vision wavering on the verge of semiconsciousness, Natalie could scarcely believe human beings had ever wanted to cross these miserable mountains. It appeared, though, that the Incas and their ancestors had domesticated the entire Andean range, terracing every square inch of arable farmland and blazing a path over every peak. Feats of engineering upon which their descendants still relied centuries later.

An entirely different example of ancient construction awaited Natalie as she started down the tortuous series of switchbacks that led down the mountain. As the sky brightened to a gray twilight, she spotted a square stone tower about two stories high, rooted on a plateau that overlooked the valley below. Silhouetted against the rising mist of morning, it resembled a chess game's black rook.

A chullpa*!* Wilcox exclaimed, jarring Natalie out of her somnambulant shuffle. *We can rest there.*

"What's a chalupa?" she asked, not really caring as long as it meant she could sleep.

I'll be charitable and assume that was a joke. A chullpa *is a funerary tower of the Chavin period. Pre-Incan, from about a thousand years* B. C.

Natalie halted, as if a sniper in the tower's turret had just aimed his rifle at her. "Wait. Is that 'funerary' as in 'funeral,' as in a place where they put dead people?"

Correct.

She shook her head. "No way. I can't do my protective mantra while I'm asleep, and if all those souls start knocking at once, I'll have a seizure."

Maybe. But I'd say dead people are the least of your worries, wouldn't you?

Natalie glanced eastward, where the bleak horizon presaged daybreak. Nathan Azure, she knew, rose at dawn. How long would it be before he sent Trent to rouse her from her cot? How long would it take them to form a search party once they discovered her tent was empty? Despite the night's grueling trek, she had probably traveled fewer than three miles from camp—a distance they could cover in a fraction of the time on horseback.

She drew a deep draft of the insubstantial air and contemplated the sentinel pillar of stones before her. Perhaps she would be safe there for a few hours, especially if Wilcox continued to inhabit her. Whenever she used to summon Dan, he'd been able to keep other souls from invading her.

"All right, we'll go there, on one condition: you can't leave me while I'm asleep, even for a second."

Don't worry. A deal's a deal—I'm not going anywhere.

The mention of the deal she'd struck with him chilled her...or perhaps it was the morning damp combined with the sheen of clammy sweat now drying beneath her coat and poncho. Natalie shook off the feeling and left the trail, stalks of brush licking at her ankles as she headed toward the *chullpa.*

The tower stood about twenty feet tall, the masonry of its walls thin and simple compared with the hulking geometric bricks of the Ransom Room and other Incan constructions she'd seen. Rough slabs, pasted together with crumbling mortar and small rocks, formed walls less than a foot thick. Tufts of stiff grass bristled from its overgrown cornice. The tower's two levels each bore a low, open doorway, the entrance to the upper story elevated a few feet above Natalie's head. She passed through the lower door into a dim chamber about eight feet square and six feet high.

Something cracked beneath her boots as she stepped onto the stone floor, and reflex made her stumble back. As her eyes adjusted to the shadows, she could see that the gray and brown trapezoids scattered at her feet were shards of shattered pottery. For an instant, she thought the white fragments were bits of broken ceramic as well. Then awful comprehension stopped her breath.

They were bones. Tibiae, femurs, vertebrae, ulnae and radii, knuckles and toes. Natalie's right foot teetered on a rib, and she jumped back. Human remains were the most powerful touchstones possible, and souls could leap from them the way an electric spark could arc from a tesla coil.

"The Lord is my shepherd; I shall not want," Natalie stammered. *"He maketh me to lie down—"*

Stop! Wilcox yelped, his presence in her mind already receding as she invoked the protective mantra. *What're you doing?*

Natalie snapped her mouth shut. "Sorry. But if anyone knocks, tell 'em there's no room at the inn. My body isn't a Motel 6."

I know. Three's a crowd.

"*Two's* a crowd. Three's a disaster." She kicked bones out of her way, inching forward as if the floor rippled with crawling rats. When she'd made her way to the room's left front corner, she used her foot to sweep a space clear on the floor, out of view of the door.

With the oasis of sleep in reach before her, Natalie felt the last of her adrenaline evaporate. Relieved of duty, her legs folded, dropping her into a sitting position. Her empty stomach rumbled, but she couldn't imagine mustering the strength to eat. Her head nodded forward, shaking her awake before she even realized she'd closed her eyes.

After setting aside her bag and water jug, Natalie placed the folded blanket on the floor for a pillow and stretched out on the tomb's glacial, unyielding floor. As a precaution against despairing dreams, she tried to think of Callie, of her father's recovery, of the comforts of home, but her consciousness collapsed like a condemned building, burying her under its ruin.

Abel Wilcox waited for almost an hour after Natalie dozed off before he cautiously opened her eyes. The light dilated her pupils but did not penetrate her dreamless slumber.

When her will did not restrain him, Wilcox slowly lifted her slack body upright. He studied her hands, which were graceful even when filthy with chalk dust and dirt. He spread the fingers, closed them—once, twice. For practice.

He did not risk moving any more on that occasion, but instead lay back on the blanket and shut her eyes again. Unlike the living, however, he had no need of sleep, so he occupied the vacant hours of Lindstrom's dormancy by listing every item of Incan gold or silver he could recall from the Spaniards' catalogs of their conquest.

18

The Carrot and the Stick

TRENT DID NOT SMILE THAT DAY. AFTER REPORTING to the boss that Natalie had escaped, he didn't dare. Nathan Azure boiled with a rage beyond all hope of appeasement.

They stood together in the center of camp, arms folded in impotent suspense as they waited for their appointed posse to return with news. "We've accounted for all the horses," Trent said in weak consolation. "She can't have gone far on foot."

"Really!" Lethal sarcasm serrated the casualness of Azure's tone. "Well, you didn't think she'd get away from us in the first place, but she did, didn't she?"

You didn't think she'd have the cojones *to do it, did you, you arrogant twit?* Trent thought, although he'd never say so out loud. Instead, he bowed his head, commiserating with the boss in judicious silence. Inside, he didn't know how he should feel—whether to be glad that Natalie was out of Azure's clutches or to be devastated by the thought that she had recognized him for the impostor he was.

Honorato and Alberto cantered into camp from the south. They had a third horse tethered behind them, but its saddle was vacant.

"*Nada,*" Honorato reported. His face betrayed neither disappointment nor fear.

"Brilliant." The frown lines at the corners of Azure's mouth deepend until he looked like his grimacing burial mask. "Assemble the men. Then prepare Juan and bring him here."

Azure hadn't deigned to look at his chief lackey, but he had spoken the command in English. Controlling his breath so the boss wouldn't hear him sigh, Trent went to round up the Peruvians. That was easy enough, although he couldn't find Romoldo, damn him. Romoldo could have handled Juan—it was his kind of job. Now Trent would have to deal with it.

Or, rather, Nick would.

Approaching Juan's tent, Trent inhaled deeply, hardened his features as he went into character. Problem was, he had nothing against Juan. The man was hardworking, obedient, and harmless—a small-time coca farmer with a family of seven children, all under the age of ten. Really, it was only bad luck that he happened to be guarding the supply tent the previous night. It wasn't his fault Natalie had escaped, yet Azure wanted to make an example of him in front of the other men.

The fact made Trent's task harder. So did his rudimentary fluency in Spanish, for, try as he might to ignore it, he could still understand Juan's pathetic begging as he pinioned the man's arms and cinched a rope tight around them.

"*¡Por favor, señor! ¡Por el amor de Dios!*"

Come on, Nick, Trent thought. He stuffed a dirty

washcloth in Juan's mouth to stifle his pleas before dragging him outside. He made sure the rag didn't block Juan's windpipe, however, for the boss would be furious if the man choked to death.

"As you know, the *bruja* has escaped." Although Azure addressed the gathered hirelings in perfect Peruvian dialect, his Spanish still dripped with British condescension. "I will give three hundred thousand nuevos soles to the man who finds her. *She must not be harmed.*"

He cued Trent with a glare, and the latter muscled Juan up in front of the crowd, ripped open the front of the condemned man's shirt.

"Three hundred thousand nuevos soles to you if you bring the *bruja* back alive." Azure hammered the words like spikes. "But if you kill her or allow her to escape again..."

He stepped back from Trent; the experience with Wilcox had taught the Englishman to keep his distance from bleeding men.

Trent drew a bowie knife from the sheath on his belt. He would have preferred the quick efficiency of a gun, but the boss insisted on an execution that would "make an impression."

Do it, Nick. It's only another job.

Tightening the chokehold he had on the Peruvian's neck to stop his wriggling, Trent slit a series of wheezing red gills between the ribs of Juan's bare chest. He carefully avoided piercing the heart or the aorta, for the goal was to delay the end until Juan either bled to death or asphyxiated from his lungs' inability to draw breath.

Trent let go of the bound Peruvian, who staggered

toward his countrymen, leaking life and beseeching them with bugged eyes. They shrank from him, and Juan toppled to the ground. Nathan Azure was the only one who didn't watch him gasping there, thickening the dust beneath him to maroon mud.

"Are there any questions?" The Englishman arched his eyebrows expectantly, like a manager at a staff meeting.

"Your money is mine, *gringo*," a voice shouted in Spanish. "I have found your *bruja*."

Trent and the other men tore their attention from Juan to see Romoldo standing at the north end of the camp, grinning.

"I am not in a mood for jokes," Azure said.

"Neither am I," Romoldo shot back. "Come. I will show you."

Azure refused to move for a moment, as if unwilling to comply with anyone else's command. He relented, though, and the rest of the men trailed him as he followed Romoldo out of camp. As Trent slipped out of the cold detachment of Nick's character, he cast a queasy glance back at Juan, who still quivered in the dirt like a flayed rabbit.

About thirty feet outside the camp's clearing, Romoldo sat on his haunches among the pincushion patches of grass. He raised his hand to halt Azure and the others before they trod on the moist soil in front of him. "You see?"

He pointed at the tracks imprinted there—the tread of what were probably the only Doc Marten boots in Peru.

Trent masked his concern. *Move fast, Natalie,* he thought.

Azure's lips whitened, and he squinted at the mountains

to the north. "Where the devil are you going, Lindstrom?" he murmured in English.

"I will find her," Romoldo answered in Spanish, as if he'd understood Azure's question. "I will bring her to you alive." He drew himself up to his full height, an inch taller than the tycoon. "Have the money ready when I return."

"He has not found her yet." Honorato nudged his way to the front of the crowd, locked eyes with Romoldo. "The money should go to the one who gets the *bruja* first."

Nathan Azure evaluated both of them, looking almost pleased. "Very well. May the best man win."

19
Sikiyta Muchay

THEY'RE COMING, NATALIE.

The words shivered her out of sleep, as if someone had yanked a set of bedcovers off her. Moaning, she rolled onto her back, pinching her eyelids shut to filter out the unwanted light. "What?"

They'll be here soon, Wilcox said. *We've got to move.*

She tried to sit up, but every joint in her body squealed with Tin Man stiffness. Allowing her head to sag back onto the folded blanket, Natalie wanted nothing more than to crawl back into the womb of sleep. "Please...just a few more minutes."

I'm not a snooze alarm. Get up.

She levered herself upright, her entire body aching as if it were one enormous bruise. "Do I get breakfast at least?"

You can eat and walk at the same time, can't you?

"Yeah. I suppose I can." Natalie took out a couple of energy bars, then shouldered her bag and the water bottle. They weighed on her like a milkmaid's yoke.

And put the skirt on, in case they see you.

She snatched up the gray blanket and shook it. "It slows

me down! And if they *see* me, this 'skirt' isn't going to save my sorry hide."

No, it won't—I *will. Now put it on.*

"Fine!" She swathed her legs with the blanket, stuffed the hem under the waist of her jeans. "Satisfied?"

Not while Nathan Azure walks the earth. But all things in good time.

"Whatever." Taking care to step only on the path she'd cleared of bones, Natalie left the *chullpa*'s burial chamber. Outside, she tore one of the energy-bar wrappers open with her teeth, wolfing its contents so fast that she coughed half-chewed morsels as she tramped back to the trail down the mountain.

Her limbs loosened up a bit as she got moving, but her calves and shins smarted from resisting the constant gravitational drag of the slope. The slant also wedged her toes into the fronts of her Doc Martens, which chafed her skin until it blistered. A mile of back-and-forth hiking along the switchbacks equaled a descent of only a few hundred feet, making progress almost imperceptible.

This is good, Wilcox assured her. *The incline will be treacherous for the horses. They'll have to slow down, maybe even dismount to lead them by the reins.*

"Swell. I'll—keep that—in mind." She paused at a curve, gasping to inhale enough air before forging down the next slope. Every time she even thought about stopping to rest, Wilcox whipped her on, reminding her that "they" would soon nip at her heels like a pack of baying bloodhounds.

Instead of dissipating during the day, the morning mist in the valley congealed into a thick coal-dust fog that dampened Natalie's face and clothes as she passed into the cloud layer.

Poor visibility will only help us, Wilcox promised.

"Funny how everything that sucks seems to be good for us." Natalie switched on her flashlight to make sure she didn't lose the trail. "Imagine how wonderful an earthquake or flood would be."

Careful what you wish for. It looks like rain.

"Perfect! I thought fall was supposed to be the *dry* season in Peru."

That's a generalization, Wilcox informed her, *not a guarantee.*

"Now you tell me." Natalie started on another nutrition bar, her fourth of the day. *Two for breakfast, two for lunch… and a sensible dinner!* she thought, already sick of the sludgy chocolate coating and mealy filling.

A trickle of pebbles hailed down from above. Natalie shot a glance up the mountainside but could see nothing through the fog. She listened, but the mist seemed to deaden sound. Still…was that the hollow scuffle of a horse's hooves on stone?

Let's get a move on, Wilcox said. He needn't have bothered, for Natalie was already hiking down the trail faster than ever.

At last, the trail bottomed out in a ravine, through which a narrow river meandered. Now below the timberline, Natalie began to see a few scattered banana and eucalyptus trees growing wherever the ground leveled off. A twitch of brown along the riverbank caught her eye, then another and another. A dozen or more animals lifted their triangular heads to look back at her, pointy ears pricked up. They possessed bodies like deer, but their breasts and bellies were covered with shaggy white wool. "What are those?" she wondered aloud.

Vicuña! Wilcox murmured. *I didn't think any wild herds existed this far north. Finest wool in the world, so they tell me.*

As Natalie marveled at them, the herd turned as one and fled. "But I thought you said alpacas had the finest wool."

The professor seemed nonplussed. *I never said that.*

"Oh. My mistake." Natalie flushed as if she'd shrieked the wrong man's name while making love. For an instant, she'd forgotten which Wilcox had given Callie her stuffed alpaca. The similarities between the two of them...all the things that so attracted her to "Abe." If Abel Wilcox were still alive, would she have been as attracted to him as she was to Trent?

She would never know now. Nathan Azure had seen to that.

Taking a swig from the water bottle, Natalie was alarmed to see that she had gulped more than half its contents during the descent, and she had no idea how much farther she had to hike to get to another supply of pure drinking water. *Water, water everywhere, nor any drop to drink*, she thought, recalling "The Rime of the Ancient Mariner."

"Well, bwana, where do we go from here?" she asked.

Head east. You're bound to hit the road to Chachapoyas eventually.

"How do you know that? You don't even know where we are."

There aren't that many roads in this part of the country, Wilcox explained. *If the camp was north of the route from*

Cajamarca to Chachapoyas, as you described, traveling east should take us there.

"If that's true, how long will it take us to get to the next town?"

I don't know. Maybe hours. Maybe days.

"I see." Natalie had to lock her knees to keep her rubbery legs from collapsing. Her toes stung with each step, their blisters popped and skinned from the flesh, so that she hobbled as if walking on stilts. She craved a few minutes' rest but didn't sit down for fear she might not be able to get up again. The possibility that she might have to walk another twenty or thirty miles made her want to wait there for Nathan Azure's goons to pick her up. At least then she'd get a ride.

A soft dripping on the brim of her hat signaled the arrival of a thundershower.

"Fabulous." Natalie bowed her head to shield her eyes from the raindrops and shuffled forward, her face twitching from the pain in her feet, the soreness in her limbs.

Following a trail that paralleled the river and ran roughly perpendicular to the northern face of the mountain, she came to an ancient stone bridge that spanned the stream. The shower thickened to a downpour, the machine-gun rhythm on her hat so deafening that Natalie couldn't distinguish the plash of the horses' hoofbeats until they were right behind her.

Don't run and don't look back, Wilcox said. *Just keep walking.*

Natalie doubted whether she could have run at that point, much as instinct impelled her to flight. Instead, she trudged onto the bridge, clutching her duffel bag and water

212 0 Stephen Woodworth

bottle close to her sides and hoping no part of them stuck out from underneath the canopy of Honorato's poncho.

"*¡Ai, bruja! ¡Alto!*" Natalie recognized the vulgar familiarity of the voice behind her.

Romoldo.

Ignore him, Wilcox urged. *Keep walking.*

She heard the clop and splash of the horses—two of them—as they stepped onto the bridge behind her.

When she didn't respond, Romoldo evidently began to doubt whether she was the *bruja* he sought. "*¡Ai, chica!*" he called with relative courtesy. "*Alto, por favor.*"

Please... let me talk to him.

The request rattled Natalie. She still didn't entirely trust Wilcox and had so far resisted ceding full control of her body to him. But she couldn't speak Spanish well enough to fool a native like Romoldo. The professor was her only chance of making her Peruvian disguise work.

With no time to debate, Natalie focused on her spectator mantra, which had been looping through her brain for so long that it had become background noise to her thoughts. A seductive reprieve from pain followed as she disconnected from the sensation in her flesh.

Life is but a dream...

"*Ai, chica—*"

"*Sikiyta muchay!*" Natalie heard herself say, shouting loud enough to be heard without turning her face to the men. She didn't understand the words but knew it wasn't Spanish.

Perhaps it was that tongue used by the locals in Cajamarca—the language of the Incas.

Romoldo must have comprehended the exclamation, for he laughed and made rude smooching sounds with his lips. He barked a question at her, and Wilcox replied in rapid Spanish as he continued to walk. Natalie saw that she was approaching the end of the bridge, but she no longer commanded the feet that moved her.

Behind her, Romoldo swapped heated words with his companion, whose voice Natalie couldn't place. A moment later she heard the snap of reins and a whip. When Wilcox inclined her head to glance back, she saw the two Peruvians trotting their horses back up the trail toward the mountain.

They're gone now, Natalie told Wilcox. *I'll take it from here.* She detested peering out through the mask of her own face, seeing and hearing everything yet powerless to act.

Wilcox gave a good-natured chuckle. "I thought you'd appreciate the break. But suit yourself."

She concentrated on the mantra again, and Wilcox slipped back into the recesses of her mind. The renewed misery of cold, weary, aching flesh weighted Natalie like sopping wet clothing. "What did you say to them, anyway?"

Sikiyta muchay. It's Quechua. I figured it would fool them because they'd never believe that a gringa like you would know how to speak it.

"And what does it mean?"

Kiss my a—

"Charming. What other garbage did you put in my mouth?"

They asked if I'd seen anyone else on this trail. I told them

I'd been walking it for hours and saw no one. They must have thought you didn't make it this far and decided to backtrack.

"Thank heaven for small favors."

They'll be back, you know. Azure won't give up, ever. If worst comes to worst... Wilcox paused, either from indecision or for dramatic effect. *We might have to kill him.*

Natalie halted, her damp skin goose-pimpling beneath the piled layers of her disguise. Wilcox had spoken the unspeakable.

In the abstract, Natalie had admitted to herself that, in order to escape, she might have to take someone's life. But the reality of killing anyone—even a monster like Nathan Azure—appalled her. In all her years in law enforcement, she had never killed anyone, not even Evan Markham, the Violet Killer, who had abducted and nearly murdered her. For a Violet, taking a human life meant forging an implacable quantum bond with that person's soul. Just as Horace Rendell now returned to persecute Callie, Nathan Azure would come to Natalie in ceaseless retribution, to knock and knock and knock.

Still, she needed to get home, back to Callie. If that meant killing Azure...

"I don't want to hurt anybody," Natalie pleaded, gazing glumly at the trail turning to slop in front of her. "I just want to get out of here."

She stomped on through the mud, trying to think of nothing but the next mile toward home.

20

Room for a *Bruja*

WILCOX WOULD NOT LET HER FORGET ABOUT Nathan Azure, however. Much as Arabella Madison had done, he spoke to Natalie in the rational, concerned tone of an older sibling, implanting ideas that seemed like her own to her weary brain.

I'm afraid you won't be able to get away from Azure by making it back to the States. He knows where you live. You... and your daughter.

"He killed you. He'll go to jail." Natalie trained her flashlight beam on the trail immediately in front of her, scanning for a safe place to step amid the cascade of runoff pouring down the incline. A bead curtain of rain dripped from the brim of her hat, obscuring her view.

He won't go to jail if he gets to you or your family first.

Natalie slipped, wobbled, sank her hands in the mud to steady herself. *"Shut up about my family!"*

I'm sorry. I just thought I should be honest with you. He'll do whatever it takes to get you to cooperate.

She got up, chest heaving, and held her quivering arms in the downpour to wash the slime from her hands and flashlight. Wilcox's arguments began to burrow into her brain:

Hadn't it really been luck more than scruples that had kept her from killing anyone before now? If she'd had to, wouldn't she have killed Evan Markham in order to save her own life? If the only way to keep Vincent Thresher from murdering Callie had been to kill his puppet Violet Lyman Pearsall, wouldn't she have done so, without hesitation? How was Nathan Azure any different?

Too tired to silence Wilcox by force, Natalie tried to defuse his reasoning with logic. "Even if I wanted to kill Azure, how could I? He has at least twenty men guarding him."

Simple. We set a trap for him.

Natalie plunged her right foot ankle-deep in muck and waded forward. "And how do we do that?"

We lure him with the thing he wants most.

"Me?"

No. Pizarro's gold.

"That would be swell if we knew where it was."

That cave you drew from Pizarro's memory. Azure will believe the treasure is there, whether it is or not.

"And how do we find the stupid cave?"

There are ways . . .

The silt beneath Natalie's boot gave way, and she flopped facedown onto the flooded path, drenching her already sodden poncho.

It's almost dark, Wilcox observed as she pushed herself upright. *We'd better find shelter for the night.*

"I *KNOW* THAT! JUST GIVE ME A MINUTE!"

Sorry.

Although not given to weeping, Natalie sagged on her knees with the water swamping her skirt and wailed. Her skin felt as shriveled and rubbery as a deflated balloon, and she couldn't stop shivering from the cold water that soaked into every crevice of her body. If she died out here tonight, her corpse might never be discovered and identified. The next time she saw Callie would be when her daughter summoned her from limbo...provided she even *wanted* to summon Natalie. Callie might spend the rest of her life hating the mother who had abandoned her, the way Natalie had resented her father for surrendering her to the School.

Courage, Natalie, Wilcox quietly urged. *You've made it this far. Don't give up now.*

His gentle comfort reminded her of Dan—braced her. Without bothering to wipe the tears from her rainswept face, she slogged forward, making a solemn vow to herself. She would *not* die here. She *would* get home to be a mother to Callie—no matter what she had to do to get there.

Natalie had followed the trail through the gorge and almost a thousand feet up the side of another mountain when she caught sight of the row of squat stone dwellings built flush against the mountainside. For a moment, she thought that they must be abandoned ruins like the *chullpa*...or possibly an illusion invented by her desperation. But these houses possessed doors of galvanized sheet metal and thatched roofs that shed the rain, and the walls proved solid when she stumbled up to touch them.

Maybe you should let me handle this, Wilcox suggested when she moved toward the door of the first house in the village.

"No." Natalie dug through her bag, dribbling yellow illumination into it from the fading flashlight and whimpering when she couldn't find what she wanted. Finally she located the pocketbook containing her Peruvian currency, which she kept folded in her fist as she pounded on the door of the hut. "*¡Socorro!* Help me, please!"

The door opened outward half a foot and a man with slicked-back black hair peered out at her over the flame of the candle in his hand. "*¿Qué quieres?*"

"I'm lost. Uh...*estoy perdida. Quiero una habitación.*" She held up the cash, the bills already limp with rainwater. "*Tengo dinero.*"

Showing little interest in the money, the man lifted the candle to her face. His dark eyes widened and he stepped back from the door, beckoning her inside.

Other than a faint orange glow from the embers beneath an earthenware cooking pot, the man's candle was the only light source in the one-room abode. As he moved toward the opposite corner, the flame revealed the dim outlines of two metal-frame beds, upon which sat a stocky young woman and two round-faced children, all wearing knitted sweaters. They all stared at Natalie, the younger of the kids rubbing her eyes as if still half-asleep.

The woman—presumably the man's wife—babbled a question to him, her fearful gaze fixed on the stranger now dripping water on their dirt floor. He responded in a low tone, indicating his eyes with his fingers and then pointing to Natalie. His wife nodded, regarding Natalie with something akin to awe.

Items of clothing lay draped over the wooden rafters that

supported the roof, and the woman pulled down a sweater and skirt and presented them to her guest. Shivering convulsively, Natalie wavered about whether she should take the clothes, for the woman spoke too quickly for her to understand.

She wants to know if you'd like to change out of your wet things, Wilcox translated helpfully.

"Uh…" Natalie scanned the room for a private place to undress, then cast a bashful glance toward the children.

Their father evidently sensed her discomfort. Pouring wax from the candle's tip to fix its base, he planted it upright on an adjacent table and tapped the boy and girl on their shoulders, commanding them to emulate him as he faced the wall.

Natalie took the sweater and skirt and bowed her head to the woman. *"Gracias."*

Despite the family's courtesy, she left her bra and panties on when she disrobed. The woman set aside Natalie's duffel bag and hung her damp clothes on the rafter above the cooking fire where they would dry faster, then gestured to the pot below. *"¿Tienes hambre?"*

Natalie nodded, her body already warming beneath the dry woolen garments. She didn't care what was in the pot as long as it was edible.

The woman spooned some kind of soup into a bowl and passed it to her. The room lacked chairs, but a long plank placed across two large bricks served as a bench where Natalie sat and scooped soup into her mouth. She was so intent on consuming the watery potato concoction that she had nearly emptied the bowl before she noticed that the entire family was staring at her again.

Abruptly recovering her manners, she put her spoon down and cleared her throat. *"Me llamo Natalie Lindstrom. ¿Como se llama?"*

The woman, who had returned to her husband's side, exchanged a glance with him, as if conferring about whether they should divulge such personal information.

"Felipe Avila." He put a hand to his chest, then pointed to his wife, son, and daughter in turn. *"Santusa. Julian. Rafaela. Y Isabel."* He patted one end of a tiny hammock stretched between the two beds, which Natalie had not noticed before. A sleeping baby girl evidently nestled in its fold.

Natalie smiled, hastily riffling through her mental file of phrases gleaned from her Spanish CD lessons. *"Yo soy de los Estados Unidos."*

Felipe nodded. *"Sí."*

The conversation stalled. Natalie struggled to put together words to express her gratitude to the family for giving her shelter, but before she could speak, the boy, Julian, piped up, an excited grin on his face. The only word Natalie caught was *bruja* before Santusa shushed her son with a reproachful look. He must have overheard his parents discussing the witch who had entered their home.

He wants to know if you're really a bruja, Wilcox said when Natalie failed to answer. *Since they've offered us this hospitality based on the belief that you* are *a* bruja, *I suggest you answer yes.*

She briefly debated the matter with her conscience. Fear

of being cast back out into the storm outweighed her aversion to lying. "*Sí. Estoy una bruja.*"

The girl, Rafaela, chirped a question over her parents' scolding.

"*Can you cast a spell on Pablo Sarete?*" Wilcox translated, warm amusement in his rendition. "*He's always teasing me and pulling my hair.*" *Are you sure you don't want me to speak for you?*

No, Natalie silently replied. *Be my interpreter. Tell me how to say what I want to say.*

As you wish.

The system was awkward, rather like the time-delayed dubbing in low-budget foreign films. The Avilas gave Natalie odd looks whenever they had to wait for her to reply, but at least she was able to communicate with them without giving mastery of her mouth to Wilcox.

As she suspected, the family had just retired for the night when she arrived. Natalie was only too happy to go straight to sleep after her supper. Felipe and Santusa insisted that she should take their bed, but she refused, assuring them that she would be more than content to lie on the floor for the night. Santusa gave her a heap of extra ponchos to spread over the dirt and to cover her for warmth.

Despite the padding, the floor was hard on Natalie's back, but it was better than napping among the bones in the *chullpa*. Cocooned in the woolen security of the ponchos and lulled by the humanity of the Avila family, Natalie allowed her battered mental barricades against exhaustion to collapse. She dropped into unconsciousness even before Felipe extinguished the candle.

* * *

For more than an hour, Abel Wilcox allowed Natalie's sleeping body to remain still. He did not stir until he heard a chorus of snoring from the other side of the room.

Satisfied that the Avila family had all dozed off, Wilcox eased Natalie into a sitting position. With adolescent guilt, he ran her hands down the shapely curves of her body. She was a beautiful woman—smart, kind, and witty, too, from what he'd gathered so far. If things had gone differently...

Her face tightened with his bitterness. Azure had denied him that treasure, too.

Wilcox paused to make sure that the movement had not roused Natalie to consciousness, then rose and padded over the dusty floor to the corner where Santusa had placed Natalie's bag. Only a few embers still smoldered in the adjacent cooking fire, providing scant light for Wilcox to find what he needed. Working mostly by touch, he snaked Lindstrom's hand into the duffel until he located the flashlight.

Wilcox darted a glance toward the two beds hidden in darkness across the room. Would the light wake them? Then he smiled at his own skittishness. He kept forgetting that he now looked like Natalie. If Santusa and Felipe woke, they would see the *bruja* going through her own belongings—and what could be more natural? "My feet are cold," he would tell them, "and I want a pair of socks."

Nevertheless, Wilcox hunched over the flashlight and dipped it deep into the bag to block as much of the sickly yellow glow as possible. He didn't want to risk an interruption that might jar Lindstrom into awareness.

When he failed to find the item he sought in the duffel's main compartment, he searched the zippered side pocket until he felt the rectangular edges of a frame. An instant under the flashlight's beam confirmed the photo's subject.

A pretty girl with brown hair and violet eyes, grinning over six candles on a birthday cake.

Seeing Natalie's daughter made him wince. He didn't want any harm to come to either the girl or her mother. But they were already involved—already in danger—whether they liked it or not.

You'll be doing them both a favor, he told himself.

The picture in his grasp, Wilcox zipped up the duffel, put the flashlight back in the bag, and crept over to the plank bench. Crouching there, he placed the framed photo on the floor beneath the plank—out of view, but not too difficult for Azure's men to find. Another bread crumb in the trail he was leaving for the tycoon to follow.

Although he could not enjoy the slumber of the living, Wilcox settled into the sleep of the just as he reclined on the floor, pulled the ponchos up to Lindstrom's chin, and shut her eyes. He *would* find the ransom that Francisco Pizarro had plundered from Atahualpa. It was his right—he had sacrificed his life to save that piece of history. And he would do whatever it took to make sure that Nathan Azure never possessed it.

21

The *Brujo* Will See You Now

NATALIE WAS SO EXHAUSTED THAT SHE DID NOT HEAR the bang of the hut's door as it flew open in the hours before dawn. It took Santusa's shriek to rip her from the snug isolation of sleep.

"*¿Dónde está la bruja?*"

Without sitting up, Natalie glanced in the direction of the voice. Two bright flashlights swept the room. One beam came to rest on Felipe, who stammered in fearful indignation as the baby caterwauled in the hammock beside him. Natalie scanned for an alternate way out, but the stone house had no windows and the intruders blocked the only door.

The second flashlight beam darted toward the floor, fixed upon Natalie's face. She snapped her violet eyes shut but not before she caught a glimpse of the broad-shouldered outline of the man behind the flashlight.

"*Nada,*" his gruff voice intoned.

The reddish glare faded from Natalie's eyelids and she chanced a look toward the man, who had now turned his back to her. His companion sputtered a protest, shining his own light on the damp jeans and black T-shirt that hung above the cooking fire. The first man shook his head, scoffed a terse dismissal, and herded his partner out the door, coincidentally blocking his view of Natalie.

Honorato, she thought.

On the opposite side of the room, Santusa cooed to the yelping children while Felipe struggled to strike a match with his shaking fingers. When he finally got the candle alight, he brought it within a foot of Natalie's face, stuttering at her faster than she could comprehend, much less answer.

He wants to know who those men were, Wilcox said. *If they mean to harm his family, he orders you to leave now.*

It's about time you spoke up! Natalie complained. *Where were you when I needed you a minute ago?*

Sorry. You said you wanted to do all the talking. Speaking of which, I think you'd better give Felipe an explanation soon. He looks like he's about to have a coronary.

She let her mouth fall open, but Felipe kept shouting at her, his eyes quivering as if he were afraid to blink. *What should I tell him?* she asked Wilcox.

You'd better let me talk. It's too complex to dictate.

She inhaled a breath and focused on her spectator mantra. *All right...*

Her mouth closed as her expression firmed from befuddlement to confidence. A stream of fluent Spanish flowed from her lips, of which Natalie understood about one word in five.

Her sudden eloquence only agitated Felipe, as if a burglar he'd apprehended turned out to be a demon in disguise. He fired several questions back at her that Wilcox calmly answered, pointing to her violet irises to underscore his assertions. A look of capitulation on his face, Felipe sighed a command to Santusa, who rose and reignited the cooking fire. Although it could not have been past four in the morning, there would be no more sleep for any of them that night.

What did you tell him? Natalie demanded as she wrested control from the professor.

The truth. I said that evil gringos *had come to steal Peruvian gold and that you needed the help of another* brujo *to stop them.*

I do, do I?

Yes. That is why Felipe will help us obtain transportation to Tingo, where the nearest local brujo *lives.*

And how can he help us stop the "evil gringos*"?*

He will help us bait our trap with Pizarro's gold.

Wonderful.

Santusa offered her a couple of triangular rolls and a bowl of coffee. The coffee was thin and laced with sugar, but Natalie savored it as if it were a triple espresso. She needed all the strength the weak caffeine could offer and even wished she could supplement it with a cup of coca tea.

Since her clothes had not completely dried, Santusa permitted her to keep the sweater and skirt she had borrowed the previous night. Natalie pressed her to take all the cash she had as compensation, but Santusa would accept only a couple of the scraggly bills. "You will need money for the horse and the truck," she said as Wilcox translated for Natalie.

Santusa was right. Only one man in the village owned a pair of horses, and he extracted a fee to help her ride to the only man in twenty miles who owned a motorized vehicle.

He, in turn, charged for the privilege of chauffeuring her down the long dirt road to Tingo in a dented Ford pickup with busted shocks.

Hardly more than a village itself, Tingo boasted such civic landmarks as a church, a school, and a "health post," a tiny cube of whitewashed walls in the center of town that served as a medical clinic. Felipe had instructed Natalie to seek the *brujo* there, so she asked the pickup driver to drop her off at the post's door.

You'd better let me do the talking, Wilcox advised her as the truck drove off.

"How did I know you were going to say that?" Natalie adjusted Honorato's poncho to make sure it covered her duffel bag.

If the brujo *thinks we're trying to find the gold for ourselves, he won't help us. I have to convince him that we need to get to the gold first in order to prevent the* gringos *from getting it. Besides... only I can speak Quechua.*

"The *brujo* only speaks Quechua?"

No. But the Incas only speak Quechua.

"The *Incas*? What do you think you're doing?"

Never mind. You'll see.

"That's what I'm afraid of." A passing woman stared at her for talking to herself; Natalie gave her an awkward smile. "I'll let you talk, but only if you translate *everything* for me." To avoid arousing the *brujo*'s suspicion, she made the transition to Wilcox's control before they entered the office.

Inside, the health post was little more than a room with an examining table, a medicine cabinet, a doctor's scale, and a set of mostly barren shelves. A boy no older than five lay on the table, his eyes half-lidded with the lassitude of illness. An aged man in a white smock stood over him, swinging the cross of a rosary over the boy's body and keening either a prayer or an incantation. A woman in a plaid skirt and orange cardigan, presumably the boy's mother, watched from the side, head bowed, hands clasped before her mouth.

When the man finished his ritual, he went to the medicine cabinet and took out a small plastic vial of pills. He tapped the bottle and gave instructions to the woman, holding up two fingers, when he happened to glance at Natalie for the first time.

The purple eyes shone in his brown face as bright as twin orchids.

He's a Violet? Natalie asked Wilcox in shock. She had been expecting some charlatan medicine man.

Of course, the professor said. *Registered with the government, same as with the N-double-A-C-C, which is why Azure didn't use him. Because of their spiritual status in the community, conduits in Peru tend to get pushed into careers as healers, too. People think they have magical powers.*

The *brujo* appeared to be as surprised to see Natalie as she was to see him, for he broke off his directions to the boy's mother and it took him several seconds to recover his train of thought.

"Do I have the honor of addressing Señor Topa?" Wilcox asked him once the woman had departed with her son. The professor mentally converted the ensuing conversation to English for Natalie's benefit.

"Yes," the *brujo* answered. "And I am pleased to make your acquaintance, Doña...?"

"Lindstrom. Natalie Lindstrom." Wilcox nodded toward the medicine cabinet with a wry smile. "I see you do not rely on the saints and spirits alone in your healing."

"The medicine can heal," Señor Topa replied, "but only if the saints and spirits allow it. How may I help you?"

"Some *gringo* archaeologists have come to plunder the tombs of your ancestors. They wanted me to help them, but I refused and escaped. Now I fear that they may find the tombs on their own."

The creases at the sides of the *brujo*'s mouth deepened. His jet-black hair contrasted with his crinkled eyes and weathered forehead, suggesting that the duties of his position had aged him prematurely. "You tell me nothing new. People are always defiling the graves of the Incas. What can I do to stop it?"

"You can help me find the tomb first. I will seal it so that no one will ever desecrate it."

"How do I know you are not trying to help the people you say you want to stop?"

"Because they are trying to kill me. Soon they will come to ask you about me, to threaten you until you tell them where I am. That should be proof enough that what I say is true."

Wait a minute! Natalie interjected. *Is that a lie? How would Azure know where we are?*

Wilcox did not take time to answer her questions. "I need to speak to an Inca who knows the land of the Cloud People," he insisted to Señor Topa. "Will you help me?"

The *brujo* exhaled, his features growing older still. "Yes. But not here. You will have to come with me."

22
Sacrifices

AS HIS MEN DRAGGED THE SHRIEKING MEMBERS OF the Avila family from their miserable hovel, Nathan Azure sighed. He had proved again the truth of the hoary adage: if one wanted something done right, one had to do it oneself.

Romoldo and Honorato, whom he had once considered his most competent hirelings, had taken separate paths to track the Violet, each taking along one man to assist in apprehending her. Romoldo had permitted some local woman he encountered on the mountain trail to mislead him, while Honorato had ignored compelling evidence that Lindstrom had visited this peasant shack. Fortunately Alberto, the former drug runner who had accompanied Honorato, returned to tell Azure about the black T-shirt and woman's jeans he'd seen hanging from the hut's rafters.

The Avila woman snarled and thrashed but could not break free of the man who restrained her. Her husband was too afraid to move, for Romoldo had thrown him to the ground and jammed the barrel of a shotgun against the back of his head. Three of the tycoon's other henchmen held the children a few yards apart from their parents. Shirking the real work, Trent bounced the baby in his arms as if he were the girl's uncle. Azure could barely hear himself think over the brat's yowling.

After a few minutes of ransacking the house's interior, Alberto emerged, exultant. *"¡La bruja! ¡La bruja!"*

He handed the framed photo of Lindstrom's daughter to the big *gringo*.

"Interesting." Azure's brow smoothed as a novel idea struck him. He turned to Trent, who still played with the baby. "You know where this girl is staying, don't you?"

Trent seemed to catch what he implied, for he hemmed and hawed and shook his head. "I don't think so, boss. It'd be hard to get her out of the States..."

"We could go to her." Azure gazed into the shining violet irises of the child in the photo. "If it becomes necessary to kill Ms. Lindstrom, we could have the daughter summon her to tell us where the treasure is. With the girl in our grasp and Lindstrom a helpless ghost, she could hardly refuse us, could she?"

"I wouldn't do that if I were you. Too risky." Trent still projected Wilcox's academic timidity, as if pathetically clinging to the role of professor even though Lindstrom had rung down the curtain on him.

"Let's hope it shan't be necessary," Azure said, concerned more about the inconvenience than the unpleasantness of the plan. He sauntered over to the Avila woman, displaying the photo and addressing her in Spanish. "We know the *bruja* was here. Where did she go?"

She wriggled and yelped. "I do not know!"

Azure made a *tsk-tsk* sound with his tongue, signaled Alberto with a glance. The latter snapped his fingers to call another hireling to come forward and stand beside those who held the children. This man cradled a lamb with dirty wool, which he had captured from a herd that grazed on a nearby terrace of land.

Azure did not know whether the sheep actually belonged to the Avilas. That would have been ideal but hardly necessary for his purposes.

Alberto unsheathed a hunting knife. The lamb bleated like a newborn as its captor clasped it to his chest to hold it still. With slaughterhouse efficiency, Alberto jammed his blade in the right side of the animal's downy neck and yanked it across to slash the throat. The hireling heaved the dying lamb onto the soil at the Avila woman's feet, where its severed head flopped askew on its stalk of vertebrae, gushing.

The woman screamed and her husband quivered on the ground, howling with impotent rage. Their neighbors leaned out of their doorways to stare, none brave enough to intervene.

Azure stepped close enough to the mother to feel her ragged breath on his face. "Tell me where the *bruja* is or I shall kill all of your lambs."

He swiped the air three times with his hand, each gesture lower than the last to indicate the descending heights of the children. Alberto placed the tip of his knife, still sheened with sheep's blood, underneath the right ear of the Avilas' son, causing the boy to squeal.

"*No!*" His mother strained forward, but the man who pinioned her tightened his grip. "She went to Tingo to see the *brujo!* That is all I know."

"Señor Topa," her husband muttered through clenched teeth, still afraid to lift his head from the dirt. "He will know where she is."

"Excellent. You have been a great help, and I thank you." Azure made a light sweeping motion with his fingers, and the men holding the older children released them. They ran to their mother, who bent to embrace them. Weeping, she rose to reclaim her baby from Trent, peppering the mewling girl's forehead with frenzied kisses.

Still pressing the children's father to the ground, Romoldo drew back both hammers of the shotgun, seeking approval from Azure with darkening eyes.

"Do not trouble yourself," the Englishman said. "We have more important work to do."

Romoldo grunted, but eased the hammers back against the firing pins. After jabbing Avila once more in the back of the head with the shotgun barrel, he permitted the man to race back to his family. Avila immediately hustled his wife and offspring back into their house and slammed the door.

Azure clapped his gloved hands together and turned to Trent. "How far is it to Tingo?" he asked in English.

"About forty miles. Ten on horse to get us back to the Range Rover."

"Smashing! I think Honorato could do with a ride in the fresh air, don't you?"

At the mention of his name, the dozen men Azure had brought with him all pivoted toward Honorato. He stood at the back of the group flanked by two of his comrades, who'd previously tied his arms behind his back with rope. They feared he might interfere with the interrogation of the Avila family, but he had merely shut his eyes and whispered, either to himself or to God. Now, as Azure approached him, he seemed to be the only man whose eyes were not bright with fearful anticipation.

"I warned you what would happen to anyone who let the *bruja* escape," Azure told him in Spanish, tapping the framed photo. "Perhaps you will talk to us now."

"Nothing I say will save my life, yes?" Honorato sneered in English. "So I say nothing."

Azure reverted to his native tongue, narrowing his eyes. "You're just full of secrets, aren't you? Pity we won't hear them all."

He nodded at the men guarding Honorato, who looped a noose around his neck and tightened it.

The condemned man's face contracted into an expression of such contempt that Azure took a step backward. "I say, you're not going to *spit* on me, are you?"

Honorato lifted his chin. "I would not waste my saliva, *señor.*"

"Thank heaven! Enjoy the scenery."

Azure gave him a mock salute and withdrew a few feet. Romoldo walked his horse forward and tied the end of the noose's rope to his saddle. As he climbed onto the stallion's back and whipped its flanks, Honorato shut his eyes, his lips pulsing with silent words.

The horse charged down the ten-mile trail toward the main road. The rope's slack uncoiled, became taut. The noose yanked Honorato off his feet, stretching his neck without breaking it, sandpapering his body along the gravel-strewn path.

Nathan Azure watched until the horse disappeared behind an outcropping of rock, Honorato still kicking his feet as his body bounced out of view.

23

The Cloud People

THE BUS TO LEIMEBAMBA WAS OLDER THAN NATALIE, the grinding of its crankshaft so loud that it made conversation impossible. That was just as well, since neither Señor Topa nor Professor Wilcox seemed eager to talk to one another. They gazed straight ahead to avoid eye contact with the other passengers, who gaped at the spectacle of two violet-eyed sorcerers sitting side by side on the same cramped, hard seat.

Relegated to the status of a hitchhiker in her own skull, Natalie faded in and out of awareness. She'd had a total of about seven hours' sleep in the past two days and was almost happy to delegate custodianship of her aching body to Wilcox in exchange for a half hour of restful oblivion.

They were lucky the bus was so decrepit, for it made the trip between towns only once a day. Ordinarily it would have departed by the time Señor Topa agreed to close the health post early and take Natalie to the Museo Leymebamba, but the scheduled stop in Tingo had been prolonged by a blown tire. Natalie avoided dwelling on the condition of the other three tires as they lumbered along the steep, rutted dirt road.

The museum was a few miles' walk from the center of

town, where the two *brujos* disembarked from the bus. Natalie had spent so much time among the ruins of pre-Hispanic Peru that the facility stunned her with its modernity. Cushioned by a carpet of verdant grass, the cluster of buildings resembled contemporary Spanish villas, with white columns supporting peaked roofs of red tile. Moss-covered stone walls enclosed a serene botanical garden, and Natalie wished she could dally among the bright spattering of flowers—orchids, fuchsia, begonias, and other species so exotic she didn't know their names. Dr. Wilcox refused to waste time with such frivolities, although he acquiesced to her demand to use the first real bathroom she'd seen in weeks, even washing her face and hands for her.

When they rejoined Señor Topa in the museum's lobby, he was poring over Natalie's drawing of the cave with a man with horn-rimmed glasses and a pencil-thin mustache, dapper in a double-breasted suit. Topa introduced him as Luís Pacampía, the assistant curator, for whom he had summoned Incan subjects during archaeological research.

Pacampía bobbed his head once to Natalie in brusque acknowledgment, then glanced between her and the picture, brows frowning over the frames of his glasses. "I am not familiar with this site, Doña Lindstrom," he said in Spanish, which Wilcox translated for her. "There are hundreds of such burial ledges in Chachapoyas, most of them undiscovered. How did you learn about this one?"

Burial ledges? Natalie asked.

Wilcox responded to Pacampía instead. "I found out about this tomb from a group of thieves who intend to loot it. In order to stop them, I must discover where it is before they do. I thought an Inca native to the region might be able to tell me where to find it. Can you provide a touchstone for us?"

The curator's expression shifted from suspicion to shrewdness. "Perhaps…on one condition. If you locate this ledge, you will notify the museum's staff immediately and permit them to preserve the site."

"You have my word on that." The fervor with which Wilcox said it told Natalie he was speaking the truth.

"Very well. I will see what I can do. Please follow me."

Pacampía conducted Natalie and Señor Topa among the visiting tourists and glass cases of artifacts in the Ethnographic Hall and into one of the museum's private examining rooms. A few pieces of pottery and primitive figurines sat on a long table, each with a small sticker bearing a number that corresponded to a computer-printed catalog lying open-faced beside them. Pacampía indicated the wooden chairs beside the table. "Please wait here."

During his absence, Wilcox took the opportunity to pull the rest of Natalie's drawings from her duffel bag, which she had set aside along with the down jacket and Honorato's poncho.

So who are the "Cloud People"? Natalie inquired.

The residents of the Chachapoyas cloud forest, Wilcox replied as he sat next to Topa. *"Chachapoyas" means "Cloud People" in Quechua. They were tall, fair-skinned warriors—not-so-neighborly neighbors to the Incas.*

And this cave is another burial chamber?

Well…yes.

I should've known. Natalie wondered if she should just

take up residence in a sepulcher, since she always seemed to end up in one anyway.

Wilcox straightened her body in the chair as Pacampía carried a gold figurine about six inches high into the room and set it on the table before them. It looked like a miniature of one of the statues in the cave's mouth, with a flat face, a long triangular nose, and a hawkish fierceness in the eyes.

"We believe this to be a product of the Chachapoyas culture," the curator said, "but we discovered it among Inca ruins at Cochabamba. Whoever obtained it must have been familiar with the cloud forest."

Wilcox and Señor Topa stared at each other like restaurant patrons, each waiting for the other to take the check. "You can call the spirit," Topa pointed out. "You do not need me."

"If I let the spirit occupy me, I will not be able to write down the directions to the burial ledge." Without giving the *brujo* a chance to object, Wilcox turned to Pacampía. "Do you have a pen I can borrow?"

Both curator and sorcerer sighed, but the former produced a ballpoint from his coat pocket while the latter cupped the idol in his hands and began to mumble. Watching Topa's face for the first sign of inhabitation, Wilcox flipped over one of the drawings and poised Pacampía's pen on the paper. "Leave us, please."

The curator, realizing the request was directed at him, huffed with indignation as he stepped out of the room.

The grooves of age in Señor Topa's face smoothed to

youthfulness, as if effaced by the hand of an unseen sculptor. When he glanced back up at Natalie's face, his eyes widened with an acolyte's reverence. *"Viracocha?"*

Wilcox smiled.

Viracocha? Natalie repeated. She racked her memory, trying to recall what Abe—that is, Trent—had told her about the name.

He thinks you are the white demigod who created the Incas, the professor told her. To the Inca now residing in Señor Topa, he said nothing to dispel the impression of Natalie's divinity. *"Imamtam sutiyki?"* he asked instead.

The Inca tapped Señor Topa's chest. *"Manco Suyuyoq."*

Tell me what he's saying, Natalie nagged.

Relax. He only told me his name. From then on, however, Wilcox dutifully interpreted the conversation's Quechua.

Manco Suyuyoq goggled at the surrounding miracles of fluorescent lights and white stuccoed walls as if he'd truly entered the realm of the sun, and the professor had difficulty keeping his attention.

"How did you get the gold?" He indicated the figurine that the Inca absently held in Señor Topa's hand.

Manco gasped when he saw the idol. "Do not be angry! I took the gold to save our Father Inca from death."

"I understand. Do not be afraid. Where did you find the gold?"

"The Cloud People. We did not want to disturb their cities of the dead. The bearded enemies—they eat gold! They told us that if we gave them gold, they would spare the Inca. I went to get gold from the Cloud People, from their dead." Manco's expression hardened like cooling lava. "The bearded enemies deceived us. After they killed the Father Inca, we hid the gold we gathered." He grinned. "We taunted the bearded ones. We took a kernel from a pile of maize and told them, 'This grain is what Atahualpa has given you from his treasures and what remains is the other!'"

Too bad we can't find that hoard, eh? Wilcox wryly murmured to Natalie inside her head. *It makes even Pizarro's little stash sound paltry.*

"You have done well," the professor told Manco. He favored the Inca with a beneficent smile but plucked the idol from his grasp. "Viracocha wants to return this gold to the Cloud People. Do you know where to find this city of the dead?"

He showed the cave drawing to Manco, who grinned and nodded, eager to please, unaware that he was showing them where the most ruthless "bearded one" of all had hidden his gold. Wilcox grinned, too, and as he teased specific details out of the Inca, the tip of Pacampía's pen skittered over the page.

By the time the session ended, the professor had to shake a cramp out of Natalie's writing hand. With the energizing ghost of Manco Suyuyoq gone, Señor Topa hunched forward in his chair, rubbing the hollows of weariness that once again circled his eyes.

Wilcox stood and gathered the drawings, folding the directions to the Chachapoyas burial niche inside them. "I cannot thank you enough, *señor*. Because of your help, I will ensure that the treasures of your ancestors will go to the museum rather than the black market."

"I hope what you say is true, Doña Lindstrom." His gaze seemed abstracted, as if he were reliving past betrayals.

The professor moved to collect the duffel, coat, and poncho. "Have no fear. I can handle these thieves—"

The soul's knock fell like a hammer-blow. Taken unaware, Wilcox dropped Honorato's poncho, but too late. The coarse wool's fibers fairly vibrated with the spirit's electric current, sparking to discharge the moment it contacted Natalie's fingers.

Natalie also did not anticipate the invasion of another soul. Not here in this modern museum, far from *chullpas* and burial chambers and scattered human bones. Preoccupied with proctoring Wilcox while he controlled her body, she did not have time to switch from her spectator to her protective mantra before the seizure slammed her to the floor. As three souls vied for dominance of its neural network, her body quivered in a delirium tremens of incapacitation, lungs dry-hacking and unable to draw breath.

"Doña Lindstrom!"

Through fogged eyes, she saw Señor Topa straddle her midsection and push her flat against the floor to retard her thrashing. With the calm of one inured to crisis, he took Pacampía's pen and jammed it like a bit between Natalie's snapping jaws, forcing her to bite on it to keep her tongue down and her airways open. As both a physician and a Violet, he had doubtless dealt with the situation many times before.

Perhaps he had even received the same treatment when racked by the fit of a multiple inhabitation. While the *brujo* might be able to keep the body alive, however, he could not minister to the psyche now cleaved by horror.

Rocks gouge flesh already pulped by jagged miles of grinding gravel. The noose constricts both blood and air without eliminating either—endless choking without the final relief of strangulation. The face barely blinks, its eyes swollen almost shut, its skin grated away, the blood matted with dust. And still the body drags on, the fusillade of hoofbeats trampling all other sound...

Please, no, God! Natalie thought, the danger to herself forgotten. *Not Honorato!*

Whether by design or capitulation, the soul of Abel Wilcox absconded from her head, fleeing Honorato. Natalie almost wished she could do the same, for she had no idea how to answer to this man who had died for her.

Her body slackened beneath Señor Topa, became still. He took the cracked pen from her mouth and made no attempt to interrupt as she spoke in a distant voice, her eyes gone glassy.

"Sweet Jesus. What did they do to you?"

De nada, Honorato replied. *It is over now, yes?*

Tears leaked from the corners of her eyes. "Forgive me."

How can I forgive you for something I did alone?

"It's my fault. If you hadn't tried to help me—"

The choice was mine. It still is. That is why I have come.

"But your family. Your wife, your boys. What will they do?"

She felt his angry sorrow well within her. *Yes... I grieve for them. They should not suffer for my sins. You are my only hope for redemption. I knew it when I saw the picture of your little girl.*

"What can I do?" Natalie pleaded. "Anything."

Live. Go back to your little girl. His soul yearned for hope, as if its hell might only be purgatory. *In the Shining Path, I made bombs. Some of them killed mothers, little girls. Perhaps it is not too late for me to save the life of a mother, a little girl. But I must warn you: the big* gringo *found a picture of your girl in the house where I saw you hiding. If he does not get his gold, he will hurt her.*

"A picture? But how—" Color returned to her blanched cheeks. "*Wilcox.*"

The big gringo *said he will kill you if he must. Then he will use your girl as his* bruja.

"He won't be able to." She clenched her jaw, and the drying tear-trails made her face go cold. "Thank you, Honorato. I owe you...everything."

Live. That is all I ask.

Honorato remained a moment more, but neither he nor Natalie could express their sentiments in words. By the time she initiated her protective mantra, he was already gone.

When she returned to external awareness, she found Señor Topa kneeling beside her with patient attentiveness. "Doña Lindstrom? ¿Está bien?"

He made further inquiries about her well-being in words that no one translated for her, but his aged joints prevented him from getting to his feet before Natalie stormed from the room.

Bursting from one of the museum's side doors, Natalie stomped through the tranquility of the botanical garden, circulating her spectator mantra in her mind and hissing Wilcox's name through her teeth.

He slunk back into her mind like a prisoner awaiting his sentence. *I know you're upset...*

"You left Callie's picture for him." She rasped the accusation. "For Azure."

Yes. But I had to give him a trail to follow.

"He killed Honorato."

I didn't mean for that to happen.

"Goddamn you!" She shrieked at the sinking sun as if it were the professor's face. "He's going to kill Callie!"

Not if he dies first, Wilcox replied. *That's what I tried to tell you. It's the only way to stop him.*

Natalie's throat still stung from the scream as she breathed in and out to quiet herself. Perhaps there was still another way. What if she went to the local police? They would most likely arrest her for conspiring to steal Peru's national treasures, or worse, they might be corrupt officials on Azure's payroll. What if she left the country? Assuming she escaped, Azure's reach was global—he could pursue her and her daughter anywhere and always, for the rest of their lives. She and Callie could go into hiding, of course...but Azure would be able to find her father or Ted and Jean Atwater or dozens of other people Natalie cared about. What if she simply gave Azure the directions to the treasure? Would that satisfy him, make him leave her and her family alone? No, she would still be a threat; she could report him to the authorities, jeopardize his possession of the gold. For his own peace of mind, he would eliminate her as surely as he had eradicated Wilcox.

Every scenario she played out led to the same endgame. Binding her soul to Azure's by killing him would be horrific, but there were even worse fates, and Natalie refused to let him make Callie an orphan or to force her into a life on the run.

"Yes, I'll do it," she told Wilcox at last. "But not for you. For Honorato. And my little girl."

24
Birthday Wishes

SEÑOR TOPA PEERED AT HER AS IF WONDERING whether her recent epileptic episode had damaged her brain. "Stay here tonight? In Leimebamba?"

Natalie waited for Wilcox to translate his words, then asked him to feed her the proper Spanish for the reply she wanted to make; she was determined not to give him control over her again. "Please, *señor*. I will pay for your room."

"But my wife—she will worry when I do not come home."

"I know, but I need time to escape the evil men who want to kill me. They will be waiting to question you when you get home."

The *brujo* put his hands to his temples in agitation. "If that is true, my wife is in danger."

"No. They will not harm her because then you will not help them. By the time the bus takes you back to Tingo to-morrow, I will be gone. When you meet the men, give this to the *gringo* with the gold hair. Then they will leave you and your wife alone."

She gave him the drawing of the cave; she no longer needed it, for that black mouth with its snaggletoothed figures now yawned in her dreams. On the back of the sketchbook sheet, she had used Pacampía's pen, now fractured and scarred with deep bite marks, to transcribe the directions that Manco Suyuyoq had given to Wilcox.

Señor Topa frowned at the picture and what she had written, shaking his head. "I do not understand. You say you want to keep these men from disturbing this tomb, then you tell them where to find it."

"They will kill me and my daughter if I do not give them what they want. Tell the *gringo* with the gold hair that I have fled the country and that I left this paper for you to give him in exchange for our safety." She squeezed the hand in which he held the picture. "Please, *señor*—our lives depend on you."

He studied her eyes, as if gauging their sincerity, before folding the drawing and sliding it in his pants pocket. Still, he shook his head. "I do not know what has happened to you, Doña Lindstrom. You are…*different* than you were."

"Yes." Natalie thought of what she was about to do, whispering to herself in English. "Yes, I am. God help me."

She obtained beds for herself and for Señor Topa at Leimebamba's local hostel, a tiny but clean place, then spent the waning hours of daylight obtaining necessities for the following day's journey: fresh food and water; a bottle of the strongest alcohol she could find, a particularly potent variety of the Peruvian brandy *pisco*; and a pair of cheap plastic binoculars she bought from a street vendor catering to tourists. She could already feel her rump aching as she arranged to rent the mule she would ride in the morning.

There did not seem to be a pay phone anywhere in town, so, after dinner, Natalie bribed the concierge to let her make a credit-card call on the hostel's phone. She kept making mistakes while entering the interminable series of digits to dial the Atwaters' number, for she could not help glancing over shoulder. At any moment, she expected to see Azure and Trent frowning and smiling at her, respectively. Finally, she got through to Dan's father.

"Hello?"

"Ted! Is Callie there?"

As it did during her call from Cajamarca, satellite transmission delayed his reply, as if they were shouting at one another across a canyon. "Natalie? Where the heck are you? We've been crawling the walls worrying about you."

"I'm still in Peru, and you were right to worry. Is everything okay there?"

"Well, one of those Corps Security guys came around, asking where you were. I told him you went back east to visit your dad again." Ted paused like a priest awaiting confession. "He also asked if I knew how that lady agent got herself killed."

Natalie's face went cold. "Bella? Killed?"

"Yeah. They found her body down in Frisco. Read about it in the *Chronicle*."

She remembered how Trent had reassured her about Bella the night before they left the country. *I've made all the arrangements*, he'd told her, his words now laced with poisonous new significance. *She'll be gone by morning...*

Natalie could never have imagined feeling sorry for Arabella Madison before then. As much as the agent had tormented her, though, she had never wished Bella dead. She might still be alive if Natalie had somehow recognized Trent as a killer...

But there was no time for remorse. Bella's murder made it all the more urgent for Natalie to get home, before the NAACC took away her daughter.

"Is Callie there?" she asked, needing the sound of her little girl's voice more than ever.

"No, Jean took her out shopping for tomorrow. We were hoping you'd be here to join us."

She knit her brows, trying to think of what he could possibly be referring to. "Tomorrow?"

"Callie's birthday. You said you were going to be back by then."

"Yes. I was." Natalie covered her face. How could she have forgotten? Had she really lost track of so many days? "I'm sorry, there's been trouble. The men who hired me, they're criminals and they're trying to kill me—"

"Say *what?*"

With no patience for interruption, she went on. "I'm afraid they might try to hurt you, Jean, and Callie, too. Can you go away somewhere for a week until you hear from me again? I'll pay you back."

"Don't worry about the money, for God's sake. We'll go. But, for heaven's sake, Natalie, who *are* these people?"

"They work for a British businessman named Nathan Azure. If you *don't* hear from me in a week, report him to the cops, the Feds, Interpol, and anyone else you can think of."

"Sure, sure. But how're you going to get out of there?"

"I've got a plan. Wish me luck."

"There must be more I can do than that."

"Yes. Wish Callie happy birthday for me." Natalie shut her eyes, picturing how her daughter would fume and sulk at receiving nothing more than a secondhand greeting from her only parent. It wasn't hard for her to imagine. She only had to remember her own reaction every time her father had claimed to be too busy to visit her at the School. "Tell her I'll be there whether she sees me or not. And I owe her a trip to Disneyland when I get back."

"I'll hold you to that." The gravity in Ted Atwater's tone implied more concern than he could verbalize. "Come home, Natalie. Call me on the cell when you get back."

"I will." As if she didn't already have enough guilt, the memory of her father reawakened the image of Wade lying alone in the convalescent home as he recuperated. "Have you heard from my dad?"

"He called last Wednesday, but he was still in the nursing facility and sounded pretty weak. We haven't heard from him since then. He said to give you his love."

"Thanks. If he calls back ... give him mine."

She *would* have had the courage to say it this time, she told herself. If Wade had been on the phone at that moment, she could have told him she loved him and she would have meant it. But part of her knew that it was far too easy to espouse love through a go-between. The true test would be what she said when she next looked into Wade's tired blue eyes, and for that she had to survive long enough to see him again.

"I've got to go, Ted. You...may not hear from me for a day or two."

"Call as soon as you can."

"I will. Soon." She hung up and went to take her bunk in the hostel room she shared with Señor Topa.

But the more important sleep became to her, the more elusive it seemed. She needed rest now more than ever, yet the following day's crushing significance merely made her wriggle in agonized insomnia. With only a few hours to go before sunrise, she slipped into a light doze, her last conscious thought devoted to the photo she had now lost: Callie, happy with her birthday cake and with the mother behind the camera. The mother who was, now as then, out of the picture.

25

The Stairway inside the Mountain

NATALIE KNEW THAT NATHAN AZURE ALWAYS AWOKE
at dawn, for that was the time he'd demand to begin their session with Pizarro. She therefore rose an hour before the sun
to prepare for her final confrontation with the Englishman.

"Happy birthday, baby girl," she whispered as she opened
her eyes in the blue darkness.

Although she had planned to leave while Señor Topa was
still in bed, she discovered that the *brujo* was already up and
dressed. Natalie had slept in her black T-shirt and jeans, so
she put on her scuffed Doc Martens and shared a dispirited
breakfast of rolls and coffee with the sorcerer. Topa spared
her the trouble of employing Wilcox as a translator, for he
said nothing. Natalie appreciated his presence nevertheless.

Afterward, she donned her down jacket, then whispered
her protective mantra as she draped Honorato's poncho over
her shoulders. Though the touchstone warmed and comforted her like a security blanket, she didn't want him knocking before she'd had a chance to summon Professor Wilcox
for the journey to the cave.

The bus back to Tingo would not arrive for another hour
or more, so Señor Topa remained with Natalie as she packed

her duffel bag and fetched her rented mule. When the yellow rind of the sun at last peeped over the eastern Andes and she was ready to depart, he made the sign of the cross.

"*Vaya con Dios.*"

Natalie did not need an interpreter for the blessing or for her response. She gave her hand to Topa. "*Gracias. Y vaya con Dios.*"

He nodded and waited as she struggled to heave herself onto the burro's back. Although it took more than a quarter of an hour for her to clop down the road out of town, the *brujo* was still there when she glanced back for the last time. He had raised his right hand and appeared to be muttering either a prayer or an incantation.

Compared to the rolling ocean-wave movement of the mare Natalie had ridden, the mule felt like a log between her legs. This might have been partly due to the fact that she didn't have a saddle beneath her this time, only a folded woolen blanket. She found the burro easier to control than a horse, and its small size made it feel safer, but the plodding regularity of its steps became maddening as it took an hour to cover each mile or two. Wilcox had insisted that traveling by donkey would get them where they were going faster than any other mode of transportation, but Natalie quickly began to doubt him.

Are you sure you wouldn't rather have me do this? the professor asked her when she repeatedly asked him for pointers on the proper way to ride and command the animal.

"Yes, I'm sure." Natalie shrugged to work the kinks out of her neck and shoulders. "Just tell me what to do."

After the first few hours' instruction and practice, she became proficient enough to manage on her own. For a while, they enjoyed the cobbled certainty of an Incan road that wound between chess squares of terraced fields and crops in varying shades of green. But then they came upon an overgrown dirt path that branched off from the road like a stagnant tributary.

There! Wilcox said. *Take that one.*

Natalie halted and consulted the directions Manco Suyuyoq had given. "Are you sure?"

Yes. It's the third peak after the river.

Casting a dubious glance up at the mountain, she steered the burro toward the trailhead. Was it really the right one? Did Manco's landmarks still exist after five hundred years? More important, was his memory still accurate now that he'd spent half a millennium in the netherworld?

Shoving the directions in the duffel behind her, Natalie could not help but calculate how long it would be before Azure and his men caught up with her. It might have taken Señor Topa as much as an hour to reach his home in Tingo. They would have been waiting for him when he arrived, ready to interrogate him. As soon as he gave them the directions she had copied for them, they would follow her. How long would they need to procure horses or burros? Another hour, perhaps. Did the experienced trackers among them know shortcuts through the sierras that would get them to the cave before she reached it? Would Natalie have any time at all to prepare for their arrival, or would she be the one walking into a trap?

The vegetation grew thicker as the path crawled up the side of the mountain, palms and alders crowding the strip of soil that marked the trail. By midmorning they ascended into cloud, the fog draped like gossamer between the limbs and fronds of the trees. Even the unshakable authority of Dr. Wilcox began to show hairline cracks of doubt as the lacework of mist obscured the way forward.

Bear left here. No, wait! Right…

More than once, his indecision led them down the wrong fork to a dead end barred by tree trunks. Every minute wasted backtracking made Natalie sure that at any moment she would meet up with Azure and his henchmen on the trail, their pale horses materializing before her as if made of the mist itself.

Grateful that she had the burro to bear the burden of the duffel laden with propane tanks, Natalie did not stop except to eat an energy bar, to take a drink of water, or to consult the directions. The incline grew so steep in some places that she had to dismount and lead the mule up the slope by its reins.

Around noon, they crested the rim of a valley that framed a looking-glass lake, its silvered surface upending the sky above it. The black sickles of circling condors sliced through the haze that hovered over the still water. Trapped moisture nourished a lush forest that grew like moss on the valley's walls. They had entered the realm of the Cloud People.

Through Natalie's eyes, Professor Wilcox viewed the panorama with increasing excitement as they wended their way down to the edge of the lake. *Yes…yes! Quick, get out the binoculars!*

Natalie reined the mule to a halt and dug the field glasses out of the bag.

There! In the cliff across the lake.

She directed the binoculars as he commanded. Through the cheap plastic lenses, she could make out the blurred forms of several stone towers clustered together inside a niche in the cliff wall. Natalie had once slept in such a tower.

Chullpas! A city of the dead by the lake of the condors, Wilcox said, referring to one of the principal landmarks Manco Suyuyoq had cited. *We're almost there.*

"Good," Natalie replied, "because my butt is *almost* dead." She shifted her weight to relieve some of the pressure on her tailbone.

"Almost" turned out to be a lot farther than the professor made it sound. They traversed almost the entire length of the lake until they came to a shallow stream that fed the lagoon. The creek led them through a cleft that it had etched in the limestone over the eons, leaving sheer cliffs of crumbling rock on either side. Natalie had to climb off the mule again so that she and the animal could pick their way over the rubble piled along the shores of the stream without stumbling. Every few hundred yards, Wilcox urged her to get out the binoculars again and scan the cliffs for the cave she'd drawn from Francisco Pizarro's memories.

Where is it? he fretted when she saw nothing but empty shelves of alluvial stone. *We should have come to it by now.*

"Maybe we took a wrong turn." Natalie did a yoga stretch to try to restore circulation to legs cramped from almost nine hours of continuous donkey riding. "Or maybe the thing doesn't even exist."

No. It has *to be here. Pizarro knew it was the perfect place for his treasure cache: an abode of the dead that none of the Incas would dare to disturb and that none of his fellow Spaniards knew about. A cave with easy access for moving the gold in and out and distinctive landmarks to make it easy to find again.*

"Yeah. Either that, or the old sadist was just playing with our heads."

Keep looking.

"Fine." Natalie reread the directions for the twentieth time, hoping that maybe she'd overlooked a few key words. "I don't suppose our friend Manco mentioned whether the cave was on the left or the right."

No...

"And you didn't think to ask him."

Well... it's huge! It should be clearly visible—

"Uh-huh. That's what I thought." She surveyed the cliffs on either side of the chasm again. More than a hundred yards above, a ledge of rock jutted out directly over her head. She backed up to the bank of the stream but still could not see past the overhang.

Natalie looked up- and downstream for a dry way to cross, then cast a dubious glance into the water. "Hope there's no piranhas..."

Without rolling up the legs of her jeans, she waded out into the stream until the water rose to the level of her hips. Gasping as the icy water bit at her skin, she turned around and trained the binoculars on the ledge.

The short scalp hairs that had grown beneath her wig

prickled with déja vu as the warrior faces of the white figures seemed to leer at her through the binoculars' eyepieces.

That's it! Wilcox exulted, his excitement only increasing her apprehension. *That's it!*

"I know." She lowered the field glasses to gawk at the niche a skyscraper's height above where she stood. "You sure we can get up there?" she asked, kind of hoping that they couldn't.

Absolutely. The Chachapoyas not only had to get their mummies to the ledge for burial, they had to return to bring gifts for the dead.

"*Mummies?*" Natalie was certain he had never mentioned mummies before. She would definitely have remembered if he had mentioned mummies.

He did not seem inclined to discuss them now. *Manco Suyuyoq laughed when I asked him how the Chachapoyas scaled the cliffs. "The Cloud People do not fly like birds," he said. "They burrow like guinea pigs."*

Natalie dragged herself, dripping, from the brook back to the burro, where she unfolded the directions again. "Is that what he meant by the 'stairway in the mountain'?"

Yes. The entrance is behind the stone marked with the petro-glyph Manco copied for me at the bottom of the page.

Natalie studied the sigil, which Manco had traced with a shaky hand unused to ballpoint pens. It was a stylized bird—a condor, perhaps?—abstracted in the same fashion as the animals she'd seen on Peruvian pottery and rugs.

Her legs cold and clammy beneath her wet jeans, she scanned the side of the ravine beneath the cave but couldn't spot any graffiti. Finding the mark would be akin to locating a postage stamp stuck to the wall of a stadium, and the sun had already drifted far to the west. It would grow dark soon.

She drew a long breath. "I guess I'd better get started."

The staircase would be straight, Wilcox suggested. *Winding stairs would be too difficult and risky to excavate. Therefore, the entrance should be a hundred yards or more to one side of the cave or the other.*

Natalie considered the cliff face, imagined a staircase slanting down from the ledge at a forty-five-degree angle to form the hypotenuse of a right triangle. If the height of the ledge was about a hundred yards, then the other leg of the triangle should be about the same distance.

Starting directly beneath the cave, Natalie paced off the length of a football field to the right of the overhang. She scoured the surrounding stones for either the bird symbol or a doorway into the cliff wall but found neither.

"Can't even win a fifty-fifty bet," she griped, jogging back to the ledge.

This time she strode a hundred yards to the left of the cave and came up against an enormous pyramidal block of broken limestone. A configuration of white lines had been etched into one planar surface of the rock. Natalie brushed the accumulated dust from the glyph, revealing the hooked beak and spread wings of a bird of prey.

The block rested flush against the cliff wall, and she did not see any doorways in the surrounding rock. However, when she walked around to the other side of the boulder, she saw that the leaning stone formed a rough arch that hid from view the hole beneath it. Submerged in a shallow pit a couple feet below ground level, the irregular opening brimmed with a palpable darkness that seemed ready to gush from the fissure like crude oil.

A feverish chill shuddered through Natalie as Wilcox's eagerness melded with her dread.

What are you waiting for, a red carpet? he panted. *This is what we came to see!*

"Wait until I hide the mule. We need the advantage of surprise."

Although hiding places were scarce between the barren walls of the ravine, Natalie led the burro a couple hundred yards farther downstream and tethered the animal with a feedbag on its snout behind a largish boulder. With her duffel bag on her shoulder, she returned to descend into the pit of the cliff's secret portal.

Having refreshed her flashlight with a new pair of batteries, she shone it down the gullet of the tunnel before her. The beam revealed little more than rough-hewn walls and a set of irregular steps that made an immediate right-angle turn. "Are you sure this is safe?"

The ancient Peruvians were among the greatest engineers in human history, Wilcox averred. *Some of their mines are still being worked.*

"Uh-huh." Natalie inched into the passageway, wanting more than the professor's testimonial to keep from imagining the entire mountain collapsing on her.

The stairs varied in thickness and depth, for the builders had simply hacked wedges from the limestone's alluvial layers to fashion the individual steps. She kept her gaze and flashlight downcast to make sure she didn't trip or stumble. Every few feet, thick wooden timbers braced the arch of the tunnel, and Natalie avoided dwelling on how dry and brittle they looked after more than five hundred years.

After its initial right turn, the stairway ascended in a linear and apparently endless succession of slabs. Whenever Natalie paused to shine the flashlight up ahead of her, the beam still could not reach the top of the staircase, and she began to feel that she was climbing a Neolithic escalator that produced the illusion of progress without getting her any closer to the summit. The acoustics of the stone tube amplified the claustrophobic echo of her footsteps and labored breath, and the immured air was icy and caustic with the scent of lime dust.

Winded by the climb and the chalky atmosphere, Natalie was relieved when the flashlight beam finally produced a dim yellow spot on a distant wall. The spot grew larger with her approach, and she saw that the chiseled wall formed the corner of another right-angle turn. When she reached the bend in the staircase, the final steps brought her to the floor level of a doorway that opened into a dark chamber whose dimensions, though unseen, felt vast.

As she advanced into the room, Natalie was momentarily blinded by the daylight that filled the open mouth of the cave some fifty feet ahead of her. The silhouettes of the warrior totems spiked the ledge like giant tusks, giving her the impression that she was peering out through the jaws of Leviathan. Would the monster spit her out or swallow her forever?

Raising a hand to block the brightness from outside, Natalie swung the flashlight beam to the right to see what occupied the room. A luster like a solar flare glinted the light back at her.

Gold.

26

The Sweat of the Sun, the Tears of the Moon

THE STATUE WAS TALLER THAN NATALIE, AND IT could not possibly be real. It had to be painted or gilded or hollow, for there simply couldn't be that much gold in the entire world. And yet, when her quivering hand joggled the flashlight to the left, she saw an identical figure next to the first.

Wonderful things. Even in her mind, Wilcox spoke the words with a reverential hush.

"Huh?" For an instant, Natalie had forgotten the rest of the world: Wilcox, Azure, Trent, Honorato, Peru, Callie, Wade, home, herself—all vanishing before the glamour of gold, like the firework that dazzles before it blinds you.

"*Wonderful things,*" Wilcox repeated. *What Howard Carter said when he first looked into Tutankhamen's tomb.*

He sounded humbled by awe, a man who had received the miracle for which he prayed. Although the gold itself was worthless to him now, he had returned from death just to venerate it—a splendor that no one had witnessed since 1532, that the world thought was lost forever. For him, it was a sacred privilege simply to stand in the presence of the history he cherished.

Even Natalie could not speak. The sight of the twin idols had struck her dumb, obliterated all thought but adulation.

The statues depicted a pair of Incan nobles, their heads elongated to the point of grotesquerie and their elephantine earlobes distended by the heavy gold discs that marked their elevated rank. Engraved necklaces on their chests were inlaid with the blue of lapis and the aqua of turquoise. The oval pits of the eyes flashed with the translucent clarity of polished green gems, and it took more than a minute for Natalie to realize—or to acknowledge—that the stones were enormous emeralds.

In a kind of trance, Natalie ambled toward the twin idols, her free hand outstretched, but something banged her knee before she could reach them. She cried out and aimed the flashlight beam at the object she'd run into. A gold urn two feet high overflowed with rough, uncut crystals ranging in size from pebbles to pigeon's eggs. More emeralds than Harry Winston had seen in his lifetime.

Natalie looked for a clear path to the twin statues, but no matter where the flashlight beam fell, artworks of gold and silver lay heaped like so much scrap metal. Francisco Pizarro had little respect for the craft of heathens, so he had shoved his hoard into this man-made cavern with all the care of someone storing junk in his garage. Sacred idols and jewel-encrusted burial masks like the one Nathan Azure had paid more than a million pounds for at Sotheby's glared out from piles of silver pitchers and gold washbasins.

Priceless necklaces and earrings sequined the floor like pennies, as if the person who dropped them wouldn't stoop to gather such trifles.

Natalie moved toward the center of the chamber, swinging her flashlight to and fro, needing to see it *all*. She and Wilcox gasped together as the beam alighted on what seemed to be a menagerie tended by King Midas.

The fabled garden of the Sapa Inca! the professor exulted, his boyish delight making her giddy as well.

Cast in precious metal, dozens of animals of all sizes appeared to have been gilded alive. Golden snakes coiled around silver mice, golden foxes chased silver rabbits. Incan smiths had fashioned a life-size alpaca, its golden fleece combed straight with vertical grooves. Beside it, a silver fountain sprayed fine wires of golden water over the gold birds that bathed in its pool. Stalks of silver sprouted nearby, unfolding their sterling leaves to unveil ears of gold maize, the corn silk rendered with minute golden threads.

As the flashlight beam penetrated beyond the glittering zoo, Natalie saw two figures slumped against each other along the wall. At first she assumed them to be identical, like the twin Incan nobles. Both were androgynous, posed in similar sitting positions, their knees pushed up under their chins, their bodies enfolded in heavy blankets of ornate design. Faded with incalculable age, the woolen cloth looked as if it would disintegrate to dust at the slightest touch. The head of the first figure gleamed with the gold complexion and unchanging stoicism of a sculpted idol, and Natalie wondered if the face of the second had simply tarnished with time.

Gold does not tarnish, however. When she fixed the beam on the second face, she started backward.

The skin shrunken against the skull, crisp and crumbly as an onion peel. The eyes shriveled to slits above a nose that was nothing more than a spur of bone. Natalie had seen faces like this in Pizarro's memories.

Instinctively she babbled her protective mantra. *"The Lord is my shepherd; I shall not want—"*

Wilcox cut her off before she inadvertently expelled him. *Whoa! Easy, girl—it's only a mummy.*

Only a mummy. The professor still didn't seem to understand that, for a Violet, a dead body acted like a lightning rod for the soul that once occupied it.

Spellbound by the magnificence surrounding her, Natalie had forgotten that this chamber was originally a crypt. She now noticed the bundled mummies scattered throughout. To make way for the hoard, Pizarro and his native bearers had wedged the corpses into corners, jammed them between heavy idols, crushed them beneath avalanches of gold and silver plate. The desiccated visage of each cadaver served as a reminder that death lurked here, that only the treasure itself was in no danger of dying.

Natalie stalked away from the gold toward the ledge overlooking the ravine, Wilcox begging her for another look. *Wait! Where are you going? There's more—*

"We don't have much time." She swung the duffel bag off her shoulder and pawed through it in the better light. "How do we make this booby trap you dreamed up?"

What? Oh, that. I figured we could take those propane tanks and—

The sounding board of the opposite cliff reflected the scrabble of many hooves and feet, the murmur of many voices in the ravine. Natalie snatched up the field glasses and crept to the edge of the cave's mouth, but she didn't need to see the crowd massing below to know who they were.

"Too late," she said. "They're here."

Through the binoculars, she saw a dozen fedoras milling about below her with Nathan Azure's golden hair in the center of their circle, the target's bull's-eye. Standing beside him, Trent, the only other hatless figure, displayed a large sketch of the bird symbol that marked the entrance to the mountain's stairway while Azure barked orders to the Peruvians.

If I only had a gun...

Natalie recoiled from the thought, attempted to disown it, but Professor Wilcox heard it.

Ordinarily I wouldn't suggest this, because I hate to see any relic destroyed, he said, as if to absolve himself of responsibility. *This being an emergency, however...we could push these sarcophagi down on top of them.*

"*Sarcophagi?*" she breathed, retreating behind one of the totems so she wouldn't be seen.

Yes. You're leaning against one right now.

Natalie lurched back from the figure. Did *everything* around here have to have a corpse in it?

Her drawing hadn't done justice to the row of seven icons that loomed from the cave's lower lip like druidic standing stones. Three feet wide at the base, each sarcophagus stood nine feet high or more, its white clay body painted with a cape of red feathers that resembled the folded wings of a hawk. Their enormous, U-shaped heads dwarfed the human skulls that had been mounted on the walls to either side of them, and the diminishing orange light of dusk made their scowls more fearsome, drilling the pits of their eyes even deeper with shadow.

They looked heavy enough to crush a man.

Natalie got to her feet, peeked over the rim of the ledge again with the binoculars. The fedoras were nodding, their orders received and understood. Nathan Azure crossed his arms with dictatorial authority while Trent refolded the drawing of the bird petroglyph. In a minute, they would all disperse to search for the symbol. When they found it, they would climb the stairs inside the mountain, enter the treasure chamber, and kill her.

With Azure gone, the rest of them will be like a body without a head, Wilcox counseled her. *But if you're going to do it, do it now.*

She pressed up close to the sarcophagus directly above Nathan Azure's swirl of blond hair.

Do it before he kills your little girl . . .

Natalie did not know whether those words were the professor's or hers. It hardly mattered.

"Please forgive me," she whispered. A plea both to the coffin's occupant for desecrating its resting place and to God for the sin she was about to commit.

She backed up a few steps to get a running start and high-kicked the sarcophagus, stamping her boot on its back and pushing. Recoiling from the force threw her off balance, and she landed flat on her back against the ledge.

A loud *crack* resounded as the clay broke loose from its stone foundation and the top-heavy figure listed forward with the slowness of a timbered tree. A puzzled exclamation rose from the ravine below when the sarcophagus snapped the wooden poles that had held it upright, sending it into free fall.

Natalie didn't wait for it to hit. She sprang to her feet, and by the time she heard the first crash, she had shoved two more sarcophagi off into space, the momentum nearly carrying her over the edge with them. In quick succession, the statues impacted the ground with the basso crunches of a bombing run, and the confused exclamations turned to curses and cries of panic.

In a berserker frenzy of destruction, Natalie launched four more figures off the cliff, leaving nothing but a row of splintered shafts and fractured masonry along the ledge. Only then did she hunker at the cave's lip to peer down at the enemy with her binoculars, like a soldier in the trenches.

Starbursts of shattered clay and exploded mummy bundles spattered the ground beneath her. An intact sarcophagus face frowned up at her, turning the scene into a surreal Dalí landscape. The Peruvians all shied far back from the ledge, some shielding their eyes with their hands as they tried to see where the statues had come from and whether any more were about to fall.

Natalie scanned with the field glasses, searching for Azure. A hideous feeling of disappointment niggled her when it seemed that she hadn't actually killed anyone.

Then a still-twitching body swept into the binoculars' stereoscopic view, the torso pinned beneath the oblong body of one sarcophagus. The victim's internal organs had burst under the weight, spraying the sepulcher's white clay with crimson, while the mummy bundle's withered corpse had sprawled with its bony arms around the man's legs, as if dragging him into death with it.

But when Natalie sighted the dying man's face through the binoculars, it was not Azure's. Instead, Trent stared at her with white-rimmed eyes that bulged beyond their lids, his mouth agog. Perhaps it was only a figment of her guilt, but he seemed to bear an expression of incalculable loss and sorrow.

The instant he stopped quivering, Natalie braced herself, knowing that she had become a touchstone for him the moment she shook his hand for the first time. Memories of his faux friendship—the little fabricated acts of kindness that had so beguiled her, the touch of his hand on her cheek—flooded her, and she was sure that he *must* be knocking.

Yet he did not come. While he was alive, he'd never had the courage to face her, to confess how he'd deceived her, to let her see who he really was. Could shame alone keep him from seeking her now? Or was he really dead? Natalie squinted through the field glasses at his whitening face to make sure.

One down, Abel Wilcox said. *One to go . . .* But his tone had gone from bloodthirsty to uneasy, as if his conscience had leached the poison of revenge from his spirit.

A pair of spit-polished black boots stepped up beside Trent's body, and Natalie raised the binoculars' view to encircle Nathan Azure's blond head.

He appeared to sense that she observed him, for he craned his neck to shout to her. "Splendid shot, Ms. Lindstrom! I can't thank you enough for ensuring that we all enjoy a greater share of the spoils."

Azure waved the Peruvians off with curt orders in Spanish. With the last light of sunset deepening to indigo, the henchmen dispersed, each of them carrying an illuminated lantern or flashlight with which to search the cliff wall for the bird sigil.

Natalie threw the binoculars back into her bag, for they would be useless in the encroaching night. "How long do you think it will take them to find the entrance?"

An hour, Wilcox estimated. *Unless they get lucky.*

"Then we better get started." She slid two of the propane canisters out of the bag, hefted them in her hands. "So how do I make this bomb you talked about?"

The professor didn't answer right away; Natalie felt her cheeks burn with his embarrassment. *It's obvious,* he said at last. *You simply heat them until they explode. See, it says right there on the label: DANGER: FIRE / EXPLOSION HAZARD.*

The pitch of Natalie's voice sank along with her hope. "Heat them *how?*"

That's what the hard liquor is for. Douse the tanks with alcohol and set them on fire.

"Yeah. And to play a flute, I just blow in one end and move my fingers over the holes." She set the cylinders down with a *thunk.* "You had me lug these stupid tanks all the way from Azure's camp, but you have no idea how to build a bomb, do you?"

What makes you think it won't *work?* Wilcox retorted. *If you know so much about bombs, why don't you make the damn thing yourself?*

Natalie sighed. "Because I *don't* know anything about bombs. But I know someone who does."

Her hands squeezed the folds of the poncho that shrouded her shoulders.

27

Gamble the Sun before Sunrise

CAN'T I SEE IT ONCE MORE BEFORE I GO? ABEL Wilcox pleaded, sounding like a boy unwilling to leave an amusement park. *Just one more look.*

Natalie glanced in the direction of the cave, where Atahualpa's ransom awaited the study and admiration of the world. Could anyone blame an archaeologist for wanting to stay with a discovery that would itself make history?

"I'm sorry. There isn't time...Abe." It felt strange to her to use the name again—especially after killing the man she most associated with it. But wasn't it the real Abel Wilcox, reflected in the mirror of Trent's impersonation, that she'd developed feelings for?

I guess I'm doomed to fall for dead guys, Natalie thought with sad humor.

"I need Honorato to help me make the bomb," she told the professor, "and you can't both be in my head at once."

Yeah, I know. I'm grateful just to be here, really. It's been a lifelong dream. The choice of words made him pause in bittersweet contemplation. *I owe you.*

She smiled. "We're even."

Not yet. Don't let him get it, Natalie. Don't let him get you.

"I won't."

Okay... ready when you are.

She didn't want to use her protective mantra, for if he left voluntarily she might be able to summon Honorato quickly enough to avoid being uninhabited. Otherwise, the dead Peruvians of this burial chamber might all start knocking at once, inundating her with souls that would overload her nervous system. Sitting cross-legged on the ledge where only the fragmented bases of the sarcophagi remained, Natalie evened out her breaths and concentrated on her spectator mantra to ease the transition. She didn't have to shut her eyes, for she could barely see the duffel bag before her on the stone floor.

> *Row, row, row your boat,*
> *Gently down the stream...*

Natalie could almost picture Abe withdrawing from her mind with one of his gallant bows... or were the bows one of Trent's improvisations? She couldn't let herself think about that now. The second she felt her mind clear of him, she gripped the poncho with both hands and called to Honorato.

> *Merrily, merrily, merrily, merrily!*
> *Life is but—*

The pinpricks of a million acupuncture needles stippled her skin. Natalie gasped but found she couldn't exhale. Unwelcome voices collided in her skull, chattering in languages she did not understand. Some, she knew, spoke Quechua, but there were others who spat angry syllables not heard in centuries—the nameless language of the Cloud People. She pictured the mummies from the cave unfolding themselves from their bundles and shambling out to embrace her, to enter her...to become her.

Since she did not have Pacampía's pen to bite down on, Natalie snapped her jaw shut and hunched forward as the spasms rocked her.

Come on, Honorato! she prayed.

The cacophony of voices diminished as she pruned spirits away until she had eliminated all but a single familiar presence. Her body relaxed, comfortable with the shared ownership of the two souls who looked out through her eyes.

You are not home with your little girl, Honorato grimly observed when he saw the arch of the cave's mouth.

Natalie rubbed her arms for warmth. "I'm afraid not. There's something I have to do first, to make sure I still have a home and a little girl to go back to."

She described how she and Wilcox planned to use the treasure to lure Azure into a trap. Showing Honorato the bomb-making materials she had brought with her, she expressed her doubts regarding the archaeologist's explosives expertise.

It was difficult to tell whether Honorato was amused or disgusted by Wilcox's naïveté. El profesor *knows his books better than bombs, yes?* he remarked. *Setting these tanks on fire would not kill. Probably the alcohol would burn away before the tanks got hot enough to blow up. Even if they exploded, unless the person was very close, the blast would only knock him unconscious.*

Natalie's shoulders slumped. "So we can't use them to kill Azure."

No ... we can make them kill. Is that what you want?

Natalie thought of Trent's gaping eyes and mouth— how she would continue to see that face in her dreams for the rest of her life and beyond. Could she stand to have Azure, Romoldo, and perhaps a dozen more men haunt her that way?

"The big *gringo* ... he's going to hurt Callie." It was her answer, the only one she could give.

It satisfied Honorato. *We must build a fire. We need wood, sticks, paper, cloth—anything dry enough to burn.*

Glad to have something constructive to do, Natalie retrieved her flashlight from the duffel and combed the ledge for flammable material. She spotted the jagged shafts that still marked where poles had once supported the sarcophagi. By stomping on them with her boot, she bent them enough to break off a dozen short sticks. These she gathered and took into the burial chamber, along with the remaining sketchbook drawings she'd kept and an extra T-shirt she had with her.

Selecting a spot that seemed to be at the center of the room, Natalie constructed a small pyre, crisscrossing layers of sticks and stuffing the kindling of crumpled paper and cloth between them.

Honorato surveyed the structure with satisfaction. *This will apply direct, continuous heat to the bottom of the tanks. Now we must bind the tanks together for explosive force.*

Natalie went back out to the ledge and emptied the duffel bag of its contents. "What if we put them in here?"

Yes, good.

She arranged the four propane cylinders in the duffel in a square formation. "So how do we make the bomb kill?"

There must be some sort of... what is your word? "Shrapnel," *yes?*

Natalie remembered the war photos she'd seen of soldiers torn apart by grenades and land mines. "Yes. Shrapnel."

In the Shining Path, we used nuts, bolts, nails. That kind of thing. Honorato's own memories preoccupied him briefly. *They worked... very well.*

Before he could suppress the image, Natalie caught a flash of a man in a city square, wailing as he embraced the limp body of a woman. Welling red gouges pocked the woman's pastel tank top. Police and paramedics attempted to pry her away from him, but the man refused to let go.

Natalie could not afford to ponder the effects of shrapnel. She snatched up the bag with the tanks and hurried back into the burial chamber.

"Would these work?" she asked, indicating the urn full of rough emeralds.

The idea darkly amused Honorato. *An expensive way to kill a man... but, yes, they will cause enough damage.*

Natalie shoveled handfuls of the gems into the duffel, stuffing them into the space around the tanks so that they would be blown outward by the blast. When the bag was nearly swollen to bursting, she froze, a final scoop of emeralds still in her palm, and glanced toward the door of the mountain's stairwell.

A tiny scuffling sound had echoed up the tunnel... or had she only imagined it?

Whether the noise was real or not, Natalie hastened to pour the last of the gems into the duffel and zip the bag shut. With the bomb prepared, she splashed a bit of *pisco* over the pyre as lighter fluid and struck a match, which she touched to the kindling in several places. Small flames shriveled the paper and began to lap at the latticework of sticks. She was about to douse the bomb itself with *pisco* and pitch it on the rising fire, but Honorato interrupted her.

No, no, no! he chided. *You do not want the bag to burn away before the tanks explode. Otherwise, all the rocks will fall out. You want to* cook *the tanks to build heat and pressure, like a pot of water with a lid on it.*

"Okay." Natalie set aside the *pisco* and moved to set the bag into the fire's flames.

No! No! No! Honorato repeated with the impatience of a maestro whose orchestra persists in playing flat. *Not yet. The bomb will explode too soon. You must wait until they are almost here before putting it in the fire.*

She groaned. "How the heck do I know when to do that?"

I will help.

"*Gracias.*" Hefting the bomb in one hand, she listened at the entrance to the stairway again. There *was* a sound: a soft, multitudinous scraping, as of the scuttling of rats in a sewer.

Natalie turned back toward the chamber to search for a shelter to protect her from the coming blast. Although she'd already seen several of the room's treasures individually, she gasped anew, for the shimmering flames of the fire now illuminated the entire hoard at once, causing the air itself to glow with the reflected warmth of silver tears and golden sweat.

And there, centered against the wall six feet from the fire, commanding a view of the lesser artifacts as a lord surveys his subjects, rested the pièce de résistance: Atahualpa's throne. The one he rode on that day in Cajamarca when Francisco Pizarro dragged him off his royal litter by his ankle as if he were a fugitive slave. Natalie recalled reading that Pizarro had claimed the throne as his personal trophy when the conquistadors divided the ransom.

There was no question that this was the seat of the Son of the Sun. Cast from solid gold, the armless chair stood almost six feet high and must have weighed more than three hundred pounds. The tall back fanned out into an arc at the level where the proud Inca would have held his head, fiery sculpted sun rays radiating out from his crown. Natalie could easily understand why Atahualpa's people believed him divine, why the nobles carried this throne on their shoulders, and why the peasants prostrated themselves before it.

The throne would not help her, however. It was too close to the wall for her to hide behind and far too heavy to move. Tearing her attention from its magnificence, Natalie found a better shield. An enormous representation of the sun god Inti leaned against a wall to the right of the throne. A beaten gold disc five feet in diameter, Inti's visage bore an expression of impassive supremacy.

Looks like he can stop a few flying emeralds, Natalie decided, and listened at the doorway again. The footfalls in the stairwell became more distinct, grew louder as she harkened to them.

She held the bomb above the crackling fire. "Now?"

No! Honorato replied. *Not yet. A little longer…*

Natalie drew the bag away from the flames. " 'Wait till you see the whites of their eyes,' " she muttered.

What?

"Never mind." She moved to gaze down the steps at the wall where the stairwell cornered to join the burial chamber. A small circle of faint yellow light appeared there. "Honorato... what is your last name?"

Velasco.

The circle of light expanded as it had when Natalie ascended the stairs, its brightness intensifying. The asynchronous patter of feet swelled in the tunnel's gramophone horn.

"Where does your family live?"

Pisac, near Cuzco, Honorato said. *Why do you ask?*

"For future reference. Provided I *have* a future."

The flashlight spot sharpened to crispness, and several lesser lights jiggled beside it on the wall.

NOW! Honorato told her.

Natalie hurried to the pyre and set the bomb on it. The flames curled to embrace the sack.

Snatching up the bottle of *pisco* as a weapon of last resort, she barely had time to duck beneath the slanting roof of the Inti sun disc. As camouflage, she hooded Honorato's weathered woolen poncho as a cowl over her face and hunched in the fetal posture of the mummy bundles in the chamber.

Natalie angled her head to watch the stairwell's doorway. Through the narrow gap between the poncho's drooping hems, she saw Romoldo lean into the chamber, a flashlight in one hand and a pistol in the other. His vulpine eyes widened as he took in the room's riches, and for an instant he appeared to lose his perpetual wariness. Finger flexing against the gun's trigger, he let out a grunt when the fire caught his attention. Natalie tensed as he motioned an unseen party forward, pointing at the blaze and shouting, "*¡La bruja! ¡La bruja!*"

No, please, no, she thought.

"*SILENCE!*" Romoldo's clamor evidently so affronted Nathan Azure that he momentarily forgot his Spanish. "*¡Cállate! ¡Cállate!* We'll find the witch soon enough. But nothing must spoil this moment."

The Englishman entered the chamber as if he were a pilgrim in a cathedral, his glacial demeanor melting into infantile wonder. His eyes misted as he pivoted his head this way and that, frustrated and delighted that he could not capture all the glories in one glance.

"*I knew it,*" he croaked. "*I knew it.*"

His hands palsied with eagerness, he fumbled to remove his driving gloves, which he cast on the floor not more than three feet from the fire that licked at the sack containing the propane tanks.

C'mon! Natalie telepathically shouted at the bomb. *Boom! BOOM! Before they see you...*

Romoldo snarled and swiped an arm at his fellow Peruvians as they crammed the doorway, jabbering and vying for the best view of the rewards they would soon reap. Maintaining a respectful distance from his boss, Romoldo advanced toward the pyre and prowled the room with his gaze.

Engulfed in a dream, Nathan Azure seemed to have forgotten the men entirely. He laid bare hands on the statues, burial masks and bowls, alpacas and maize stalks, in a gathering frenzy, moving faster and faster, as if it might vanish in a blink like fairy gold.

"*YOU SEE THIS, FATHER?*" He shook fistfuls of jeweled necklaces at the ceiling. "*HERE'S TO YOUR BLOODY WASHING POWDER!*"

Still, he did not smile. He raved in an ecstasy akin to that of a rapist, a desolate gratification of desire devoid of human warmth or joy.

Then he saw Atahualpa's throne, and rapture overcame his ranting. Azure crept up on the shining seat in trepidation, his palms hovering over its surface as if touching it would strike him dead. When at last he pressed his palms flat against its sheen, a shudder of hideous consummation rippled his wiry frame. Eyes glistening, he lowered himself onto the throne with the deliberateness of a monarch awaiting coronation.

Hurry up! Natalie pleaded to the bomb. *Blow, baby, blow.*

Romoldo gaped at his boss and fidgeted like a third party on a date. Averting his attention from the big *gringo*, he scowled at the fire. He shoved his flashlight into his back pocket and bent to examine the duffel that baked in the flames.

NO! Natalie started forward, grasped the neck of the *pisco* bottle.

Romoldo grabbed the top of the bag to lift it from the pyre, but dropped it and flinched back, licking his fingers to cool them.

Natalie froze, the poncho closed tight around her head, but it was too late. Romoldo must have seen her move, for he aimed his flashlight at the Inti sun disc and squinted, cocking his gun as he advanced toward it.

Natalie tensed, unsure whether to make a break for it or to hold still and try to look as much like a mummy as possible. Before she could decide, a thunderbolt *CRACK* deafened all thought.

She cringed and covered her head with her arms as the gong of the sun disc rang with a spitting hailstorm of projectile hits. The clangor nearly buried the shrill keen of a man's shriek in the room beyond.

The chamber darkened to an infernal reddish gloom, lit only by the smoldering sticks and embers that the blast had scattered. An abrupt silence followed, or perhaps Natalie simply could not hear whatever noises there were over the tuning-fork hum in her ears.

The bomb worked, yes? Honorato asked after a few minutes passed with no apparent movement in the burial chamber.

We'll see, Natalie replied, afraid to speak aloud.

She eased out from behind the sun disc but shrank back when she heard a rattling gasp. A couple yards away from her, Romoldo pushed himself onto his knees and crawled across the floor like an infant, a thread of bloody drool dangling from his mouth.

He teetered to a standing position, and Natalie clutched the liquor bottle in readiness. But he did not attempt to find her. He lurched instead toward the stairwell, groaning with the effort. His compadres had evidently fled the explosion, so Romoldo braced himself against the wall and stumbled down the stairs, blotching the wall with black spots and smears wherever he collapsed against it.

When he had descended from view, Natalie noticed that his flashlight still glowed where he'd dropped it. She was willing to bet his pistol still lay somewhere near it.

As she ventured out from behind the sun disc, she kept an eye on Atahualpa's throne and the dark shadow that seethed there. Natalie scampered the few feet to the flashlight and with its help located the gun. Armed with both, she went to face Nathan Azure.

Slumped back in the Inca's seat, his arms hanging straight down at his sides, Azure made no sound but a labored gurgling. When Natalie shone the flashlight on him, she saw why. Meteors of green crystal cratered his chest and stomach, blood leaking over and around the gems, and when Natalie raised the light to his face, emerald translucence glittered in the socket where his left eye had been.

For a second, Azure's remaining eye rolled up to glare at Natalie, but he seemed to reject her as unworthy of his final moments. Instead, he swiveled the eye left and right, focusing beyond her, so that his last sight might be the glinting glory of his one true love.

Then the eye came to rest in an empty stare, and his bobbing mouth fell open and did not close. A golden boy on a golden throne, now studded with jewels, Nathan Azure had become a part of the treasure he craved.

That is that, yes? Honorato said. *It is over.*

"No, it's not." Natalie stared at Azure's inanimate face, at the green twinkle in its new eye, and felt no triumph, no relief, no closure, only exhaustion. She knew what awaited her, for she had slapped him with her bare hand. Unlike Trent, Azure hated her enough to come back.

Spots of cold stung her skin like melting snowflakes. She meant to turn away from the throne, to collect her passport and other belongings, to *leave,* but she found herself as rigid and rooted as one of the Cloud People's sarcophagi. Honorato tried to say something but interference fuzzed his words, as if he were a radio station slipping out of tune.

As the seizure started, Natalie toppled toward the throne, landing on Nathan Azure's lap. The blood that had run down his torso and onto his pants daubed her left cheek, and the knocking intensified.

You killed me in my moment of victory! he sobbed in her head. *You took my life just when it began to* mean *something.*

Her hands contracted on the flashlight and pistol with an electrocution death grip, as if they were live power lines. Of its own volition, her right hand raised the gun toward her head.

I'll show you what it is to deprive someone of all that he loves...

Natalie sought Honorato for help, but Azure had forced him out. Spilled blood was too strong a touchstone.

Fighting for mastery, Natalie forced her numbed mouth to bleat the Twenty-third Psalm. "The—Lord—is—my—shepherd...*I shall not want.*"

The pistol's barrel quivered at her temple.

As she went on, the words came more easily. *"He maketh me to lie down in green pastures! He leadeth me beside the still waters!"*

She uncrooked her finger from the trigger, lowered the gun.

NO! Azure shrieked.

Natalie stood and wiped the blood from her cheek, shouting. *"HE RESTORETH MY SOUL! HE LEADETH ME IN THE PATHS OF RIGHTEOUSNESS FOR HIS NAME'S SAKE!"*

You shan't get away with this, you witch! Azure sniveled, his thoughts already dimming as the protective mantra flushed him from her mind. *I'll come back again and again until I get in. You hear me? I'll be with you forever!*

"I know," Natalie said softly, with genuine regret. "But *I will fear no evil.*"

She resumed reciting the psalm, whispering it for comfort even when she was certain Azure was gone.

Returning to the ledge, Natalie recovered her passport and other necessities for the long trip home. She switched to her own flashlight but kept Romoldo's pistol in hand to defend herself in case any of Azure's timid lackeys came back.

The Peruvians did return, their lanterns bobbing through the doorway as they cautiously explored the burial chamber. They paid little attention to Natalie, however. Leaderless now, they had come to loot the cache for themselves, and when they were reasonably certain no other bombs would detonate, they dove at the treasure like a flock of hungry buzzards, stuffing valuables into sacks, pockets, shirtfronts, as much as they could carry.

Natalie made no move to stop them, nor did she take anything for herself. The blood-ransom gold was as good as cursed for her, and she already had enough angry souls to plague her the rest of her life. When she got back to

Leimebamba tomorrow, she would contact Luís Pacampía at the museum and give his staff explicit directions on how to find the cave. Plenty of treasure would remain for them to preserve; there was simply too much for even Azure's pack of small-time crooks to carry away in one day.

On her way down the stairway inside the mountain, Natalie came across Romoldo, lying faceup along the steps. He hadn't gotten very far, although, given his condition, it must have taken a superhuman effort to walk at all. One of his enterprising countrymen squatted beside him, and at first Natalie thought the man was ministering to Romoldo's wounds. Then she saw the Peruvian pluck his scarlet-slicked fingers from one of the puckering holes in Romoldo's side, grinning as he held the damp emerald up to his lantern to admire it. Natalie hurried past him while he pocketed the gem and probed a gash in Romoldo's abdomen.

Under the accumulated weight of her responsibility for what she had done, for what she had yet to do, her feet seemed to grow heavier with every step of the tedious descent. She emerged from the stairway's hidden entrance with a sigh of surrender—her weariness would let her go no farther that night.

With the flashlight and a half-moon to illuminate her way, she retrieved her patient burro from behind the rock where she'd tied it and led the animal downstream. The mule stopped to lap at the creek's water, and Natalie sank onto the rocky bank to wait out the hours until dawn. She lowered her face into her open palms, wanting the balm of sleep but unsure whether it could ever restore the peace she had just sacrificed. Yet there was still so much to do before she could get back to where and to who she had been less than a month ago. So far to go, so many promises to keep, and nothing about home would be the same as when she had left it.

Tonight, then, she would weep the tears of the moon and mourn for everything that had been lost. Tomorrow she would sweat in the sun to save the invaluable treasures that remained.

28

Another Home, Not Her Own

IF I EVER GET HOME, I'M NEVER TRAVELING AGAIN, Natalie swore as the cramped bus disgorged her and its other passengers into the center of Pisac.

It was Sunday, market day, and the cobblestoned plaza teemed with buyers and vendors. The interweaving colors made the square resemble an intricate Peruvian blanket as men and women in vibrant clothes haggled over food and handicrafts. The crowd flowing around her, Natalie hugged the thick bundle of Honorato's folded poncho to her chest and surveyed the plaza's side streets.

"Which way?" she asked him under her breath.

There, on the right, between those white buildings. Follow the road out of town.

She headed down the road he indicated, her stomach tightening with his anxiety. Honorato feared this encounter more than he had feared his own death.

Natalie well understood his dread. She had deliberately waited until late at night—well past Callie's bedtime—to call Ted Atwater on his cell phone at the L.A. motel where they were hiding to let him know that she would not be able to come home for several days. "The Peruvian authorities want me to answer some questions," she lied to excuse the delay. She couldn't bear to tell Callie directly that Mommy would not come to her as soon as possible.

After she made it back to Leimebamba, Natalie wanted nothing more than to catch the first flight to the U.S. she could find. But she knew that if she left now, she would never return to Peru—could never leave Callie again—and there was a duty she needed to perform here before she departed forever.

The paving stones ended not long after the road left the marketplace, and Natalie hiked up the dirt lane toward the grassy hills striped by the dark green striations of ancient agricultural terraces. The air felt drier and dustier here than it had in the northern part of the country, chapping her lips and chalking her skin with fine powder. The bristles of real hair beneath her wig itched from perspiration, and she couldn't wait to get back to her hotel in Cuzco, strip bare, and wash the paste of sweat and dirt from her body.

A small stone hut with a thatched roof came into view on her left. Three boys between the ages of four and eight kicked a soccer ball around the patch of rough ground in front of the house. Halfway up the hill behind them, a middle-age woman chopped at the soil with a wooden hoe while carrying an infant in an orange sling on her back. None of them wore shoes.

The grim obligation that awaited her made Natalie ashamed of her petty complaints. "Is that them?"

Yes. My boys, my wife. Honorato said it with the heaviness of a man who has lost his life savings on a bet. *My Celestina...* *she will never have her girl now.*

Natalie drew a deep breath and trudged up the slope toward his widow. Intent on her toil, the woman did not look up until Natalie's shadow crossed the handle of her hoe.

"Señora Velasco?"

Celestina possessed a stout, stolid figure, with a broad, flattish face that seemed to have been baked as hard as the soil she tilled. When she saw her visitor's violet eyes, however, her impassive expression turned fearful.

Natalie waited for Honorato to tell her how to say "Your husband is dead" in Spanish, but it proved unnecessary. The poncho in Natalie's arms signified as much to Celestina as a triangular folded flag would to a soldier's mother. She dropped the hoe to clutch her plump cheeks, mewling in a voice slurred by grief.

She says she knew this would happen, Honorato translated, his tone more hopeless than before. *Every time I went away, she expected it.*

For a while, he refused to speak, even when Natalie prodded him to serve as her interpreter. Finally he consented to give her the words she wanted to speak to his wife.

"He died while saving my life," she said in Spanish. "I owe everything to him, including the happiness of my child. That is why I have brought you this." She lowered the bundled poncho from her chest. "He wanted you and your boys to have it—to take care of you since he cannot."

Natalie lifted a fold of the woolen cloth, unveiling scores of tightly bound stacks of crisp nuevos soles, worth a hundred thousand U.S. dollars—half the money Nathan Azure had wired to her savings account. She'd had to go to the biggest bank in Lima to withdraw the sum in cash. She owed

Honorato her life and would have given his widow all of Azure's money, but she had to keep at least enough savings to help Dad with his medical bills and to buy herself some time to get out of debt.

Her eyes brimming, Celestina shook her head as she stared at the currency Natalie offered, as if unwilling to accept good fortune spawned by tragedy. Natalie lowered the cloth to cover the money and urged her to take the poncho. When she wouldn't, Natalie laid the bequest at the widow's feet.

The two women regarded each other in solemn silence as Natalie waited for Honorato to relay what he wanted to say. When he said nothing, Natalie drew upon her limited vocabulary to speak for both of them. "I am sorry," she told Celestina. "May God be with you and your family."

She turned away and started down the hillside.

Wait, Honorato implored when they neared the three boys. *Wait here, yes?*

"Yes. Of course."

She watched the lads at play, trailing laughter behind them like airborne kites. The two older boys kicked the ball back and forth to each other as they ran down the impromptu soccer field, then deliberately allowed their tiny brother to steal it from them and make the goal.

Natalie smiled. "You have handsome sons. What are their names?"

Abimael, he is the oldest. Then Modesto and Victor. José is still on his mother's back.

She felt him yearn for them. "I would let you speak to them. To her."

No. No, I cannot. Without the mask of a face to conceal it, his soul trembled, its helpless despair exposed to her. *What could I say? How could I explain my mistakes?*

"You can give them your love. They will give you their forgiveness."

I don't know. I think this was another mistake. Seeing them...I should not have come back. So many bad choices. But you have given them hope for the future, yes? I will carry that hope with me as well.

Natalie swallowed to loosen the knot in her throat. "Honorato, I—"

But he was gone, leaving Natalie alone with her own bad choices.

29

Return to the Golden State

ALTHOUGH NATALIE MADE SURE HER TRIP TO LOS Angeles was not on a Daedalus Aeronautics jet, she worried less about the flight than about what awaited her on the ground when she arrived. She had called ahead to arrange for Ted Atwater to pick her up at the airport, and Callie had demanded her turn with the phone.

"Are you *really* coming back this time?" she asked.

"Yes, baby girl," Natalie had assured her. "And I won't leave again. Ever."

Her voice sharpened with doubt. "Promise?"

"Promise."

"That's what I thought."

Before she could respond, Natalie heard scuffling in the background and Ted Atwater came on the line to make apologies.

"Don't let her upset you," he advised. "She's still a little out of sorts about the whole birthday thing."

So am I, Natalie thought, recalling the conversation while she reclined in her aisle seat on the plane. Her hair still looked like a military buzz cut but it had grown out enough to cover the node point tattoos, so she'd ditched her dusty, bedraggled wig back at the terminal in Lima. She'd also bought a fresh pair of sunglasses in order to keep her violet irises from drawing stares. However, she'd still gotten strange looks when she went through ticketing, customs, and security carrying only a tote bag containing a miniature Peruvian flag and a stuffed toy llama for Callie. Other than her passport and purse, she'd thrown away what little she had left from her Andean adventure.

With her eyes shut behind her shades during the flight Natalie did not realize she had dozed off until she heard the captain's voice over the passenger cabin's public-address system.

"Flight attendants prepare for arrival…"

Natalie sprang upright, gripping the buckle of her safety belt to make sure that it was still fastened—that she hadn't moved without her knowledge.

The Lord is my shepherd, she quoted. *I shall not want…*

A flight attendant touched her shoulder, causing her to jump.

"I'm sorry, ma'am," he said, "but we need you to raise your seat back to the full upright position."

"Oh…right. Sorry." She did as he asked, but kept reciting the protective mantra in her head. Even though Azure had knocked only once since that night in the burial chamber, she needed to be careful. In her Lima hotel room, she awoke early one morning to find herself sitting upright with the contents of her purse dumped on the bed in front of her. In her hand, she held the nail clippers, the sharp point of the nail file poised on the pulsing skin over her carotid artery.

Then a rolling spasm ran through her body, and she

realized what had jarred her from sleep. Someone else was knocking, attempting to muscle Azure out of her head the way Dan had once purged Callie of unwanted souls. Her mind caught in a tug-of-war between the opposing invaders, Natalie twisted on the bed, her flailing hand flinging the nail clippers across the room.

Let me alone, you imbecile! Azure sputtered, his thoughts already growing fainter. *It's my right! She denied me the only thing I lived for…*

Natalie's body unwound from its contortions as the usurping soul asserted its dominance. As soon as it had displaced Azure, however, the newcomer withdrew, leaving Natalie only two words to determine the soul's identity: *I'm sorry.*

Nathan Azure had not knocked since then. If Trent was the one restraining him in limbo, it meant he really had cared about her—perhaps even loved her.

Natalie still grappled with all the implications of that possibility. When Dan had died, she had secretly feared that he was the only man who could truly love her, the only one capable of looking beyond the violet eyes into the mind and heart behind them. But if even a hardened criminal like Trent could develop feelings for her, then perhaps there would come another man—a *good* man—one she could love in return. The prospect both terrified and exhilarated her.

When she deplaned at LAX, Natalie feared that her worst-case nightmare had come true. No smiling relatives waited to welcome her at the gate the way Dan had when he reunited with her in an airport terminal. Had Callie refused to come? Were the Atwaters angry with her for all the trouble she'd caused them?

Forlorn, she scanned the crowd and noted that her fellow travelers all proceeded alone to baggage claim. Of course! She'd forgotten that airport security allowed only ticketed passengers to the gate nowadays.

A new, deeper fear struck an instant later when she heard the cultured, Indian-accented voice that suddenly spoke from behind her.

"Ms. Lindstrom! Welcome back to Los Angeles. I hope that you had a most enjoyable trip."

Although she had never heard him speak before, Natalie was not surprised when she turned to find Chameleon Man approaching her.

"May I have the pleasure of presenting myself?" He flipped open his ID with a small bow of his head. "Sanjay Prashad, Corps Security."

So he has a name after all. She cast a cursory glance at the booklet's photo, in no mood for pleasantries. "I presume you want to know where I've been."

"That would be most helpful, of course." He tucked the ID back in the jacket of his gray suit. "But what we truly require is information regarding the fate of my colleague Arabella Madison. Given the synchronicity of your disappearance with hers, we thought you might know something about her murder."

Natalie's face went cold, but she kept her gaze steady.

"I'm sure you've heard about the Incan gold discovered in Peru last week," she said. Since the Museo Leymebamba crew had recovered the remaining treasure, headlines about the hoard had splashed across newspapers around the world.

Prashad nodded in impatience. "Yes, yes. Remarkable. What of it?"

"Nathan Azure, the millionaire whose body was found at the site, abducted me and forced me to help him locate the treasure," Natalie continued, reciting the story she'd rehearsed for this occasion. "When his men mutinied and killed him, I took the opportunity to escape."

"That is a most fascinating fiction, Ms. Lindstrom." A harshness edged the agent's singsongy accent. "However, it does not explain why my former counterpart in the Corps' northern California division admitted to accepting a bribe to allow your departure. He also said you left voluntarily."

"Because Azure had threatened my family."

"Your family lied to Security agents regarding your whereabouts—"

"—in order to protect my daughter from Azure's men."

Prashad's mouth flattened. "You have still not accounted for the death of Agent Madison."

"I'm afraid she was killed in the line of duty while trying to prevent my kidnapping." Natalie adopted the appropriate tone of sober regret. "If you want to recommend her for a posthumous commendation, you have my full support. Now, if you'll excuse me, my family is waiting."

She headed off toward the escalators that led down to the baggage-claim area, quickening her steps as Prashad hastened to trail her.

"This is not the end of this matter, Ms. Lindstrom!" he

called after her. "You still have many questions to answer. Many questions."

She did not look back.

Natalie descended to the luggage carousels even though she had no bags to collect. There, just beyond the baggage claim checkpoint, she saw Ted Atwater holding Callie against his chest so that she could peer over the harried travelers criss-crossing in front of them.

Mother and daughter spotted each other at the same time, and Callie tugged her grandfather's shirt collar until he set her down. Unburdened by luggage, Natalie rushed through the checkpoint to catch her little girl, who sprang into her open arms.

"You *came*," Callie cried, nuzzling her cheek. "You're really here."

"Yes, honey." Natalie tightened her embrace. "I'm so sorry."

"I was so afraid you wouldn't come back."

"I know, baby girl. So was I."

Ted Atwater gave them a long moment together before interrupting. "Hey! Do grandpas get hugs, too?"

Unwilling to let go of Callie, Natalie hoisted her daughter into the crook of her left arm and curled her right arm around his shoulder. "Ted, I can't thank you enough for everything you and Jean have done. If there's anything I can do—"

"It was our pleasure. But you're not done with the grandpa hugs yet." He nodded to his left.

Natalie's heart stuttered even before she turned to the

man who stood patiently a few feet to the side. His suit hung on his wasted frame like the sails of a becalmed ship and his complexion looked almost as gray as his hair, but a broad smile lit his wan face.

"Hey, kiddo."

"*Dad*." She practically slammed into him as she rushed to greet him. "How...?"

Squished between Natalie and Wade, Callie giggled. She must have almost burst trying to keep the surprise a secret.

"I had to come." Wade chuckled, his blue eyes watery. "Doctor's orders. Nothing does my heart as much good as seeing my two favorite girls in the world."

"Oh, Dad." Natalie kissed his cheek, whispered in his ear. "*I love you.*"

There it was. After all her agonizing, it came out naturally, without thinking, almost by mistake, but its lack of premeditation was what made it feel so good, so right. Yet it seemed too easy somehow. Had she really said it or only thought it, as she had so many times before?

Wade answered that question in the best possible way. "I love you, too, sweetheart," he said. "More than I can say."

After a respectful pause, Ted broke in again. "Well, what say we get out of this madhouse, pick Jean up at the motel, and go get some grub? My treat!"

Wade raised his hand like a traffic cop. "No way, Ted. This one's on me."

"Don't be ridiculous! You came all the way from the East Coast. The least I can do is give you a hot meal..."

The grandfathers managed to fight over the tab all the way back to the parking garage where Ted had parked his car.

Natalie and Callie just laughed at them, loving them, loving each other. Only when they rode away from the airport, Callie nestled under her mother's arm in the backseat, did the two of them become moody again. Out the rear windshield, Natalie could see Sanjay Prashad's car tailing them onto the freeway, a gadfly reminder of the problems that still pursued them.

"I missed you on my birthday," Callie said, then lowered her voice, aware that Ted could hear her from the driver's seat. "It wasn't any fun without you. But don't tell Grandpa that."

Natalie rested her head on top of her daughter's. "I know, honey. I'll give you a makeup birthday, I swear."

"It's okay. I'm just glad you're back." She twisted her mouth as if attempting to hold in some words she didn't want to escape. "Um...Grandpa Ted said there were some bad men who kept you in Peru all this time."

"That's right, honey."

"Are they...gone now?"

Natalie looked into those eyes that were so like hers. *Yes, honey, they're gone now,* she wanted to say. *I got rid of them.* But that would be a lie—and one Callie would recognize immediately. She would sense that Natalie could not rid herself of her bad men any more than Callie could expunge Horace Rendell and Vincent Thresher from her nightmares.

"No, sweetheart, they're not gone," Natalie admitted. "But if we help each other, we can keep the bad men from hurting us. Will you help me?"

"Uh-huh." Callie's eyes shone with anxiety, but also hope. "And you'll help me?"

"Always."

They swayed together with the gentle turns of the car, and Callie heaved a sleepy sigh. "So can we go to Disneyland now?"

Natalie laughed and ruffled her daughter's hair. "Sure, birthday girl. Anything you want."

Acknowledgments

In researching this novel, the author has relied upon many excellent information sources. He is especially indebted to the following books: *Children of the Incas* by David Mangurian; *The Conquest of Peru* by William H. Prescott; *The Conquistadors* by Jean Descola; *Cut Stones and Crossroads* by Ronald Wright; *Detectives of the Sky: Investigating Aviation Tragedies* by Michael Dorman; *Incredible Pizarro: Conqueror of Peru* by Frank Shay; *Insight Guides: Peru,* edited by Pam Barrett et al.; and *Valverde's Gold: In Search of the Last Great Inca Treasure* by Mark Honigsbaum.

The author also wishes to thank the following people for their essential contributions to and support of his work: Anne Lesley Groell, my editor, and the entire crew at Bantam Dell; my intrepid agent Jimmy Vines; my foreign-rights agent Danny Baror; my family and friends; and, more than ever, Kelly.

About the Author

STEPHEN WOODWORTH is the author of the previous Violet novels *Through Violet Eyes* and *With Red Hands*, and he is currently at work on the fourth book in the series. A graduate of the prestigious Clarion West Writers Workshop and a first-place winner in the Writers of the Future Contest, he has published short fiction in such publications as *The Magazine of Fantasy & Science Fiction*, *Weird Tales*, *Aboriginal Science Fiction*, *Gothic.Net*, and *Strange Horizons*. He lives on the West Coast with his wife, writer Kelly Dunn.

AND BE SURE NOT TO MISS

FROM BLACK ROOMS

by Stephen Woodworth

The next thrilling novel
in the Violet universe, and the continuing
adventures of Natalie Lindstrom . . .

Here's a special preview:

FROM BLACK ROOMS
on sale fall 2006

On the day Bartholomew Wax had selected to kill himself, he called in sick at work so he could spend part of the day saying good-bye to his children. He would enjoy their company as he ate his last meal.

With the strains of a Vivaldi violin concerto issuing from the speakers of his home's built-in sound system, Wax uncorked his finest bottle of Beaujolais and prepared himself a plate of Brie, *foie gras*, cracked wheat and rye crackers, and fresh grapes. Once the wine had had a chance to breathe, he placed it on a sterling silver tray along with the platter of food and a cut-crystal goblet and carried the tray from the kitchen to a door in the hallway. Setting it on the adjacent mahogany side table, he punched in a seven-digit combination on the door's digital keypad, and the carbon-steel bolts slid back into the jamb with the *shuck* of shells being pumped into a shotgun barrel.

Wax pulled the door open, revealing the foot-thick depth of insulation and metal behind its mundane wooden façade. The walls of the basement had been similarly reinforced. The plaster and drywall hid tungsten-carbide plates and sandwiched layers of concrete, steel, and Sheetrock—making the shelter impervious to fire, drills, and explosives. The vault had cost his employers at the North American Afterlife Communications Corps a couple of million dollars to build, but no price was too great to pay for his children's safety.

They glowed in welcome as he descended the cellar steps with the silver tray. Sensors detected his heat signature and switched on the lamps that illuminated his family. Warm yellow rectangles seemed to hover in the darkness of the black-walled room. Basking in their individual spotlights, the children smiled at him—as precious to him as if he'd given birth to them himself. Wax had positioned the spots to light each canvas on the wall to best effect, precisely calibrating the intensity so as not to fade the colors. Although a blistering New Mexico heat broiled the exterior of the house, climate control systems kept the cellar at a constant seventy degrees, with just enough humidity to keep the paintings from cracking.

An office chair and a small table in the center of the floor provided the chamber's only furnishings. As the vault door automatically sealed him inside, Wax set the tray on the table, unwound the bread-bag twist tie he'd used to hold back his hair, and shook out the ponytail until it fell down around his shoulders in a gray mane. Popping a grape in his mouth, he seated himself in the chair, which he could swivel to view the artwork hanging on any of the cellar walls. There, with forced air and piped music swathing him in a cool swirl of Vivaldi strings, he spent his last hour with the only real family he had.

An only child, Bartholomew Wax had virtually grown up among paintings. His divorced mother couldn't afford a babysitter during summer vacation, so every morning she would drop him off at the Isabella Stewart Gardner Museum while she went to work the day shift at a Dunkin' Donuts shop in downtown Boston. Back in the seventies, when parents were still naïve about pedophilia and when day care was considered a luxury, Bartholomew's mother told herself that it would do the boy good to spend his days surrounded by high culture rather than at home watching television.

A withdrawn and frail boy with an autistic's love of routine, little Barty came to cherish his hours in the dim galleries of the Italian-style palazzo. The docents all knew him by name, and he would eat his sack lunch among the white lilies and Greco-Roman statuary in the peaceful courtyard, alone with his thoughts. But what he loved most were the paintings, each of which remained exactly where Mrs. Gardner had decreed it should stay forever. On some walls, masterpieces of different sizes and themes were jammed so closely together that their frames butted against one another, resembling a patchwork of postage stamps on an enormous envelope. Each one silently whispered its story to Barty, and when no one else was in the room, he would talk to each in turn, telling them all his secrets and his grand plans for the future. They were his family, after all.

Several members of that family now hung before him in this vault. Munching a cracker spread with Brie, Wax basked in the delicate glow of *The Concert*—one of only thirty-six Vermeers in existence. The artist's muted use of light gave a preternatural tranquility to the scene; Wax could actually hear the music a young Flemish girl played for her parents, the quiet strains of the harpsichord calming the frenzy of thoughts in his capricious mind. Next to the Vermeer, *Storm on the Sea of Galilee* churned in an endless, frozen tempest. Rembrandt's only seascape, it depicted Jesus' disciples clinging to a sailboat that cresting whitewater threatened to overturn. Golden sunlight touched the wave-tossed boat as a hole of blue sky opened in the coal-smoke clouds, the promise of God's salvation for the faithful. Now more than ever, Bartholomew Wax needed the promise of peace and redemption.

His meal finished, he rose from his chair and strolled past the remainder of his collection, sipping wine from his goblet. Here were the other siblings from the Gardner—a tiny Rembrandt self-portrait, *Chez Tortoni* by Manet, *La Sortie du*

Paysage by Degas, and more. Alas, those barbarians from the Corps had savagely cut the pictures from their frames, and Wax himself had had to remount the canvases on stretchers and find suitable replacement frames for them. He also made sure that the NAACC took greater care the next time they procured children for him to adopt.

Wax had always dreamed of having such a family. Reproductions would not do, for even the finest lithographs could not capture the play of light upon the actual brushwork, the depth and textures of the swirls and ridges, the translucence of the glazes. As a boy, he decided that he would have to become very rich so that he, too, could buy a mansion full of artworks like Mrs. Gardner's. His need for money drove him into medicine, for weren't all doctors well-to-do? Yet as he matured and learned more about the rarefied world of art auctions, Wax discovered that the paintings he wanted—the ones painted by the artists while they were alive, not the posthumous "collaborations" created by government Violets—sold for millions of dollars each. He considered starting his own biotechnology company to make his fortune in the stock market, but soon realized that even the wealth of Bill Gates could not purchase the works he truly wanted: the priceless treasures that hung in the Gardner and other museums around the world. And that was when he made his bargain with the Corps, offering his services in exchange for their promise to accumulate the unattainable collection he craved.

Wax lingered before each item in the gallery as he made his way around the vault, attempting to delay the inevitable. After more than fifteen years of effort, his work for the Corps was near an end, which meant that so was he. Ironically, success rather than failure spelled doom for him. As soon as the

NAACC obtained what it wanted, it would take his family away and eliminate him to protect its secrets.

He paused in front of da Vinci's *Madonna of the Yarnwinder*, raised the goblet to his lips, but found only a dribble of wine left. Once again, he toyed with the idea of sealing himself up with his treasures like a pharaoh in his tomb. But Wax knew better than anyone that you could take nothing into the afterlife. The Corps would no doubt breach the vault sooner or later, and Wax could not bear to think of his children ending up in the hands of a ghoul like Carl Pancrit.

He contemplated Leonardo's rendition of Mary and the Christ child, which had once adorned the home of the Duke of Buccleuch in Scotland. In the painting, the baby gazed at the T-shaped wooden spindle in his hands, a symbol of the cross that awaited him—the end prefigured in the beginning. Mary's right hand hovered uncertainly over the infant, as if she longed to hold her son back from his destiny yet knew she could not. Certain sacrifices had to be made.

Wax approached the final and most recent acquisition in his collection with reluctance. His time was almost up, but that was not why he dawdled. The last picture frightened him. Although he had seen countless copies and parodies of *The Scream*, none had prepared him for the terror portrayed in the original, brought here all the way from the Munch Museum in Oslo. Beneath a sky as red and fluid as an arterial hemorrhage, a solitary androgynous figure shivered on a bleak seaside boardwalk, its eyes and mouth gaping, its grotesque, distended hands pressed to its temples.

Most people who saw the picture did not realize that it was not the humanoid figure screaming. No, Wax mused, the mutant being was struck dumb with fear as it vainly covered its ears to shut out the eternal cosmic wail of the universe—"a loud, unending scream piercing nature," as Edvard Munch had put it.

With its indigo eyes and bald, skull-like head, the figure might have been a Violet, its scalp shaved to accommodate the electrodes of a SoulScan device.

The resemblance filled Bartholomew Wax with both revulsion and a renewed sense of urgency. What would it be like to hear that awful shriek of transcendental agony…and never be able to shut it out? What if everyone could hear it? Would the human race be able to withstand the constant sound of its own inescapable mortality?

The questions preyed on Dr. Wax, hastening him into action. Tying his hair back into its ponytail, he did not take the trouble to clean up the remains of his last meal, but left the cheese and pâté to rot on the silver tray beside the uncorked wine. His remaining time was too valuable, and he would never return to this place, anyway.

Instead, he began taking the paintings off the wall one at a time and meticulously packing them into the special reinforced shipping crates he'd accumulated in the cellar for that purpose. Custom-cut Styrofoam brackets held each frame motionless within its box, ensuring that nothing touched the surface of the canvas, while wood inserts prevented the cardboard sides from being crushed or punctured. The crates all bore shipping labels with the name "Arthur Maven" and a false return address as well as the packages' destinations: the Munch Museum in Norway, Drumlanrig Castle in Scotland, and, of course, the Gardner, among many others.

Wax actually giggled as he imagined the astonishment on the recipients' faces when they opened the boxes and discovered their long lost pictures inside. The thought made him happy. Unlike human beings, artworks had no afterlife in which to perpetuate their existence. A painting that no one saw ceased to be, and his children deserved to live.

The CD changer on his stereo system switched from Vivaldi to Mahler's Ninth. Opening the vault door, Wax began the laborious task of carrying the crates up the stairs and out to his Ford Explorer. He left the engine running and the air conditioner on full blast while loading the SUV, which barely contained his collection. At last ready to depart, he grabbed the antique black doctor's bag that usually carried only his lunch. On the way out the door, however, he tapped his brow to chastise himself for his forgetfulness.

Hurrying to the Steinway baby grand in his living room, he opened the piano bench and took out a thick score filled with computer-printed musical notes. Wax ripped a fistful of pages from the book as he carried it into the kitchen and threw it in the stainless-steel sink. He used a burner on the gas stove to ignite one corner of the torn pages, then used them to set the rest of the score on fire. The smoke detector on the ceiling shrilled as he left the music flaming in the sink.

The afternoon sun cast the vertical ridges of the Organ Mountains in sharp relief, the craggy gray range resembling the pipes of a church organ as its name implied. Dr. Wax lived in a desert housing development a few miles outside Las Cruces, and he had to hurry to make it to the shipping office before the cutoff time for overnight delivery.

"You want more than fifty bucks' insurance on any of these?" the thick-fingered clerk asked him when she weighed in the packages.

Wax smiled at the folly of assigning a dollar value to an irreplaceable work of genius. "No, that'll do."

With the members of his adopted family safely on their way back to their original owners, Dr. Wax drove his SUV back onto U.S. 70 headed east. He now had to attend to his other progeny—the misbegotten ones.

Dusk tanned the chaparral along the road a dirty orange color and the scattered houses at the city's edge grew more infrequent. Wax wound his way through the deepening shadows of a cleft in the mountains until he passed the turnoff for Route 213 South, which brown-and-white signs indicated would lead to White Sands National Monument. He turned instead on the restricted road that served as entrance to the missile range, pausing at the guardhouse to display his ID badge to the soldier on duty. The G.I., a crew-cut beanpole of a boy whose face still broke out in zits, waved him on with barely a glance. He knew mousy Dr. Wax. Everyone here did.

A herd of oryx grazed along the road toward the military base, adding a surreal touch to an already alien landscape. Distinguished by the masks of black-and-white coloration on their heads and their long, straight horns, these African antelope had been imported here as part of a program to introduce exotic game into the region, and they had thrived in the New Mexican desert. They scattered as Wax veered down an unmarked offshoot of the main road.

Before long, the desert gave way to an even more desolate landscape: stark dunes of granular gypsum, as white and coarse as ground bones. In places, the windswept mounds of sand had crept over the fringe of the pavement, attempting to reclaim the path and bury it. The SUV's tires bounced over and crunched through the occasional hillocks, which the

Army would plow aside like drifting snow. At last, Wax arrived at a large, windowless gray building that resembled military barracks. No sign identified the structure; only those who already knew its purpose were allowed inside.

Wax parked in the adjacent asphalt lot among a few scattered civilian and military vehicles and carried his black bag up to the structure's only door, which required him to slide his ID into a slot and press his thumb on a touch pad for authorization.

"Dr. Wax!" The corporal on duty at the front desk smiled as he entered the foyer.

"We weren't expecting you today. How are you feeling?"

"Much better, thanks." He smiled back, embarrassed that, although he saw her practically every day, he'd never bothered to remember the corporal's name. "Just came by to check on the subjects."

"Sure thing. You want me to call an orderly?" She nodded toward the building's auxiliary wing, where the staff lounge, offices, and laboratory were located.

"No, that won't be necessary," he replied, although he could have used the help. He'd never had to deal with the patients alone before.

"Whatever you say." The corporal tapped in a code on her computer keyboard, and the door behind her buzzed. Wax opened it and passed through into a corridor lined with identical gray doors, each with a round glass portal at eye level.

The doctor donned the white lab coat that hung on a rack to his left, but waited until the security door swung shut behind him and the buzzing ceased before opening his black bag. Instead of his usual bagel, lox, and cream cheese, it held a pneumatic vaccine gun and dozens of glass vials filled with clear liquid.

Wax drew a deep breath and set the bag on the floor. *Do no harm,* he thought, shaking his head. It was far too late for the likes of Hippocrates now. .

He took the first vial and inserted it top-down into the circular tube on top of the vaccine gun. It was the same device he'd used to inject the carrier virus into the subjects to commence their gene therapy. He hoped the gun's familiarity would keep it from spooking the patients. The doctor wouldn't be strong enough to deal with them alone otherwise.

With the vaccine gun loaded, Wax went to a wall panel beside the corridor's entrance and turned on the preprogrammed classical music he used to calm the patients during his visits. The hall filled with the sonic balm of Pachelbel's Canon in D.

Holding the gun behind his back, he approached the first room and peered through the porthole. When he'd satisfied himself that the occupant was not waiting to attack him, Wax entered the security code on the door's keypad to unlock it. The music was not quite loud enough to drown out the scream that burst forth as the door opened.

"Get away from me! Leave me alone!"

Dr. Wax knew that the patient was not shrieking at him. The plump man lay curled in the far corner of the room between the mattress and the toilet and did not even seem to register the doctor's presence. But Wax could not help fretting that the subject knew what he had come to do.

"Hello, Harold. How are you today?" Although he knew perfectly well how Harold was, Wax employed his usual bedside-manner patter to avoid upsetting the patient as he advanced, the gun concealed behind him.

Harold pounded on his head with his fists, which were

bound in padded cotton mittens. Scabs and scars still streaked his face and shaved scalp where he'd clawed the skin with his fingernails. "GO AWAY! *ALL* OF YOU!"

Fecal matter smeared the back of his loose hospital smock as he squirmed against the vinyl upholstery of the walls and floor. Unlike a true Violet, Harold could neither allow a dead soul to inhabit his body nor shut out the souls who tried. He lived, therefore, in a gray zone between this life and the next, constantly bombarded by spirits that knocked, knocked, knocked.

"Easy, Harold." Wax knelt and brought his arm from behind his back. "I can make them go away."

He jammed the point of the gun into Harold's upper arm and pulled the trigger. With a spitting sound, the needle shot the fluid under the skin, and Harold's eyes snapped open to stare at Wax.

"*You.*" His pupils, flecked with both violet and robin's egg blue, became an electric shade of lavender. "You did this to me. I'll—"

Wax stumbled back as Harold lunged for him. But the convulsions dropped Harold back onto his belly, where he quivered like a salted slug. Not one to take chances, Bartholomew Wax had put almost ten times the lethal dosage of procaine in the vaccine gun's solution.

The doctor returned to his bag and replaced the empty poison vial with a fresh one before proceeding to the next room.

Through the door's circular window, he could see a young Hispanic girl pacing the tiny cell and hugging herself. Her scalp, like Harold's, had been shaved and tattooed with the twenty node points that showed where to attach the SoulScan electrodes. When Wax entered the room, she darted her eyes toward him. One was violet, the other brown, like mismatched marbles.

"Hello? Who are you? Where am I?"

"Don't worry. Everything's going to be all right." With the vaccine gun hidden behind him, Wax edged toward her, waiting for some indication of how dangerous the soul that inhabited her might be.

The girl swiveled her head to take in her surroundings. "Is this a hospital? I remember being in an accident." She looked down at the smooth brown skin of her arms. "What's *happened* to me?"

"You'll be fine," Wax assured her. "I'm a doctor."

The problem in handling Marisa was that the person she had been no longer existed. The quantum connection in Marisa's brain that had once moored the electromagnetic energy of her soul inside her body had eroded away, leaving her an empty receptacle for any dead soul to inhabit. Another spirit might displace the current one at any moment, but if Wax could keep the present soul at bay long enough for the injection...

"You've got to call my husband," she beseeched him. "You've got to tell him where I am."

"Of course. But, first, let me give you something to help you relax—"

Before he could administer the poison, Marisa's body jerked right as if yanked. She waggled her head, her face twisted by tics, and when the fit passed, she stood with her feet spread apart, fists clenched at her sides, her brows lowered in a glare. *"So help me, I'll kill you, Wax."*

Marisa launched herself at him, seizing his throat. Strangulation starbursts blurred his vision, and he stabbed the gun's needle blindly into her torso and pulled the trigger. Only when her hands fell away from his neck and she collapsed to the floor did he look down to see that he'd pierced the thin cloth of her hospital gown, injecting her right over the heart.

Harold, he thought, rasping to restore his breath. Wax hadn't counted on the poison working so quickly, although he'd heard that procaine in sufficient quantities could cause cardiac arrest. He couldn't risk having the patients he'd killed inhabit the other subjects; he'd have to work faster.

Hurrying back to the doctor's bag, Wax transferred all the remaining poison vials to the deep pockets of his white coat. He paused between rooms only long enough to put a new dose in his gun. Each victim added bites, bruises, or bleeding scratches to his wounds.

The last one, a skinny black man named Ezra, survived long enough to pursue Wax into the corridor. The doctor stumbled and crawled across the hall, hyperventilating as the dying man threatened to topple on him. When Ezra slumped halfway through the door instead, Bartholomew Wax sprang up and reloaded his gun, swapping the vials as if changing the clip in an automatic weapon. Then he cast a sheepish glance to his right.

The corporal from the front desk stood only a couple of yards away, her .45 pistol drawn and aimed at his head. She wasn't smiling.

A tall, stocky man in a navy blue suit stood beside her. Silver threads filigreed his dark hair and thick black eyebrows, and the rumples in his face gave him a fatherly beneficence.

He tipped his head in greeting. "Dr. Wax."

"*Mr.* Pancrit." The title was a deliberate slight. Wax knew that Carl Pancrit was a doctor, too, in the technical if not the ethical sense. "I didn't expect to see you here at this hour."

"Obviously not," his colleague observed with a deep

chuckle, nodding toward the man sprawled in the doorway. "But I've been expecting you. For some time now, I've suspected that your heart wasn't quite in this project."

Wax tightened his finger on the vaccine gun's trigger. "Take a look around you, Carl. The experiment is a failure."

"Not if it prompts further research. Yet you haven't submitted a new proposal in months, and that makes me think you're holding out on us. You wouldn't do that, would you, Barty?"

Pancrit advanced, arms spread as if to embrace him in a paternal hug, but Wax swung the gun toward him. "I'm done, Carl."

The corporal cocked her pistol.

Pancrit raised his hands to placate both of them. "Please! Let's be sensible about this." He motioned for the soldier to lower her weapon, then gave Wax a sympathetic look. "I can't blame you for putting the poor devils out of their misery. I would have done the same thing myself—"

"I'm sure you would have." Wax kept the vaccine gun level with Pancrit's chest.

"—but you still owe us for those pictures of yours, Barty. We went to a lot of trouble to get them for you. Do you want us to send 'em right back where they came from?"

Wax gave a wan smile. "That won't be necessary."

He drove the needle of his gun into his own carotid artery and pulled the trigger.

As he crumpled to the floor, the corporal rushed forward, brandishing her pistol in case Wax was playing some kind of trick. He wasn't.

Carl Pancrit sighed as he watched Bartholomew Wax twitch in his death throes. "Don't think you can get away from me that easily...."